ALSO BY ALAFAIR BURKE

Long Gone
If You Were Here
The Ex
The Wife
The Better Sister
Find Me

The Ellie Hatcher Series
Dead Connection
Angel's Tip
212
Never Tell
All Day and a Night

The Samantha Kincaid Series
Judgment Calls
Missing Justice
Close Case

With Mary Higgins Clark
The Cinderella Murder
All Dressed in White
The Sleeping Beauty Killer
Every Breath You Take
You Don't Own Me
Piece of My Heart
Where Are the Children Now?
It Had to Be You

THE NOTE

THE NOTE

ALAFAIR BURKE

ALFRED A. KNOPF
NEW YORK
2025

THIS IS A BORZOI BOOK
PUBLISHED BY ALFRED A. KNOPF

www.aaknopf.com

Knopf, Borzoi Books, and the colophon are registered trademarks of Penguin Random House LLC.

Library of Congress Cataloging-in-Publication Data
Names: Burke, Alafair, author.
Title: The note : a novel / Alafair Burke.
Description: First edition. | New York : Alfred A. Knopf, 2025.
Identifiers: LCCN 2023054411 | ISBN 9780593537084 (hardcover) |
ISBN 9780593537091 (ebook) | ISBN 9781524712747 (open-market)
Subjects: LCGFT: Thrillers (Fiction) | Novels.
Classification: LCC PS3602.U755 N68 2025 | DDC 813/.6—dc23/eng/20231201
LC record available at https://lccn.loc.gov/2023054411

Jacket photographs: (pool and house) Martin Barraud/Getty Images;
(woman) Radka Janouskovcova/Getty Images
Jacket design by Jenny Carrow
Shrug emoji illustration courtesy of artemoberland/Adobe Stock

Manufactured in the United States of America

FIRST EDITION

For Liz and Nic Wolff

A real friend is one who walks in
when the rest of the world walks out.

—WALTER WINCHELL

THE NOTE

PROLOGUE

It was meant to be a harmless prank. Not even a prank, not initially. An inside joke, only for the three of them. But now she was locking her apartment door behind two departing police officers.

She had managed to sound appropriately earnest but unworried when they began asking questions. After all, why should May Hanover, of all people, be nervous around police? May was the good girl, always. The one who only needed to be told once by a teacher to open a book to a specific page. The teenager who drove strictly within the limits of her learner's permit. Even her pug, Gomez, seemed to understand at an instinctive level why he needed to break away from his neighbor buddies to ride the building's service elevator while they strutted brazenly with their humans through the lobby.

May, simply put, was a rule follower. A rule enforcer, in fact. It was a trait that had helped her succeed in life, but, as she had learned, could also lead to trouble.

Josh emerged from the bedroom where he'd gone to give her privacy when the police arrived. Gomez waddled slightly behind him. "Was that about Roland Shaw?"

Shaw was the man she'd convicted in her final in-person trial as an assistant district attorney after he was found breaking into his next victim's apartment. "How'd you know?" Could a question be a lie? That one probably counted. So many lies since she'd gotten home yesterday from her long weekend in the Hamptons.

"That was a major case for you. I recognized the big guy from the news."

The trial was before she and Josh had found themselves suddenly living together. Before they were engaged. The media coverage consisted of two small articles in the *Post,* including a photograph of a defiant-looking May flanked by two detectives in the courthouse hallway—one of them the "big guy" Josh recognized. Whereas May was obsessed with all things crime-related—in her job, the news, truth or fiction—Josh found it all, quote, "dark and depressing." But Josh was interested in all things May-related. Of course he had followed the coverage.

"The DA's Office got an inquiry from another jurisdiction and needed to clear something up," she said. Misleading, but technically true.

"They couldn't just call you?" he asked.

"Actually, he called, but I didn't see the message." That one was a full-on lie. "Guess he's training a new guy and wanted a change of scenery."

"Well, I'm glad they were quick. I really wanted a Negroni but thought the sound of a cocktail shaker might be inadvisable while you were in official law enforcement mode."

"Another reason why you should stir," she said.

"I like what I like."

"Make two? I'm getting back into my comfy clothes."

She called Lauren once she was alone in the bedroom.

"Hey there, woman. We were just saying we miss you."

"Yes, we miss you!" Kelsey called out in the background. "Come back here right now. It's boring without you."

May could hear a few drinks' worth of enthusiasm in Kelsey's voice. "You're clearly having a miserable time. Absolutely suffering." She felt a knot form in her sternum as she steeled herself to explain why she was calling. “I don’t even know how to say this, but the police are probably going to call you. Both of you.”

“What? How would they even know about us?” Lauren asked.

“They came to my apartment. They asked who I was with. I didn’t have a choice. They have your names. And your phone numbers.”

“How? Were there cameras or something?”

“No, it was because of me. I’m so sorry.”

What had she gone and done? No one was supposed to know about any of their stupidity. And now something really, really bad was going to happen—she could feel it. Something she couldn’t control. She wanted to open her mouth wide to scream—to scream impossibly loudly again, like last time.

PART ONE

THE BEST TRIP EVER

SIX DAYS EARLIER

1

May stood before her open closet, finding a reason to hate everything in it. Her clothes consisted of either suits and sheath dresses or jeans, tees, and hoodies. She was utterly unequipped for a girls' weekend at the beach.

A few years ago, everyone seemed to be purging their belongings—dumping anything that didn't "bring them joy." May had quietly judged them all. To her, the act of finding happiness through decluttering was an indulgence for people who had too much time on their hands and enough money to spend on custom organizers at the Container Store. Now that she was staring down all her sad clothes, she was pining for a little Kondo energy.

She decided her good old reliable black shirt-dress would work if she paired it with a colorful bangle and some cute strappy sandals. She rolled it neatly before slipping it into the carry-on bag she had flopped open on her side of the bed. Resting next to the bag was Josh, his back against the headboard, the reading glasses he only recently admitted needing perched low on his nose. Gomez was curled in a tight ball next to him.

For the first four years of that dog's life, she had trained him to stay off the furniture. All that changed during the lockdown, when he'd been glued next to at least one of them 24/7 for more than a year straight. No going back now.

She noticed that Josh was grimacing as he read.

"That gross?" she asked. Josh was a product manager for one of the world's largest makers of personal care products. Tonight's homework was a report on emerging trends in the personal hygiene market.

"Reviewing a complete list of places to use full-body deodorant. Want to hear?"

"Nope. People are disgusting."

Josh set the report aside on the nightstand and replaced it with the memoir he was reading by the lead singer of one of their favorite bands. They'd splurged on good tickets to see them live, the very first performance at Madison Square Garden after the world began to reopen. The date landed within those heavenly few weeks after vaccination appointments were plentiful, but before the arrival of the new vocabulary of *variants, breakthrough cases,* and *boosters*—when they believed that life was finally back to normal.

A few protesters showed up at the Garden, mocking them as sheep for complying with the venue's vax requirement. The guy in front of them had heckled back. "*Baaah,* motherfuckers. We sheep are going to dance our asses off while you idiots sweat outside."

May cried when the band broke into the first chorus. *It's times like these you learn to live again.*

Two years later, everyone else seemed fine. They were living again. But May?

May felt like she was still learning.

"You and your suitcase burritos." Josh smiled at the growing pile of compressed clothing bundles in her bag.

"Oh shoot," she said, immediately rethinking her black-dress choice. "I'm pretty sure I wore this the last time Lauren was in town. Does that sound right? When she had that gig at Lincoln Center?"

"Let me check my annal chronicling your historic wardrobe decisions across time." He pretended to reach for his iPad. "She won't remember a dress from 2019, and if she did, it's not like she'll judge you for wearing it again. Plus you just bought a new outfit for the trip. You'll be fine."

The new outfit was a purple sundress that did, in fact, bring May joy. It had that effortless just-threw-this-on boho chic look, which meant it cost as much as catering for two people on the wedding guest list they were trying to find ways to cull. She reminded herself this was only a weekend trip, and they'd probably spend most of it at the beach or sitting around the house, just the three of them. Swimsuit, shorts, T-shirts, all rolled neatly and set in place. Done.

As she finished zipping her bag, Josh stood and lifted it from the bed for her. He was old-fashioned that way. He opened car doors, took out garbage, did the stereotypically male things. When they traveled together, he insisted on pulling both of their suitcases behind him through the airport. He was a caretaker.

As he tucked the bag out of the way in the bedroom corner, she crawled into bed, nestling Gomez into her side like a football. "I'm going to miss you so much, you little pumpkin head."

"And here I was, thinking you were talking to me," Josh said.

"I'll miss you too, but Gomez can't text and call me, can you, sweetie? No, you don't have any thumbs or we'd text all the time."

Even though the trip was only for a long weekend, this would be the longest she'd been away from her dog for years. It was also her first time out to the Hamptons since she'd worked at the law firm, where some of the other associates had parents with summer houses and would occasionally invite a coworker or two to share in their largesse.

Kelsey had rented the beach house for ten days, but May was heeding the warnings she had received about using her academic summers wisely. She needed to write if she was going to get her contract renewed and eventually get tenure. She knew herself. She worked best when she kept to a routine schedule. Plan your work and work your plan. Plus, Lauren and Kelsey were both single, while May was engaged and organizing a wedding. She couldn't just take a whole week off and play with her friends in the Hamptons.

Her phone pinged from the nightstand. A text from Kelsey in the group thread. *Lauren, how'd it go today?*

He loved my initial ideas. He's paying me to watch the rough cut and come up with some initial samples. Fingers crossed!

Kelsey's ability to keep track of her friends' important plans was uncanny. It had been at least two weeks since Lauren mentioned that an award-winning documentarian had contacted her about the possibility of composing a film score. May would have never remembered that the initial Zoom meeting was scheduled for today.

Of course you crushed it, she chimed in. *Congrats!*

Climbing back into bed, Josh asked, "You're sure you want to do this trip?" He said it casually, as if they hadn't had this conversation multiple times since it was planned three weeks earlier.

"Of course. I told you. I'm excited. Do you not want me to go or something?"

"No, I promise it's not that," he said, pulling her close into a spoon position. His left hand held hers as he adjusted her engagement ring to center the Tiffany-cut diamond on her finger. "I will manage to live without you for three days. But can I just remind you that you told me on that trip to New Orleans that I was the only human being who you could share a roof with for more than two days?"

"Oh my god. That makes me sound like a total psychopath."

"Well, to me it was very romantic, because it meant that other people drive you crazy in a way that I do not. And now you've committed yourself to spending seventy-two hours with these women. Honestly, I'm not sure whether to be more worried about you or them."

She rolled over to face him. "Lauren and Kelsey are different. I've talked to them, like, every single day for more than a year." They didn't actually *talk*. But the group text thread among the three of them had somehow grown into an omnipresent conversation. "I've known them since I was twelve years old."

"No. You *used* to know them. Not the same." His lips curled into a sly smile. He knew he had a point. This would be the first time she had seen Lauren and Kelsey in person at the same time for nearly a decade.

"Well, I was super close to Kelsey for like ten years—all the way through college. And Lauren and I never fell out of touch."

"A few phone calls a year and lunch when she comes to New York is not the same as a vacation together under the same roof."

"No, but back in the day, the three of us basically lived together for weeks on end."

"When you and Kelsey were kids at summer camp a lifetime ago."

"One, Wildwood was an *arts* camp." And she hadn't exactly been a kid that final summer after college graduation, when the economy crashed and even her Ivy League degree couldn't land her a good job. Off to law school she would go instead, spending the interim summer as a counselor at the camp where she'd once been a student. She was surprised when Kelsey chose to do the same. Kelsey had a ready-made job waiting at her father's commercial real estate company, but when she found out May's plan, she asked her father if she could defer adulting to join her.

"And two," she added, "don't make me sound like such a geezer." She ran the math in her head. "Wow, that last summer at Wildwood was fifteen years ago." Not half a lifetime, to be sure, but how was that even possible?

"May, you are definitely not a geezer." Josh gave her a soft kiss on the lips. "And even when you are . . ." He moved down to her clavicle, and she felt herself smiling. "Your gray hair and wrinkled skin will be all my old man junk needs to—"

She pushed him away playfully. "Oh god, I'll never get that image out of my head."

"My OMJ will have you saying OMG."

"Stop!"

He pulled her close to him again, nudging Gomez to the foot of the bed and wrapping his arms around her. "I am going to miss you," Josh whispered. "I don't even remember what it's like to sleep without you."

"You'll have Gomez."

"You're really sure you want to go? What if your pen pals are torture in real life?"

"They won't be." She didn't know how to explain to Josh how important this trip was. A year ago, after the worst day of May's life had made her infamous, Lauren—more than anyone, more than her mother, more than even Josh—had been there for her. And then, through Lauren, Kelsey was there too, in the group thread that sometimes felt like her only tether to sanity.

Of course she was going to East Hampton tomorrow. She couldn't wait.

2

May was making her third loop around the JetBlue terminal at JFK when the next text from Lauren popped up. *Okay, finally made it outside. Pick up 4.*

As she passed the third area for passenger pickup, May had no problem spotting Lauren in the crowd, even though she hadn't seen her in person for nearly four years. There had been plenty of Zoom happy hours, but those were typically conducted with unbrushed hair, makeup-free faces, and the athleisure they had all come to live in for months on end.

Where May felt like she was having trouble readjusting to a world that expected a certain level of aesthetic attention, Lauren was apparently back in full fashion mode. She wore wide-legged peach linen gauchos with a silk paisley wrap blouse and chunky wedge sandals. Her long hair was pulled back sleekly at the nape of her neck, then fluffed into a perfectly round pom-pom. Her giant square sunglasses screamed peak Jackie O. If May tried to pull off Lauren's look, people would say how nice it was that she was able to get around by herself.

I see you! Pulling up now. May watched as Lauren read the message and then scanned the tangle of cars jockeying for space near the curb. Lauren waved enthusiastically at the sight of Josh's Subaru.

May hit the hazards and hopped out to help Lauren with her bags. She felt a familiar heat in the pit of her stomach as the gazes of two twenty-something-year-old white women followed her when she moved in to hug Lauren. When the video of May first went viral, she was convinced people were staring at her everywhere she went. Recognizing her. Whispering about her. Judging her. She didn't leave the apartment for five days straight because she was convinced that her neighbors would shun her in the elevator. And when she finally did, she was grateful to have the N95 mask as an excuse to cover most of her face.

She looked directly at the two women who had been watching her, reminding herself of the times Lauren had tried to comfort her by joking that May shouldn't worry about being recognized because "most people think you all look alike." Instead of confronting May, the young women seemed discomforted by her stare.

"Sorry, we were just admiring your whole vibe." They were talking to Lauren, not her. May was most definitely *not* a vibe.

"Your hair is amazing," the second woman added.

"Why, thank you," Lauren said, primping her hair puff with her fingertips. "Have a good day, y'all." As she threw her bag in the hatchback of Josh's car, she whispered under her breath, "At least they didn't try to touch it. That's a good way to lose an arm with me."

May studied Lauren in her periphery as they strapped on their seatbelts. Lauren had arrived at Wildwood as the lead symphony coach during May's third summer. She was twenty-three years old and had already served as the first-chair violinist in the Louisiana Philharmonic Orchestra. By the end of the first week, the camp rumor mill reported that she played five other instruments, had been identified in grade school as a prodigy, and had composed the score to an entire animated film. By week four, she supposedly had a recording contract with Quincy Jones. That part turned out not to be true, but she did land a two-year artist-in-residence gig at the Music Institute of Chicago when it wasn't camp season. She was only nine years older than May, but seemed impossibly talented and sophisticated. It wasn't only that Lauren felt an entire generation apart from May at the time. She seemed like a completely different *species.*

The age gap felt negligible now. With less than a decade between them, they were basically contemporaries, and though Lauren had landed a job as the director of the Houston Symphony, May knew at an intellectual level that she was impressive in her own right. Raised by a first-generation Chinese single mother, she graduated magna cum laude from Harvard, then did the same at Columbia Law. Until that video blew up online and she was asked to consider resigning, she had been a board member on the state's Asian American Bar Association. Now she was on her way to becoming a tenured law professor. But when Lauren was around, she felt a little like a nerdy kid again. The same excitement, but also still the same insecurities.

Lauren reached from the passenger seat for a second hug. "Oh, the way I have been looking forward to this. I need this vacation so much."

"Me too," May said. "*So much.* The Canceled Crew, finally together in person." Weeks into the text thread, May had been the one who entered a name for their group chat: *The Spelling Bee Hive.* It was a reference to the fact that May had told Lauren and Kelsey about her daily habit of completing all the *New York Times* puzzles as a distraction from her floating anxieties. Work, politics, her mother, wedding planning—all of it disappeared when she was grinding out a word game.

It turned out that Lauren and Kelsey had gotten hooked on one of the puzzles too, called the Spelling Bee, which involved compiling words from seven letters arranged in the shape of a beehive. The discovery of additional words was rewarded by increasingly complimentary levels of accomplishment: Nice, Great, Amazing, Genius, and, on that special day when the puzzler found every possible word, the elusive Queen Bee. For a dispositional grade-grubber like May, those digitized words of praise were a morning drug. Rather than get stalled at Genius, May, Lauren, and Kelsey conspired to hit Queen Bee every day by comparing word lists.

But *The Spelling Bee Hive* didn't capture the true nature of their bond, so May tried out the *Don't Judge Me Hive* before Kelsey amended it to *Three Despised Bitches* and May came back with *Three*

Non Karens. The evolving group-thread name became a game of its own until Lauren weighed in with her own suggestion—*The Canceled Crew.* Whether it was because the name was a good one or it had come from Lauren really didn't matter. It was the name that had stuck. It was what had brought them all together again as a trio—three ladies who had gone through the cancel mill.

Canceled. When had that word hit the cultural lexicon?

He got canceled.

Cancel culture.

Shhh, I don't want to get canceled.

What did it even mean? A human being can't literally be *canceled.* You're either alive or dead, breathing or not. Brain-dead, maybe, but that's still not canceled. But whatever it meant, it was why Lauren had reached out to May in the wake of that disastrous video. She and Kelsey had already been through it, their lives . . . what? Not exactly canceled, but *transformed.* And transformed in a specific way—revealed, and then reduced. Forever altered by the specific mechanism of public scrutiny and judgment. Lauren, because of the affair. Kelsey, because of her husband's murder. And May, because of a confrontation on a subway platform. Three women, judged and vilified by strangers.

"Canceled, my ass," Lauren said, reaching for the car stereo to blast Janelle Monáe while she sang along. *I'm looking at a thousand versions of myself, and we're all fine.* "We're going to have the best trip ever."

3

"We knocked it all out. I say a little reward is in order." Lauren pulled a bottle of prosecco from the refrigerator and expertly popped the cork, tipping a few ounces into two wineglasses she had laid out on the kitchen island.

Since the drive from JFK, they had managed to unpack, make supermarket and liquor store runs, and put away the cheese, crackers, chips, dips, eggs, bread, milk, coffee, and every other thing they piled into their overflowing grocery cart.

The house had three bedrooms. One was the upstairs suite with a king bed, en suite bathroom, and a deck with a view of the bay. The parents' room, which meant it was Lauren's room, no question. She was the original Queen Bee. The elder. Their glue. The one who had remained close to both May and Kelsey after the May/Kelsey BFF Duo had fallen out of touch. Even though the three of them were a hive now, Lauren somehow felt like the overlap in their Venn diagrams.

A smaller bedroom was next door, simply furnished with a full bed and a single nightstand. The first floor had a second suite with its own bathroom and a sliding glass door out to the pool deck.

May took the small room. No deck, no view, no en suite bath. She was the one who had to go back to the city early, and she was the one letting Kelsey pay. It was the obvious decision.

"The house is nice, right?" May asked, as she neatly folded the final paper bag to set out with the recycling.

May knew that Lauren generally preferred hotels when she traveled. The first time she rented an Airbnb, a neighbor had called the police to report a trespasser. When Lauren told May about it, May responded too quickly, saying she "couldn't believe anyone would do that" and lamenting what bad "luck" Lauren had had. Lauren replied under her breath that luck had nothing to do with it, then quickly changed the subject. That night after work, May googled *vacation rentals racism* and understood why Lauren avoided owner-operated rentals. Harassment from prying neighbors. Calls to the police. Claims by homeowners that the rental was suddenly unavailable, despite what the website clearly stated.

When Kelsey proposed renting a house in the Hamptons for a girls' trip, May hadn't wanted Lauren to feel boxed into an uncomfortable situation, so she suggested that hotel rooms would be less expensive than a whole house in the Hamptons. Kelsey insisted that they needed a place large enough to hang out and chill in private. She also offered to pay for the entire rental.

Checkmate. May was out of moves.

Lauren's next text, sent only to May, followed seconds later. *I appreciate what you're trying to do, but please stop. Let her pay. It will be fine. Don't overthink it.*

The next day, Kelsey texted photos, saying she had the perfect place. *Kind of small but right by this gorgeous bay beach.* Out of curiosity, May had used a reverse Google image search to find the listing.

She was grateful Kelsey was footing the bill, because the rent was fifteen hundred dollars a night. It sounded impossibly expensive to May, but apparently the market warranted it. According to the rental listing, the house was booked solid for the entire summer, and the detailed home instructions left on the refrigerator by the owner—full of exclamation points and random all caps—gave a "FIRM!" checkout time because the house needed to be turned over immediately after their departure. The long list of prohibitions and rules ended with a handwritten note. *Have a great stay, Callie!!! xox Arianna.* The *i* in her name was dotted with a heart, and she left a contact number for emergencies.

Lauren's and May's phones simultaneously pinged with a new message on the Crew thread. It was a short video that began with the view of the wake behind a boat and ending with a glimpse of Kelsey, her long hair blowing wildly around her face as she squinted against the sunlight. She had added an animated sticker of a ferryboat and the words VOLUME UP.

May unmuted her phone and heard "Let the River Run" by Carly Simon. She and Kelsey had watched *Working Girl* the summer after seventh grade and became obsessed with Melanie Griffith's transformation from sneakers and a wall of permed hair to boss of the boardroom. Rewatching became a Wildwood annual tradition as they gathered a growing number of girls each summer in front of the communal television with hoards of snacks, reciting their favorite lines from memory. *I'm not steak, you can't just order me . . . I've got a mind for business and a bod for sin.* And May's personal favorite: *Sometimes I sing and dance around the house in my underwear. Doesn't make me Madonna.*

Kelsey was driving down from Boston, which involved a ferry that would carry her first from southern Connecticut to Orient, then from Orient to Shelter Island, and then from Shelter Island to the South Fork of Suffolk County, aka the Hamptons.

May leaned in close to Lauren, snapped a selfie, and attached it to the group thread. *Yay, you're almost here! Can't wait to see you!* Send.

How's the house? Kelsey asked.

May typed in five star emojis and hit enter, then quickly followed up with *Thank you again for being so generous. What a treat.*

Have you guys done the bee already?

Nope. We were saving it for you.

Yay. Let's work on it while I'm on the ferry.

May responded with a thumbs-up and hit enter.

"Prosecco by the pool time?" Lauren asked.

As May slid open the back door to the deck, a thought suddenly came to her. "Do you think Arianna with all the refrigerator-note rules has cameras all over this house?"

Lauren laughed and shook her head. "Sometimes your brain terrifies me, May. You and that creepy imagination of yours really should write a book someday."

The first sign of Kelsey's arrival was a voice calling from inside the house. "Stash away the strap-on and get yourselves decent. I'm here!"

Lauren and May popped up from their chaise longues and headed for the kitchen, where they found Kelsey with a roller bag and an oversized straw tote embroidered with the words BEACH PLEASE. She wore slouchy denim overalls paired with a black tank top.

Lauren threw her arms around Kelsey. "You made it!"

When Lauren let go of Kelsey, it was May's turn. Kelsey pulled her into a tight hug, rocking back and forth. The feeling was instantly familiar: Whatever nervousness May had been feeling about seeing Kelsey after so long melted on contact. Kelsey's hugs always had that calming effect.

May remembered the first time they met. She was twelve years old and new to the camp, having landed a scholarship on her second try, but it was already Kelsey's third summer at Wildwood, and they were assigned as bunkmates. *Can I hug you? I feel like I already know you from your camp profile.* May was initially suspect, thinking no one could possibly be that eager to know her, but within a few weeks it became clear that once Kelsey Ellis decided she was your friend, she really meant it.

"You must be exhausted from the drive," May said.

"Friday afternoon in the Hamptons. Rookie error. I should have left Boston earlier. One of our flagship tenants in Downtown Crossing is pulling some shit with their lease renewal. They would never try a stunt like this with my father, so I'm determined to handle it myself. But—" She forced a smile and took a deep breath. "That is all totally whatever, and I'm just so happy we're finally all here."

Kelsey dropped her car keys on the kitchen island next to the open prosecco bottle. "Oh, man, you started the fun without me."

"Barely," Lauren assured her.

"So that means only one orgy in the pool so far?"

Kelsey had a unique talent for saying the most inappropriate things in a way that managed never to be off-putting. The one time she had accompanied May to Bloomington for spring break, she asked May's mother out of the blue while clearing the dinner dishes what had happened between her and May's father. When May's mother tried to sidestep the question by saying it was so long ago, Kelsey said something about smart women learning how to "take care of themselves" and then made a humming sound.

May was mortified at the obvious vibrator reference, but then Coral Hanover did something she rarely did. She laughed—loudly—like an actual, full-belly laugh. By the end of the night, May's mother had taken out an old photo album and shared the story of meeting Mitchell Hanover while she was getting her graduate degree at IU to become a teacher. How he had tried asking her out to dinner in Chinese, only to learn that her friend who had helped him study had taught him instead to say, "I am not very good at this." How surprised she was to find herself in a relationship with an American from a small Midwestern town. How businesslike he was when she told him she was pregnant, immediately asking how far along she was to make sure it wasn't too late to go to a clinic.

May's father, her mother explained, had been excited to meet someone as "exotic" as her mother, but confessed that he could not imagine himself making a lifetime commitment to a woman who "wasn't from here." May knew the rest of the story. Her mother promised to raise the child alone as long as he married her long enough for her to obtain citizenship before they divorced. But until that night, May never realized the full extent of the mean-spiritedness beneath her father's rejection of both May and her mother. It's almost as if May's mother needed Kelsey in the room as a buffer to tell the whole story.

Kelsey was looking at May now and smiling. "God, I can't believe how long it's been since I've actually seen you in person. I mean, it must have been at the wedding?"

No, it wasn't the wedding. May remembered exactly when it was—eight years ago, not long before May left the law firm for the DA's Office. She remembered because that was the beginning of the story of how she and Kelsey had stopped being friends.

4

May was excited to be traveling for depositions without a supervising partner, even more so because the work was in Boston, which meant she could meet up with Kelsey. When they were in college, they'd seen each other regularly. Harvard and Boston College were only five miles apart. But it had been seven years since they'd graduated, which meant seven years of living in separate cities. Even when May was in law school, she and Kelsey had found time to hop on Amtrak to visit each other several times a year, but they were both so busy now.

They met at a heralded steakhouse Kelsey selected, one that May never could have afforded if she didn't have an expense account at the law firm for "potential client engagement." At the time, May was single, focused on her career. She needed the firm salary to pay off her loans, but no matter how many hours she billed, the clock toward partnership consideration was the one ticking most loudly in her head.

The day before her flight to Boston, she'd had her annual review with the head of the litigation department and the two cochairs of the junior associate mentorship committee. The good news was that her reviewing partners described her as "smart," "hardworking," "a grinder."

Her billable hours put her among the top ten percent of associates by that measure. But the bad news was bad. She needed to "lean in." "Be heard more." "Show that you can lead a team and be more than a supporting player." "Demonstrate potential to bring new business into the firm." When they tried to soften the blow by saying how "agreeable" and "amenable" everyone found her to work with, she pictured herself calmly rising from her chair, throwing it across the conference table, and then walking out the door as they stared at her in shock. Instead, she nodded, smiled politely, and thanked them all for their candid and helpful feedback, promising that she would take it to heart.

The message was clear. Unless May either got a personality transplant or managed to change the elusive metrics large law firms used to measure "partnership material," no number of billable hours could save her from the inevitable day a year or two from now when she would be not-so-subtly encouraged to "look for opportunities beyond the firm." To avoid the humiliation, she had spent the entire night researching legal jobs that came with student loan relief.

All of this was weighing on May as she and Kelsey played catch-up over their matching meals of martinis, shrimp cocktails, and rare rib eyes. Not wanting to be a Debbie Downer, she told Kelsey that her hard work at the firm was paying off and that she was now entrusted to deal with some of the clients directly. In fact, she was enjoying her independence so much that she was considering leaving Big Law culture behind for a job that would allow her to handle her own cases. Maybe the District Attorney's Office, since she had always been so fascinated by crime. She might even have time to get a dog. She managed to make it seem like it was everything she had always wanted.

Meanwhile, Kelsey appeared to have jumped into her role as the third generation of the Ellis real estate empire, going on at length about a pending closing she was handling for a thirty-two-story office building in the Back Bay district and a "sexy" renovation of an old movie theater that she was planning to transform into a cinema-slash-speakeasy—no mention of her father's reputedly questionable lending arrangements and deals that seemed to breeze through the usually cumbersome Boston regulatory process, concerns that used to eat away at a younger Kelsey.

She showed May photographs of the three-bedroom high-rise condo that her father had insisted on helping her with after she had been looking at a fixer-upper in a neighborhood he didn't approve of. May also got to hear all about the lavish wedding plans Kelsey was making with her fiancé, who was in the process of opening his own restaurant. Kelsey assumed William Ellis would be paying for all of that too.

When the server asked if they were interested in dessert or coffee, May passed, saying she had an early start the next day, even though the depos weren't resuming until ten in the morning. Kelsey pleaded with her to stay longer, but May had already concluded that she and Kelsey had become different people since they'd last seen each other. As much fun as they used to have together, May should have known that Kelsey would eventually inhabit a different universe, given all of the advantages she enjoyed. Life was too short to spend it with strangers.

The next morning, May woke up to an email from Kelsey, something like *Had the best time tonight. Two years, and it felt like we were never away from each other. Hope this case keeps you coming back to Boston!*

May's response was equally effusive but ended with an abrupt *Running into depos now!*

Go get 'em!

May returned five additional times to Boston before she finally left the firm, and never once told Kelsey.

The wedding invitation—one of hundreds, May presumed—arrived the same day she interviewed at the DA's Office. The card stock was heavy. *Mr. and Mrs. William Ellis request the pleasure of your company at the marriage of his daughter Kelsey Weston to Lucas Benjamin Freedman.*

Interesting, May had thought. Another Mrs. William Ellis—making her the third. The first was Kelsey's mother, who had died of ovarian cancer when Kelsey was only seven years old. The second was Kelsey's stepmother, Jeanie, a widow whom Kelsey's father had married when Kelsey was nine. By the time May met the family, Kelsey referred to the couple as "Mom and Dad" and to Jeanie's son, Nate, as her "brother." And yet during Kelsey's freshman year in college, her father, armed with an ironclad prenup, filed for divorce. And once the divorce was final, he stopped speaking to both Jeanie and Nate altogether, destroying Kelsey's sense of family for a second time.

At the time, Kelsey and Nate were shocked, but their parents insisted it was simply time to "move on." When Jeanie was diagnosed with early-onset Alzheimer's nearly a decade later, Kelsey wondered if her father might have picked up on some early signs of her illness. But if May had to guess, the split had something to do with money, because that's how William Ellis rolled. *My dad says money is power.* She first heard Kelsey say that when she was only fourteen years old. *It may not buy you happiness but it can buy almost everything else.*

Rubbing the thick invitation stock between her fingertips, May pulled up Kelsey's Facebook page, curious to see pictures of her fiancé. Luke Freedman. He had dark spiky hair and a perfect layer of face stubble. In one of the shots, he stood in a commercial kitchen, spooning a pea green sauce gingerly onto a perfect piece of fish. The caption read "Chef Hottie."

The next post contained pictures from a Halloween party. Kelsey wore prison stripes, a pair of handcuffs dangling from one wrist. May recognized Kelsey's brother as the stern-faced police officer posing beside her, despite the fake mustache and dark aviator sunglasses. The caption read, "One of these outfits is more convincing than the other."

Attending the wedding would inevitably mean seeing Nathan Thorne, aka Nate—who, in addition to being Kelsey's stepbrother, had also been May's boyfriend for two years. She checked the REGRETS box on the RSVP card, scribbling a note that she would be starting a new job and wouldn't be able to make the trip. As the wedding date approached, she started to feel guilty and got the registry information from Lauren, but the only items within her budget felt lame. She only realized when she got a thank-you note from Kelsey that Lauren had added May's name to the martini glasses she'd purchased.

The pace of their interactions on social media or by text slowly dwindled until there was practical silence. Then, five years ago, she was in the middle of running the felony arraignment docket when Lauren texted her. *Tragic news today. I thought you'd want to know.* The embedded link led to an article in *The Boston Globe.* Lucas Benjamin Freedman, chef and owner of Bistro LB, had been fatally shot while making a bank deposit run. Police were investigating.

What do you do when someone you're not close to anymore loses her husband to violence? A text or an email felt at once both too impersonal and too invasive.

She asked Lauren for Kelsey's mailing address, but she couldn't send Kelsey one of those tacky two-dollar cards from the drugstore. She'd go to the *good* card store once she had a chance. In the meantime, she checked the news online every day for updates on the murder investigation. Still no eyewitnesses, but police were reviewing surveillance footage from the neighborhood. They were looking into the facts surrounding a restaurant employee's recent termination. A business loan that was overdue. And the victim's pending divorce from his estranged wife, Kelsey.

Interesting.

By the end of the week, Luke Freedman's murder made its way to the top threads of the leading true-crime message boards, with plenty of posters agreeing that the wife with the notorious real-estate-mogul father was a huge red flag. More than a few comments mentioned the rumors that William Ellis had inherited his father's financial ties to Whitey Bulger. The soon-to-be-ex-wife and her daddy must have hired a hit man, they insisted.

Why must it have been a murder for hire? Because at the time Luke was gunned down on his way to the bank after closing his restaurant, Kelsey had an ironclad alibi. Her father was receiving something called the Golden Plate Award at the International Achievement Summit, and when the event photographer gathered all the recipients for a group photo at the end of the evening, his dutiful daughter was at her father's side. To the crime-obsessed groupies who gathered online to crack cases from their living rooms, the evidence that should have exculpated Kelsey was a little "too convenient." In the online forums where new information was twisted and molded to conform to the preexisting narrative, Kelsey and her father had "obviously" timed the assassination to coincide with their joint appearance at a crowded event.

May had gone down all the rabbit holes, poring over every available detail and forcing herself to examine it with a lawyer's eye rather than from the perspective of a former best friend. The undeniable fact was that Kelsey had no motive to kill Luke. Kelsey and Luke were getting divorced, but he had been the one to insist on signing a prenup to prove to Kelsey that he had no interest in her father's money.

According to Luke's friends and family, it was actually his desire *not* to take money from his wife's family that ultimately drove the two apart. He found his father-in-law's involvement in Kelsey's life overbearing. William Ellis was even trying to interfere in Luke's restaurant, insisting it would be more "elevated" if it were located in one of his prestige properties, and offering to pay off his loans if he'd only follow his father-in-law's advice. Luke told his friends he felt as if he had married into an entire family—"Empire Ellis," as he derisively called it.

Luke wanted to be with a woman willing to define him and their eventual children as her primary family, instead of feeling like he was simply a plus-one. Nevertheless, a bunch of strangers on the internet felt free to claim without any factual support that Luke's selfish, greedy wife must have killed him to keep him from taking her money. These anonymous strangers psychoanalyzed Kelsey as if they had insider knowledge of what made her tick. It felt like an epic work of crowdsourced fan fiction about a narcissistic, spoiled rich girl driven to murder by her husband's rejection. But May, unlike these strangers, really did know Kelsey at her core. She knew that her eyes still watered every time she heard James Taylor's "Fire and Rain," because her mother used to call it "the song that makes Mommy cry." That she decided when she was in the ninth grade that she wanted to have children early so she could know them as long as possible. That she spent the entire year gathering the perfect holiday presents for everyone she loved. That she gave the best hugs.

Kelsey could be a little tone-deaf about how entitled she was, but she wasn't a killer. May read everything she could about Luke's murder, wondering if she might even spot a clue that could crack the case. May's personal theory was that it was a robbery gone wrong, but she had no way to prove it.

When she finally made it to the good card store, she selected the most elegant sympathy card on the rack, knowing it didn't capture the message she wanted to convey: *Sorry-your-soon-to-be-ex-was-murdered-and-no-I-don't-think-you-killed-him-but-other-people-definitely-do.*

While waiting in line to pay, she checked Kelsey's Facebook page to see if she had posted any updates, but her account was deleted. So was her Instagram. Something about those words on May's screen—*this account does not exist*—felt incriminating and confessional. The law referred to it as consciousness of guilt. What if May was missing something? She wasn't privy to everything the police knew. Kelsey's father had always seemed a little shady, keeping a private investigator on retainer, for example, to gather compromising information about his business rivals. And the last time she'd seen her old friend, she was happily following in his footsteps at Ellis, Inc.

And then there was also the very real possibility that inviting Kelsey back into her life would mean being around Nate at some point, too. As close as May had once been to Kelsey, being part of her life could be a major commitment. Kelsey checked in constantly on the people she loved. It came naturally to her to follow up on every event a friend may have mentioned to her in passing. Waking up to a Kelsey *good luck with xyz today* message was a reminder that she was in your corner 24/7, despite the physical distance. But May remembered the way she had felt obliged to do the same, even when it felt like work. Suddenly, the simplest act of sending condolences felt like the opening of floodgates she hadn't even been aware of. Plus, she was an assistant district attorney now. How would it look if she was caught on a wiretap talking to a murder suspect?

May was handing the card to the cashier when she lied and said she'd forgotten her wallet. She decided to take a wait-and-see approach before reaching out. Once the police made an arrest—that would be better.

But days passed and then weeks with no arrest. And meanwhile, the internet kept piling on.

It has to be the wife.

It always is.

Just look at her. Is it just me or does she have crazy eyes?

And it wasn't only strangers who had gone after Kelsey. Her former in-laws didn't go so far as to publicly accuse her, but Luke's parents said they were "open to all possibilities" and made clear that Luke did not get along with Kelsey's father. According to them, the expected divorce was "acrimonious" and had "divided the two families."

Both *Dateline* and *20/20* had run episodes focused on Luke's case. Two years after Luke was killed, Kelsey tried online dating, only to have her profile discovered and posted online, which led to a fresh rotation through the virtual gossip mill.

May would occasionally pull up Kelsey's number, but it never seemed like the right day to suddenly call out of the blue. Then the world suddenly changed, and May was learning how to practice law by Zoom, moving into Josh's place, and preparing herself for the interview with the Fordham faculty. Somehow years flew by, even though, at the time, each day felt endless.

Then one of those days brought her to that subway platform, and May was the one getting the anonymous fan-fiction treatment. She was the one erasing herself from social media, all because of one very bad awful moment. Just as Lauren had texted May with Kelsey's news after Luke died, she had sent May's subway video to Kelsey with an explanation. Kelsey immediately called her. They talked for over an hour. It was exactly as Kelsey had said after that steakhouse dinner in Boston—like they had never missed a beat.

The morning after that call from Kelsey, May sent a text to both Lauren and Kelsey. *I can't thank you enough for your love and support. Today feels better because of you guys.* It was the very first text in what had become the Canceled Crew thread.

And in the year that had passed since then, to May's profound shame, Kelsey had never asked her—not once—why May had never even sent a sympathy card.

5

God, I can't believe how long it's been since I've actually seen you in person. I mean, it must have been at the wedding?"

May shook her head. "No, um, it was before that—when I was in Boston for depositions."

"Right, at Garvey's! It's so sad that place is gone. It was always my mom's favorite for a special occasion. She'd eat a dozen oysters all by herself with an extra-dry martini." Kelsey's thoughts appeared to drift, but she suddenly perked up as she spotted the owner's note and plucked it from beneath the refrigerator magnet. "Wow, this is extremely detailed. Arianna needs a gummy."

"Or maybe too many gummies explains why she thought the note should be addressed to 'Callie,'" May said.

Kelsey dropped the instructions on the kitchen counter and did a quick walk-through of the first floor, taking in the shabby-chic decor. The living room was bright and airy, with white furniture and pops of color from throw pillows and the vintage beach posters that lined the walls. "I hope you guys like this place. I know how busy you are."

Lauren wrapped an arm around her waist and handed her a flute of prosecco as she gestured toward the glass doors leading to the deck.

"Are you kidding? Look at this view. You can almost taste the salt from the bay."

May was rolling Kelsey's powder blue Rimowa through the kitchen when Kelsey stopped her. "Where are you going?"

"To your room."

Kelsey followed her to the suite off the kitchen. "One of the rooms is down here?" Her gaze lingered on the stairs. "I guess I didn't notice that in the listing."

May was quick to explain. "We can switch if you want to be upstairs. There's a suite and the small room I took, with a bathroom in the hallway."

"We barely unpacked," Lauren added.

"No, I'm being silly. I just want us all to be together as much as possible. If I get too lonely, I can always take May's room when she leaves. And if Nate decides to come out, I'll definitely move upstairs with you."

"Nate's coming out?" May asked. She had been preparing herself for a weekend away from her usual routine, but her ex was definitely not part of the plan.

"Unclear. I told him about the trip and that you were leaving early, so he knew I'd have an extra room. He's not sure about his schedule yet, but, Lauren, are you sure you're okay if he decides to join? This was supposed to be a girls' trip."

"Please, Nate's family. He can have temporary membership in the Crew."

Was Kelsey already counting down the hours until her departure? May stopped herself. Why did she always have to overthink everything? Kelsey seemed to be over the fact that May had been a shitty friend for a while, but May wondered if she would ever stop feeling guilty.

A ringing sound came from the back pocket of Kelsey's overalls. She glanced at the screen and then rejected the call with an eye roll. She didn't need to explain that the caller was her father. "It's nonstop, you guys. I've begged him to text, but he pretends he doesn't know how." She waited for the ping of a new voicemail message and hit play.

"Can you let me know you got to East Hampton okay? And send me

pictures of the house and the neighborhood. I don't trust those internet rentals. If you get a bad feeling about the neighborhood, go to a hotel. Use the corporate card. Don't take any chances with your safety."

Kelsey shook her head in frustration as she listened. "This is what I deal with every day. Only my father could treat a trip to the Hamptons like I'm embedding myself in a war zone."

"Do you need to call him back?" May asked. Her mother could be overbearing, but William Ellis made Coral Hanover look like an absentee parent.

Kelsey returned her phone to her pocket. "I'll do it once we're settled in."

While Kelsey was unpacking her bag, May was prone on the floor, pulling one leg into a much-needed hamstring stretch after all the time in the car, while Lauren was splayed out on the bed, her phone held over her face. "Okay," Lauren said, "our final two words both start with *L*. One is six letters and one is seven." They were on the tail end of the bee, down to the cheat sheet, which listed the number of words beginning with each letter and the length of each word.

"Wait, I think I know it," Kelsey said, sliding a dresser drawer shut. "Two words we always miss. A single and a plural."

May sat upright. "Oh, oh, I know. Three syllables. The white part of your fingernail. We've looked it up before." She began tapping at her own screen, trying various letter combinations.

"Yes, we know this," Lauren said. "*Luluna. Lunaca*? Wait . . . try *lunula*!"

"And the plural," Kelsey added.

May smiled as her phone app accepted first one word and then the other. She held up her phone in triumph. "Our first Queen Bee in the same room!"

"Oh my god," Kelsey said, "I love us so much together. Okay, I'm unpacked and ready to rumble. Let's go into the village and get the lay of the land?"

May had been hoping to take advantage of the view and the pool while it was still sunny, but waited for Lauren to weigh in.

"Sounds like a plan," Lauren said, heading toward the kitchen. "Let's do it."

The thought of traipsing around town with crowds of vacationers packed into tiny stores and cramped restaurants made May's brain itch, but she was clearly outvoted.

Kelsey pulled her tank top away from her chest and gave it a quick sniff. "I'm gross from the trip though. I need to make myself look more like an actual person."

"I'll order the Uber," May offered. "How long do you need?"

"Let's just drive," Kelsey said. "We might want to tool around. Dinner in Sag Harbor maybe? Or Montauk could be more fun."

"It's just . . . we've already been drinking," May said.

"I've had like two sips of prosecco," Kelsey said. "And after boozing it up through the bad times, my threshold is still through the roof. I can drive, but it's going to have to be your car if that's okay? Mine's a two-seater. Meet in the kitchen in fifteen all dolled up? That'll give me time to call Dad, too." She unclipped the bib of her overalls and stripped off her tank top on her way to the bathroom. The sound of a running shower followed through the open door.

As May closed the bedroom door behind her, she wondered if she was supposed to change, too. She went upstairs and slipped on her black shirt-dress. She was, in her opinion, as put together as she could be.

From the backseat of Josh's car, May found herself studying Kelsey in the rearview mirror. May didn't believe in false self-deprecation. She knew she was not the least bit unattractive. She had almond-shaped eyes, a heart-shaped face, and flawless skin she'd inherited from her mother that probably wouldn't see any wrinkles of note for another decade. Her nose was flatter and wider than she wished, but she was—by any reasonable standard—a nice-looking human.

But Kelsey Ellis? She was in an entirely different category. A lot of it came naturally—full lips, long legs, flat abs, a cute nose sprinkled with just the right number of freckles to make it even cuter.

But when she actually made an effort? Kelsey Ellis was the kind of pretty that made May wonder how it must feel to experience the world while looking like that. It helped that she had long blond hair and blue eyes, which, all things being equal in May's experience, tended to correlate highly with subjective measures of attractiveness.

But Kelsey was beyond that. She had a look that meant they never paid for drinks at their usual haunts in Boston. One time in New York, a guy had even left the hotel bar to go to the front desk and pay for their room, even though Kelsey had made it blatantly clear to him that he would not be going upstairs with them.

Kelsey was beautiful in a way that made men literally stupid.

But to May's surprise, Kelsey's current version of "dolled up" was nothing like it used to be. She had chalked up Kelsey's appearance on their various Zoom calls to the fact that she, like May and everyone else May knew, gave zero fucks what they looked like on a girlfriend Zoom party. But she could see now that the expensive highlights were gone, leaving Kelsey's hair more of a light brown than any shade of blond. And instead of the perfect tumbles of messy curls that used to fall to the middle of her back, her hair was pulled into a loose ponytail at the nape of her neck, topped with a cream-colored fedora. The only makeup she appeared to have on was a sheer rosy lip gloss. Most of her face was hidden behind aviator sunglasses that were even bigger than Lauren's retro frames.

May wasn't sure she would have even recognized Kelsey if she happened to pass her on the street. And then she realized that was exactly the point. Beautiful women turn heads, which means they get attention, which means they could be identified as the woman who may or may not have been involved in an estranged husband's unsolved murder.

What had brought May, Lauren, and Kelsey together again was the shared anguish of becoming notorious. But not all notoriety is the same. As hard as May and Lauren had been tumbled around in the media cycle, the scrutiny to which Kelsey was exposed after Luke was killed dwarfed their experiences many times over. Kelsey wasn't accused by strangers of being "problematic" or "toxic." She was accused of hiring someone to murder her husband.

As they walked down Newtown Lane through the main shopping district in East Hampton, May noticed that when they passed other pedestrians, Kelsey would turn her face away or pause to look into the window of a store she wasn't actually interested in. She kept her sunglasses on, even when they stepped inside a shop to browse around. She checked her hat in the reflection of parked cars, keeping the brim of the fedora tipped low.

Kelsey was still beautiful. She just lived her life in disguise.

6

Lauren flipped the passenger-seat sun visor closed and tucked her bright red lipstick into the bucket-shaped bag on her lap. "Wow, that man is really taking his sweet time, isn't he?"

The man in question was the driver of the house-sized black pickup that was currently occupying the primo Sag Harbor parking spot that would soon belong to them. May had been certain from previous trips to the Hamptons that they'd need to park on a remote side street and then schlep themselves back to the historic American Hotel, where Kelsey had decided they absolutely *had* to go for a cocktail. The hotel itself was small, but the restaurant, she insisted, was a "veritable institution." Lauren and May deferred because, one, Kelsey cared about where-to-eat-and-drink far more than they did; and two, she had really good and very specific taste, forsaking any place that was the least bit hipster for what Kelsey liked to call "a classic old-man bar."

Despite the hotel's location on one of the busiest blocks of Sag Harbor, Kelsey insisted that she had "good parking karma" and stuck it out in the long line of cars creeping down Main Street through the village. Apparently she had been right because just as they were approaching the American Hotel, Kelsey squealed in delight at the sight of a bearded man opening the driver's side of his pickup. They'd been hovering for a full two minutes as the man fiddled with his cell phone, reverse lights promising an imminent departure that had yet to happen. The clicking sound of the turn signal seemed to get louder with each annoyed car that maneuvered around them and the lane they were now blocking.

"Why don't you guys go in and get a table?" Kelsey offered. "I'll wait for this dude to work his way through his Tinder matches. Maybe I'll even find a way to say hi. He's a slowpoke, but he's pretty cute, right?"

May was about to open the back door when Lauren said they'd of course all stay together and that this wasn't the weekend for Kelsey to be talking to strange men.

"Finally," Lauren said as the truck began inching its way out of the space, the bed of the pickup coming so close to Josh's Subaru that Kelsey shifted the car into reverse.

As the truck's reverse lights turned off, May spotted a small white sedan approaching them in the opposite lane. "No, no, no, no," she cried from the backseat as the driver of the white car hit the left turn signal. "Don't you dare take our spot! Nooooo!"

As the pickup pulled away, Kelsey gave the Subaru horn a little *beep-beep* to underscore their claim to the spot. But reversing to make room for the enormous truck to depart had left enough space for the white sedan to make its move.

"Oh, bitch, no." Lauren reached for the car horn as she realized what was happening.

Kelsey blocked Lauren's hand as the white sedan swept cleanly into the vacant spot. Florida plates. A rental car. "Of course. Tourists."

"*We're* tourists," Lauren said, starting to roll down her window. "But they're entitled asshole tourists."

Kelsey held her right hand to the side of her face, shielding herself from the scene she obviously expected Lauren to make as she inched the car forward. The woman who stepped from the passenger seat of the rental appeared to be looking directly at them, smiling.

"Oh my god," May said, "did you see that look she gave us? She was so proud of what they did."

"You should have at least let me blast them with the horn," Lauren said. "They would have backed off."

"Look at this cute little town. I don't think people honk around here."

"Um, says the woman who literally honked at them twice."

"That's different. A little *beep-beep* isn't a honk."

"Seriously," May said, "did you guys see her actually *smirk* at us? What a total asshole."

"You guys, stop," Kelsey said, her hands gripping the steering wheel tightly. "I don't want people staring at us because we're yelling at people out of car windows."

"I wasn't sure," Lauren said, "but you're right. That girl totally knew that they were in the wrong."

"So they're awful, because people are awful," Kelsey said. "But it's just a stupid parking spot. And my good parking luck is going to come through again, I can feel it. Look, right around the corner. That convertible's pulling out. I told you."

With a few tries, Kelsey was able to squeeze Josh's car into place with only a few inches to spare. May was about to open the back door when she spotted the couple from the rental turning the corner down the block. Both tall, white, and blond, but her hair was more of a strawberry blond. His arm was around her shoulders, and hers around his waist—two happy little lovebirds.

"Oh my god," May said. "And there she is again."

Kelsey glanced in the rearview for a glimpse and then moved her bag from the console to her lap, dropping the car keys inside. "Please, you guys. Just let it go."

Lauren threw her arm around Kelsey's shoulders when she joined them at the curb after the spot-thieving couple had passed by. "Who would have ever predicted that Little Miss Kelsey Ellis, of all people, would keep us on good behavior?"

"What can I say? I've learned the art of being Zen. Besides, let's save our bad behavior for the fun stuff."

When they were offered a table on the restaurant's coveted front patio, May stepped toward the chair with its back to the sidewalk, leaving the prime people-watching seats to Lauren and Kelsey.

"Oh, do you mind if I sit there?" Kelsey asked. "My eyes are so sensitive to the sun." The sun was already coming down the horizon to the west, and Kelsey's hat and sunglasses were still firmly in place.

"Of course I don't mind," May said.

As close as May believed the three of them had become in the past year, she realized she had never allowed herself to feel truly sorry for Kelsey before. That last dinner in Boston, it would have been unthinkable. Her life had seemed so enviably privileged and perfect.

She reached over and gave Kelsey's hand a quick squeeze. "Thank you again for organizing this trip."

Kelsey placed a second hand over May's and held it for a long moment.

"Anything for my girls."

7

The cocktail they planned to have at the American Hotel had been followed by a bottle of champagne, and now they were on another round of drinks. Two hours of alcohol, and the only thing they had eaten were raw oysters and clams.

"You guys, can I admit something?" May asked.

"Ooh, yes, I love it," Lauren said. "What is it? You're having a torrid affair with the hottest faculty member? A final fling before the wedding? We want all your secrets."

"First of all, *hot law professor* is an oxymoron. And no, nothing nearly that exciting. I just have to confess that every time I look up and see that dumb rental car, it's like it's gloating at us. I wish there was an open sunroof or something. I'd dump all these oyster shells in there."

"Oh, you're not alone," Lauren said. "I don't know why I got so mad, but I really did almost lose it on them. Thank the baby Jesus you talked us down, Kelsey. The last thing we need is someone who looks like me yelling at some cute little white couple. My ass could land in a Long Island jail."

"I know exactly why it made you so mad," May said, leaning forward as a customer at the next table slid behind her to leave. "Because they *knew* we were waiting. And they didn't care. Because something is broken in people now. Rules don't matter. Basic decency doesn't matter. And it's not just that they did it. They were *proud* of it. They loved getting away with it. It's like there's no such thing as shame anymore. So it's not just about a parking spot. It's the whole fucking society." She realized that Kelsey and Lauren were sharing an amused look. "What? I'm serious. People are objectively horrible now."

Kelsey laughed first, but Lauren laughed louder. "And you're so drunk now," Lauren said.

"It's not funny. You're the one who said you didn't understand why it got you so mad. And I just explained it. And I'm totally right. Like, the-world-needs-to-pay-attention level of right."

"Oh, we didn't say you weren't right," Lauren said, shaking two big drops of Tabasco sauce onto an oyster. "It's still extremely entertaining though."

"They have to come back to their car eventually. I'm tempted to say something when they do." She leaned forward again, this time for the busser who was clearing the recently vacated neighboring table.

"Maybe you should write down everything you want to say to them instead," Kelsey suggested. "It might help to get it off your chest. At least that's what my therapist says. Or also, maybe it would just be really funny to have a pissed-off cocktail-napkin rant from Drunk Riled-Up May as a vacation memento."

"Yes, that sounds a hundred percent accurate," Lauren said, pulling a pen from her purse and resting it on a bar napkin. "I'm totally here for it."

With both sets of their eyes on her, May figured she may as well do as instructed and began writing as quickly as she could.

Hi. We were waiting patiently for this parking spot. We did not honk at or rush the person who was leaving, because we are not mean and rude. You saw us waiting yet took the spot anyway. That was extremely unkind, especially at a time when people have been through a lot and need a little more kindness. I hope in the future you will choose to be more considerate.

The napkin was almost full, so she wrote "over" at the bottom before turning to the back for more room.

Also, we could have recorded you and posted the video, but decided to be kind instead.

Her friends barely suppressed their amusement as they read the note shoulder-to-shoulder in silence.

"Don't you think that last part would scare them?" May said. "Make them realize how obnoxious they were and how we could have posted their faces on the internet?"

"I think they would make some kind of Boomer joke and throw it in the garbage," Lauren said.

"Yeah, that tracks," May said. "But down on the sidewalk because they're the types that don't give a flying fuck."

While a group of women paused next to the hotel porch for a group selfie, Lauren began scrawling on a new napkin. She finished quickly. "Now that's how you do payback."

He's cheating.
He always does.

May turned and stared at Lauren, her mouth open in a shocked smile. "Oh my god, you just thought of that?"

Lauren shrugged. "What can I say? That's just where my brain went. It doesn't make me a bad person."

"No, but it might make you a sociopath," May said.

Kelsey laughed so hard that May thought she might spit her Manhattan from her nose. "A hilarious sociopath," Kelsey added, once she caught her breath.

"Can you even imagine how delicious it would be if they came back to their car and found that?" May said. As she giddily imagined the scene, she realized that the drinks were getting to her. "Like, how could he even begin to explain it away? Some stranger just made that up and left it on a random rental car?"

"Well, they certainly wouldn't be strolling all around, hands all over each other like a couple of newlyweds," Lauren said.

May thought she heard a twinge of jealousy in Lauren's voice. To May's knowledge, Lauren's only long-term relationship had been with the man who had landed her in the public-scandal hopper: Thomas Welliver, the Dallas oilman who co-owned Wildwood with his wife.

When Lauren moved to California to pursue her dream of composing film scores, May assumed whatever had been going on between her and Welliver had ended. In the years that passed, May would occasionally ask if Lauren was seeing anyone, and the answer was always no. Too focused on her career, she said. Too hard to find a man who would love her for the right reasons. Too independent to live her life around another person at this point. Too accustomed to living alone. In short, not interested.

It was only after Welliver's involvement in Lauren's appointment to the Houston Symphony became public that it was apparent the connection between the two of them extended well beyond that final camp summer. May had no idea what if any role Welliver played in Lauren's life today, but she suspected that Lauren did not know the feeling of strolling down the street, happy and carefree, hand in hand with someone she loved.

Kelsey pulled her phone from her purse and snapped a photo of the two notes. "And I'm keeping these," she said, carefully slipping the flattened napkins into the side pocket of her bag. "Maybe I'll even make a little scrapbook or something."

"I have to admit," May said, "that was pretty therapeutic. My desire to key their car has passed."

"Excellent," Lauren said. "So no one's getting arrested today. Now what should we do?" She rubbed her palms together in anticipation.

"Find a place with more booze," Kelsey said. "And food. We really need to eat some food." She reached into her bag to apply a fresh coat of lip gloss.

"There's an independent bookstore I wanted to check out," May said. "And a donut shop that's supposed to be really good." She began looking up locations on her phone.

"Yes to books," Kelsey said, "and a triple yes to donuts."

"Sounds like a plan," Lauren said. "And May and I already talked about it. We are getting this bill."

"No, that's crazy. I'm the one who picked the place," Kelsey said.

"Which is fabulous, by the way," Lauren said, signaling to the passing waitress. "And we can go Dutch for dinner."

"Fine, you win."

May placed her phone in the middle of the table to share the map on her screen as she and Lauren handed their credit cards to the server. "Oh, this is perfect. The bookstore is at the end of this street by the water, and then the donut place is at the corner, right by our car."

"I have to pee so bad," Kelsey said, lowering her voice. "You guys go ahead to the bookstore and I'll catch up to you."

They were passing a bichon frise sharing steak tartare with his owner outside a French bistro when May asked Lauren if she thought they should get an Uber after all the drinks they'd had.

"Kelsey's responsible," Lauren said. "She would tell us if she wasn't okay to drive. And she really wasn't kidding about having a Viking's liver. That girl could drink a linebacker under the table."

May nodded, but could not silence the voice in her head telling her that something was going to go wrong.

"Hey, it's your call," Lauren said, "and if you're worried about being the enforcer, I can tell her it was my decision. Just say the word."

If they took an Uber back to East Hampton, she'd have to ask Kelsey to drive her back to pick up Josh's car in the morning or pay for another ride to come to Sag Harbor alone. "No, it's okay. I guess I'm still adjusting to not being at the prosecutor's office anymore."

She was still adjusting to everything.

8

In the origin story of their friendship, Kelsey was always the prettier, richer, bolder, brasher, more fabulous one. When they first stepped onto the deck at Showfish, May felt herself shrink, immediately feeling Plain Jane in her simple black shirt-dress and sandals compared to the Hamptons Chic that was on full display. But Kelsey seemed immediately at home, chatting up the hostess and scoring them an A-list table by the deck's edge, overlooking the marina.

Even in their primo spot, the Jimmy Buffett song that was playing over the speakers as they finished dinner was barely audible beneath the sounds of overly excited, alcohol-fueled summer voices. May had wanted to go to Rowdy Hall in East Hampton, both because it was much chiller than its name would suggest and because it was relatively close to the rental house. Lauren was the one who decided they should find a place near the water, and Kelsey decided she had a craving for lobster, so they had made the trip all the way to Montauk on the east end of the South Fork. At least Lauren had been right about Kelsey's driving skills. Not a single swerve detected.

Kelsey had just ordered a round of espresso martinis for dessert when her phone buzzed on the table.

She snuck a quick peek. "It's Nate," she said. "Bummer. He didn't get the commercial he was hoping to shoot next week." Nate was still trying to make a go of it as an actor in New York City, but May's impression was that he was nowhere close to becoming a success. If she had to guess, Kelsey was probably finding a way to supplement his income. "But that means he's free to come out on Monday. Speak now, Lauren, or forever hold your peace."

Lauren smiled and shook her head. "I already told you. I'm good. I kind of like how he acts like a little brother around me, so sweet and respectful. My brothers still treat me like I'm in middle school."

May had been expecting Lauren and Kelsey to try to convince her to stay longer. She had even packed extra underwear just in case she changed her mind. Now that wouldn't be an option with another person taking over her room at the house—especially when that person was Nate.

Kelsey made a show of widening her eyes as she scrolled through the message. "He said he's going to take the early train, so maybe he'll get a chance to see you before you head home, May. Very . . . interesting."

Lauren bumped one knee against May's, smirking. "Maybe he's coming to sweep you off your feet," she said. "One last chance for a ride on some strange before you're locked down for life."

"Gross," Kelsey said. "You did not just call my brother a piece of strange."

"Technically a stepbrother," Lauren said. "Come on, you've never noticed that Nate is fine?"

"I'm going to jump off this deck into the ocean if you don't stop talking about him like that," Kelsey said. "Seriously, what is wrong with you?"

"So apparently incest jokes are a step too far, even for you. Duly noted. I'll confess though, I'm surprised, May, that you didn't get back with Nate after he moved to New York. I really did think the two of you might go the distance."

"Really?" May asked. "A lawyer and an actor?"

"You weren't a lawyer when you first dated. You were a brilliant pianist with a big, bright, bookish brain. And Nate loved the theater but wanted to be a successful real estate developer like his dad."

"Stepdad, as my father has made it all too clear," Kelsey corrected, her voice suddenly sharp. May knew how wrecked Kelsey was after her father's divorce from Nate's mother broke apart the only family she'd really known after her own mother died, but she always seemed reluctant to talk about the details of the split. Yet the children, through their own commitment, remained siblings for all practical purposes.

"Plus you had little Miss Kelsey over here playing matchmaker," Lauren said. "She told me so many times how perfect it would be if you ended up being her sister-in-law. You and Nate just seemed to make a lot of sense. And did I mention that the man is fine AF?"

May couldn't argue with that last part. Nate was and apparently always would be the best-looking guy she had ever dated. And it wasn't only his looks that were a draw. He was smart and funny and confident. Josh was also all those things, but Josh was a nerd like May. Nate was most definitely not a nerd. He was a cool guy. He had what the kids these days called *rizz*. Serious charisma. The way Kelsey could make men stupid? Nate had that effect on women—at least in May's experience.

"In theory," she said, "but it obviously wasn't meant to be. And it's definitely not going to happen now. Josh is the one for me. From the first day I met him, we just . . . clicked." Her own words surprised her as they came tumbling out. It had been so much bumpier and complicated than that.

"Vomit," Kelsey said, a sly smile creeping across her face.

"Aw, that's so sweet," Lauren said, placing a gentle hand on May's forearm. "But is it okay for us to hate you a little bit for that?"

"Only a little," May said.

The truth was that it took the lockdown—and multiple lectures from May's mother—for May to realize she'd be crazy to risk losing a guy as nice as Josh, all because she still wasn't sure she was ready for such a serious commitment. Josh was solid. He had a good job. He was kind and reliable and loyal. And he adored her. She finally said yes, not just to Josh's proposal, but to a Fordham law professor's invitation to apply for a tenure-track faculty position. Apparently they were looking to expand their pool of candidates beyond the usual path that lawyers followed into academia. She went from having a stressful, exciting job and relatively messy relationships to having the rest of her life suddenly all planned at once.

She had no idea why she had poured it on so thick about being certain about Josh from day one. Anything for Lauren to stop talking about how Nate had seemed to be a perfect match for her. Maybe he was and maybe he wasn't, but she hated even thinking about the way she had been with him.

Kelsey's eyes widened as the waitress arrived with a tray containing three gigantic martini glasses filled so high that it took an expert hand to place them on the table without spilling. Kelsey held her phone high above the round of drinks to get a photo.

May leaned forward to take an initial sip before daring to lift the glass. She knew the dangerous mix of sweetened caffeine and alcohol would mean rolling into a new level of intoxication, but she didn't want to be the one to kill the party, and Kelsey had already promised before they ordered a bottle of wine with dinner that they'd take an Uber home.

"Kelsey, I hope you don't mind, but can you please not tag me in any posts? I don't need my 1Ls finding pictures of me getting hammered in Montauk with my besties."

"As if you need to ask me—of all people—to keep a photo private," Kelsey said.

May found herself straining to hear Kelsey over the sound of their fellow diners. Were they actually getting louder as the night progressed, or had May reached her limit for being out in public?

"I hardly even remember to take pictures anymore," May said, forcing herself to focus on their conversation rather than drawing inward the way she tended to do at the end of a busy day. "Once I stepped back from social media, I fell out of the habit. Like, what do you even do with a photo if you're never going to share it?"

Kelsey tucked her phone into her bag. "I still like to have them for my own personal memories. And I meant it about making some kind of scrapbook for all of us—and just us, I promise."

"I told Josh I wanted to ask all of our friends not to take pictures at the wedding—or at least not to tag us in their posts—but he said he thought it would be rude."

Lauren's vicious side-eye made her exasperation clear. "Maybe Josh should let you decide for yourself what you can and want to expect from the friends you choose to share your wedding day with." Lauren had only met Josh twice, so May didn't think her distaste for him was personal. Lauren simply didn't believe in shaping her life around a man's expectations. She had never said directly that she disapproved of May's decision to get married, but she didn't hold her tongue when she thought May was compromising too much of herself in order to please Josh—or anyone else for that matter.

"I told him I thought he was being pretty judgy for shutting me down so quickly, but he said he really didn't think I even needed to worry anymore. Everything has blown over by now. The guy from the subway didn't get charged for assault, and I didn't get charged for filing a false report." May knew the man's name, of course—Darren Foster—but rarely used it. She wished it were possible, in fact, never to think about him. If she could undergo a lobotomy to forget that day on the subway platform in its entirety, she'd happily sign the waiver forms. "Now I'm just some boring law professor no one needs to talk about anymore, as long as I don't write any more viral op-eds."

"Wish I could say the same thing," Kelsey muttered.

May cringed inwardly when she realized how self-pitying she had sounded. She had been able to move on from her "incident," while Kelsey's situation would never change as long as Luke's murder remained unsolved. She was wondering how she might apologize when she saw Kelsey searching for the waitress again, her martini nearly gone. This time, she ordered a cosmopolitan. Lauren and May shook their heads, gesturing toward their relatively full glasses. "Don't listen to them," Kelsey told the waitress. "Three cosmos. They're getting drunk and they love it. And no, we're not driving."

The waitress stared at May and Lauren, expecting an objection, then left when they did not argue.

Kelsey had always been a bigger partier than May. Even on their Zooms, May had noticed that Kelsey would be making a second drink—a cocktail, not wine—while she and Lauren were still working on their first glass of sauvignon blanc. But what she was doing tonight felt more like self-medication than recreational drinking. May was beginning to wonder if Kelsey was forcing herself to seem fun and carefree, just for their sakes.

When the drinks arrived, Kelsey told them that they at least had to have one sip with her. When they did have an obligatory taste, Kelsey let out a satisfied sigh. "Bless, that tastes exactly like the early aughts," she said. "And sorry, Lauren, it totally brings back the memory of that night when we thought you just might murder us. You were so pissed. It was honestly terrifying."

Lauren looked confused for a moment and then placed her face in her hands, laughing. "Oh lord, it was cosmos that night, wasn't it? Other kids, I'd catch with Bud Light or shots of Jägermeister. No, fifteen-year-old Kelsey Ellis has to host a cocktail party like she's Carrie Fucking Bradshaw. I was surprised you didn't have Jimmy Choo stilettos and a Prada handbag for the occasion."

May hadn't caught the reference until Lauren connected the dots. It was the first weekend at camp, the summer after ninth grade. Kelsey had managed to smuggle in a handle of vodka and all the fixings for lemon drops and cosmos, complete with a cocktail shaker. There were red Solo cups in lieu of stemmed glassware, but it all felt terribly sophisticated nonetheless. Even though Kelsey had sworn all the girls to secrecy and they were making a point not to be loud, Lauren had managed to bust them anyway. After threatening to call their parents and send them home for the summer, she eventually settled for marching them out to the lake and watching them pour all the alcohol into the water.

"You still owe me a bottle of Grey Goose," Kelsey said wryly.

"How did you even know to barge into our cabin like that?" May asked. "After all these years, just go ahead and tell us. It had to have been Marnie, wasn't it?"

The mention of her name—Marnie Mann—felt like a record-scratch moment. Lauren put her drink down, her smile fading. Kelsey coughed and looked down at the table awkwardly.

Their conversations over the past year never touched on Marnie. They almost always focused on the present. Their jobs. May's wedding plans. Kelsey's father's prostate cancer treatment and the trauma it had triggered from her mother's early death from ovarian cancer. Lauren's bathroom remodel. Even just the Spelling Bee. That was the Canceled Crew group thread's entire purpose—a form of steady, daily companionship, proving that life does move on.

Now that they were strolling down memory lane, May had somehow managed to pivot from Kelsey's lighthearted reference to getting busted for drinking, to the name of the girl whose death had changed everything that final summer at Wildwood.

"I'm sorry." The words were out of May's mouth before she even registered them. Josh had told her once that he was tempted to keep a tally of how many times she apologized on a daily basis. "I shouldn't have mentioned her. I didn't mean to stir up bad memories."

Lauren took a small sip of her pink cocktail, a smile returning to her face. "It's fine, May. To be honest, I really don't remember how I knew about your fancy little cocktail cabin party. It was such a long time ago."

May couldn't tell whether Lauren was telling the truth, and Kelsey quickly changed the subject. "Man, I'm going to miss this," she said, her eyes closing contentedly as she took another sip of her cosmo.

"Aw, it's only the first day of the trip," May said.

"No, I mean booze. Being buzzed is quite delightful."

"Wait, what?" May said, covering her mouth with one hand. There was only one reason she could imagine Kelsey giving up drinking.

"Are you seriously thinking about doing it?" Lauren asked, leaning forward at the table. "When? I can't believe you haven't told us until now."

"I mean, I'm thirty-seven years old. I thought Luke and I would be raising children together, and that obviously didn't happen. I've been waiting to see if the man I eventually end up with will be on board, but the fact is, I may have to do this on my own. I can't keep living in limbo."

May had so many regrets about falling out of touch with Kelsey, but the biggest one of all was that she was not around to support Kelsey when she had to make what she still described as the most difficult decision of her life. At her doctor's suggestion, she decided to get tested for a mutation in the *BRCA1* gene that greatly increases a woman's chances of both breast cancer and the ovarian cancer that killed Kelsey's mother. The test came back positive, and Kelsey faced a grueling choice: Do nothing and live with the knowledge that a fatal diagnosis could come at any moment, or do something to save her life, which meant a prophylactic double mastectomy and the removal of her ovaries. She and Luke hadn't even celebrated their first anniversary yet. Kelsey chose the surgeries, but, before the procedures, had her eggs harvested and fertilized, freezing the embryos to keep all options open for the future. And May hadn't been around to help her through any of it. She was never going to make that mistake again.

"So when is this all happening?" May asked. "I can come up to Boston to be with you."

"Oh, there's no concrete date yet, and I'll probably change my mind again tomorrow. And then again next week and the week after that. I keep thinking, you know, once the police finally find out what really happened to Luke, my life could be normal again—or sort of normal. I could get married and have a partner for this parenting thing. It's hard enough to find someone willing to date me once they do a Google search, but I'm going to be a single mother on top of it? Talk about a deal-breaker, ladies."

Part of May was tempted to warn Kelsey that it was unlikely the police would ever locate Luke's killer. The fact that Luke's glove box was found open had led to speculation that the money bag from his cash drop had been stashed there and grabbed after the shooting. There was a brief glimmer of hope for an arrest when the police linked a fingerprint on the car door handle to an ex-convict with a robbery conviction, but it turned out he worked as a valet at a restaurant Luke had gone to two weeks before he was killed. The case had been cold for five years. But May couldn't offer her professional opinion to Kelsey without admitting that she'd been following the facts of her husband's case the whole time May had been out of touch with her.

"You don't need a husband to be happy," May said.

"Says the bride-to-be planning her wedding to the guy she just clicked with the first time she met him," Kelsey said with a sad smile. "Anyway, don't listen to me. I was babbling like a messy Blanche DuBois and ruining all the fun."

"You never have to apologize for talking about your life to us," Lauren said.

"That's a really important decision," May said. "Of course we want you to tell us."

"Well, except it's not a decision. Not yet. One moment, it feels like I should just go ahead and pull the trigger. Fifteen minutes later, it feels completely impossible." Kelsey abruptly veered into party mode again, brightening up instantaneously. "Looks like they're closing down here. Let's forget all this serious stuff and go back to the house, okay?" She began to fumble with her phone, but May already had the address loaded into the Uber app.

She signaled for the bill, but when the waitress appeared with it, she dropped it intentionally in front of Kelsey, who already had a card in the palm of her hand. Even wasted off her ass, Kelsey was still on top of it, just like always.

9

Kelsey stumbled in the restaurant's gravel parking lot but caught herself as she was about to tumble onto the hood of the Toyota Camry that was their ride. She kept her balance with one hand on the car and then reached to open the front passenger door. May signaled to the back door, volunteering to sit in the middle.

"I can sit up front with him," Kelsey said, smiling at the driver. May knew from her app that the guy's name was Jackson. "You don't mind, right?"

"It's all good," Jackson said, moving a Gatorade bottle and a stack of papers from the passenger seat to a pocket in his car door.

May snapped on her seat belt in the backseat and instructed Kelsey to do the same up front.

"Okay, Mrs. Nelson," Kelsey said, the esses slurring slightly in the word *Missus*. "You're really thinking about changing your last name?"

"I don't know. Maybe. It's actually kind of dumb my mom and I are still Hanovers, but it's my name, right?" That night in Bloomington, after May's mother had told her and Kelsey so matter-of-factly that May's father never wanted May to be born, she asked her mother why she had given May her father's last name and had taken it as well. She replied without hesitation. *I didn't want my child to be seen as foreign, and I thought I deserved as much too.*

"Luke wanted me to change my name," Kelsey said, "and I wouldn't even consider it. Maybe that was the beginning of the end."

May looked to Lauren to see if she seemed concerned about the most recent downswing in Kelsey's mood, but she was typing a message on her phone, her seat belt already secured. May spotted the name at the top of the screen. *Thomas.* So there was still something between her and Thomas Welliver.

They were halfway home when an Ed Sheeran song came on, and Kelsey turned up the radio without asking the driver. She waved her hands near her head and began to bounce in her seat. *Ooh, I love it when you do it like that . . .*

May could picture her Uber rating falling with every passing moment, but when she caught sight of the driver's face in the rearview mirror, he was smiling.

At the house, Jackson the driver hopped out quickly after pulling into the driveway, rushing to get Kelsey's door. May noticed that he'd cut the engine. May couldn't find the buckle to unlatch her seat belt. By the time she managed to get out of the car, Jackson already had his arm around Kelsey's waist and was leading her to the house.

"Door-to-door delivery," Kelsey said. "Five stars for this man!"

"We've got her from here," May said, catching up to them as Kelsey fumbled to get the house key into the lock.

"Why don't you come inside," Kelsey said. "It's too nice out to be driving drunk people around all night. We're really fun." Just as Kelsey had predicted, any thoughts about becoming a single mom appeared to have floated away for the moment.

"Yeah, a real party," Lauren said sternly, "which no one else will be joining tonight. But, yes, thank you very much for the ride and the assistance. Above and beyond the call of duty."

Jackson hurried back to his Camry and disappeared into the night.

"Party poopers," Kelsey said once the door was closed behind them. May reached for Kelsey's arm to steady her, but Kelsey's balance was suddenly solid. Sobered up, just like that. Her superpower was still intact.

"I think we should all slam some water and aspirin before we hit the hay," May said.

"The only thing I'm hitting is the deck!" Kelsey said. "One day of our trip down and we haven't even taken advantage of being right on the water. I brought stuff for s'mores and there's one of those fancy smokeless-fire stoves on the back deck." Kelsey had already pulled three wineglasses from a cabinet and was positioning a wine opener over a bottle of red. "Come on, May, you know you're going to have FOMO tomorrow if you go upstairs already, and you hate FOMO."

Lauren had kicked off her wedge sandals and was fiddling with a Bluetooth speaker on the kitchen island. Obviously May's only choices were to stay awake or to leave the two of them to continue the night without her. *FOMO* wasn't a word yet when they first knew each other, but even back then, everyone knew that May was the one who hated to be left out, and she had joked many times in the Crew thread about nights when she agreed to do things she didn't even want to do just in case she missed out on something great.

"Success," Lauren declared, as the speaker began to play Prince's cover of a Joni Mitchell song. May had been the one to introduce Lauren to it, knowing that she loved Prince. May could still remember how pleased she felt with herself, impressing Lauren of all people with a piece of music.

"Come on, May," Kelsey pleaded. "We've only got you for the weekend. You can recuperate when you're back home with boring Josh." She immediately covered her mouth with one hand. "Oh my god, did I just say that out loud?"

"You think Josh is boring? You haven't even met him."

Kelsey looked to Lauren, and May did the same. Her lips were pressed together, eyes wide.

"You told her Josh is boring?"

Lauren winced and held up her thumb and index finger an inch apart, and then Kelsey burst out laughing.

Josh. Sweet, patient Josh. Josh, who had sent her multiple texts asking how things were going.

Hope you guys are having fun!

How's the house?

How was dinner?

Gomez says hi, Momma. The accompanying photo was super cute.

Okay, you guys must be having a blast. Should I be jealous?

Sorry to text bomb you all day. Heading to bed now. Love you!

She had texted him good night from the Uber, but they normally made a point to call each other before they went to sleep when they were apart. It seemed awkward, though, to leave Kelsey and Lauren waiting for her while she called her fiancé when she only had a couple days with them. And if she called Josh, she might feel obligated to call her mother, too, who had also texted her multiple times to ask how she was "handling" the trip so far. Her mother had always treated her like a child, but she was even more protective since May had tried to explain the stress that had led to the whole subway incident.

"You're right. Sleep is for the weak," she said. Kelsey and Lauren shared a high-five to celebrate their win. "But one condition: House rules from the Arianna note say to use the plastic wineglasses on the deck."

Kelsey reached for May and gave her a big hug. "I forgot how much I love you."

As they huddled around the fire, May forced herself to eat a sticky, gooey marshmallow smeared on a graham cracker with chocolate, hoping that it might sop up some of the alcohol coursing through her body.

The cushion on her chaise longue, cool from the night air, felt good against her bare legs. She was resting her eyes, listening to the sound of the water beneath what Kelsey had dubbed her "bangers" playlist streaming across the speaker they had brought outside.

The water. Drinking. Laughing. Music. Her mind felt somewhere else. Not East Hampton. Not the present. *Marnie. Has anyone seen Marnie?*

The volume of the music increased. She opened her eyes and tried to stand up, or at least she thought she did.

The song from the Uber was back, Kelsey yelling the words into the sky. *And when they say the party's over, then we'll bring it right back.*

At Wildwood, Kelsey had been an average flutist at best, but she had always been a strong singer, just a few notes shy of a four-octave range. And apparently she could still crush a pop song.

The last thing May remembered was seeing her two friends dancing together without her in the firelight, the bay waves rippling behind them.

She woke on the deck to silence, a beach towel she didn't recognize draped over her body. The lights in the house were on, but the speaker was gone. So were the wineglasses and bottles. Her legs felt stiff as she raised herself from the low chaise longue. She breathed a sigh of relief as the sliding glass door opened.

On the kitchen island, next to the speaker and Kelsey's keys, she found a large glass of water beside a container of Advil. She recognized Lauren's handwriting on the accompanying Post-it. *Take 2 and all the water. We could NOT get you to come inside.* She did as instructed and gulped down the water without stopping for breath, hoping it would prevent her from being a wreck tomorrow, and then refilled the glass to take to her bedroom. After checking all the locks on the doors, she turned off the kitchen lights, leaving the house in darkness. As she passed Kelsey's bedroom on the way to the staircase, she thought she heard a voice. No light came from the crack beneath the closed door. She craned her neck and closed her eyes, trying to make out the words. Was she . . . crying?

She reached for the knob but suddenly froze. "Kelsey," she whispered. "Are you okay?"

Silence. She stood there, monitoring her own breath, waiting to see if Kelsey would come to the door or invite her in. As she reached for the knob again, she felt a surge of water in her stomach and a sickly-sweet taste rise in her throat. She managed to make it to the bathroom upstairs and shut the door before she fell to her knees in front of the toilet.

Later, as the bedroom ceiling was spinning above her and she began to pass out, she wondered if she heard a car engine.

10

May felt herself squinting in her sleep and slowly realized that she was awake, pressing her eyes closed against the blinding sunshine flooding through the window. She was used to room-darkening shades behind room-darkening curtains, with a quilted eye-mask to assure absolute blackout status. She reached to search for the mask on the nightstand, but knocked over a glass of water instead. She opened her eyes to an unfamiliar room, a weight pressing down on her head.

Right, she was in East Hampton.

She groaned and forced herself to roll over, averting her eyes from the window. Her entire body ached, the taste of Cabernet and graham crackers in her throat, as she tried to piece together the rest of last night after leaving the restaurant.

Kelsey flirting with the car driver. Using the paper grocery bags to start the fire on the back deck. Those disgusting marshmallows. Ed Sheeran. And, oh god, heaving on the cold bathroom tile, trying to hold back her own hair. The sight of that dirty bobby pin covered in dust at the back of the basin, and wondering how dirty the rest of the house must be.

She sat up and was surprised to find that she was wearing her pj's, and her phone was charging on the floor in the corner by the only free outlet. Some rituals could be completed under the most trying of circumstances. Three texts and a missed call from Josh. Two missed calls from her mother. And lots of messages on the Canceled Crew thread, beginning after midnight:

LAUREN: We left water and Advil in the kitchen. Text us so we know you're in, okay?

LAUREN: I woke up worried and went to check. May came in. Water glass is gone. Bedroom door shut. Doors locked. I'm going back to sleep!

KELSEY: Oh good. Was just going to look. Going back to bed too.

KELSEY: I'm up FYI! Have breakfast ready to cook once you sleepy-heads are up.

LAUREN: I'm awake but moving slow. The bee is hard today.

KELSEY: What? You can't do it without us when we're under the same roof.

LAUREN: Says who?

KELSEY: New rule for the Crew. Starting today.

LAUREN: Bossy.

KELSEY: Speaking of bossy, where are you, May? WAKE UP! We want the bee. And the BACON!

She was typing a response when her phone rang in her hand. It was Josh. Based on the pace of yesterday's festivities, she worried she might not have another chance to talk to him today. "Hey, there." She wondered if her voice sounded as raspy as it felt.

"You're alive," he said. "I was starting to wonder if the entire group thread was an elaborate catfish to lure you out to Long Island to your demise."

"You were not actually wondering that," she said. "That's how my brain works, not yours."

"True. But I did wonder if you were having way too much fun without me."

"Trust me, it would not have been your scene."

"A scene, huh?"

"Just . . . a lot."

"Are you okay though?" he asked. His concern was palpable. "If you want to bail, you can blame it on me. Say something came up here and you have to leave because of my schedule."

"What about your schedule would require me to leave in the middle of a vacation weekend with my friends?" She realized how icy she sounded and wondered if the comments about Boring Josh and him telling her what to do had gotten to her.

"Okay, not my schedule. Appendicitis or something."

"I'm not going to lie to my friends and, really, I don't want to leave. We're having fun. It's just a lot more activity than I've been used to." May had long ago mastered the science of online delivery orders, but upped her game that life-changing second week of March when the rumors began that the governor was going to shut down the city. Thank god Josh's apartment had that terrace. Other than the hours they would spend there for fresh air, she literally did not leave the apartment for a month after the move-in, until Josh convinced her it was safe to at least join him for a walk outside with Gomez.

She eventually started to appreciate the permission she gave herself to stay at home in a T-shirt and joggers, the first time in her life when she wasn't working to reach for some new goal. The only challenge was to make it through the day without crying. More than three years later, she was no longer worried about getting a disease she was once certain would kill her, but that didn't mean she was back to normal. "We were on the go almost all day yesterday."

"If you need to wind down, just tell them it's too much. They're your friends. You're still adjusting. I'm sure they'll understand." How many times over the past three years had Josh needed to understand? She had abandoned the first indoor party they attended after twenty minutes. Walking up the steps of the Museum of Natural History for his college roommate's wedding, she'd had a panic attack, turning around while he attended solo. Just last month, she had made them leave Balthazar even though it was her favorite restaurant and they were almost to the top of the waiting list. And, of course, no incident came close to what had happened on the subway platform.

"Actually, being out in the restaurants and everything was fine.

To be honest, I'm just a wee bit hungover." She pressed her free palm against her temple, hoping that might relieve the tension in her head.

"Ah, in that case, well done. I'm proud of you. You deserve a break."

She felt an odd sense of relief that he wasn't resentful that she was having such a good time away from him, and then immediately wondered why she had even been worried. It had been a very long time since she did something that wasn't for work and wasn't with him, it occurred to her.

They talked a few more minutes, and May started to yearn for the comfort of their routine in their own apartment. It would only be another two days. "Go have fun with your friends," Josh said.

"I don't think they'll give me any other choice."

She used one of the towels folded on top of her dresser to sop up the spilled water beneath her nightstand before leaving her room. The smell of bacon struck her halfway down the stairs.

Lauren and Kelsey were sitting at the round dining table on the pool deck, already up and dressed in beach clothes.

"Sorry I stayed in bed so late," May said as she slid open the back door.

"Hey, sleepyhead," Lauren said, rising to give her a quick hug. "You feel okay?"

Lauren had on a brightly colored kimono-style cover-up, open to reveal a sunflower-yellow one-piece. Kelsey was wearing a royal blue bikini, also with a matching cover-up. May was still in her pajamas, but her only swimming suit was a black tank-style one-piece, and her "cover-up" would be a T-shirt and shorts.

"Yeah, if okay feels like I got hit by a bus."

"We'll fix you up in no time," Kelsey said. "I've got bacon in the oven, a pitcher of bloodies, and the scrambled eggs are all set to go whenever we're ready."

"Oof. Bloodies already?"

"Sorry, but it's the only cure for what you've got. Hair of the dog."

"We'll see," she said. "We need to go out to Montauk for Josh's car."

"Already done," Kelsey said. "I hopped into an Uber first thing this morning since it was definitely my fault we ended up leaving it there."

"Oh wow, I'm way behind, aren't I?"

"What time did you finally come inside last night?" Lauren asked.

"I'm not really sure." She was about to mention that she'd thought she heard Kelsey in her room when she went to bed, but decided against it.

"We felt terrible leaving you," Lauren said, "but we could not get you to move. We even tried sliding the lounge chair, but you definitely vetoed that idea."

May could tell from the way they were acting that there was more to the story. "Yeah? Wow, I'm really sorry." She blinked away a hazy recollection of Kelsey grabbing her arm. "I got mad at you for trying to get me to go to bed?"

"I think you were just tired," Lauren said.

"No," Kelsey said, laughing, "you were definitely mad. Like, hella mad. I've never seen you get that mad."

Lauren shot her a corrective look across the table, because they all knew that wasn't literally true. They had seen the video.

"Was I, like, yelling at you?" May asked.

"It doesn't matter," Lauren said. "We were all overserved."

"It does matter," May said. "You guys know what happened before and the reasons why. I've been working really hard to get right. If I'm still acting out like that, I need to know."

Lauren reached over and held her hand. "Sweetie, I promise you it wasn't like the video, okay?"

Kelsey looked mortified as she realized what they were talking about. "Oh my god," she said, covering her mouth, "no, not like that at all. I was only kidding. It was just kind of funny because I've never seen you that loopy. You kept talking about the water and how you couldn't leave the water and we were all jerks if we didn't stay and look at the water. Water, water, water. We finally gave up because it was clear you weren't in any condition to go anywhere."

"And, just to be clear, I did check on you," Lauren said. "My pea-sized bladder can only stay asleep so long. The first time I got up, you were already in bed. I was going to open your door to make sure you were okay, but then I heard you snoring, safe and sound and sawing some big old logs."

Kelsey pumped her hands in the air. "Moe was in the hou-ouse."

They burst out laughing, and May covered her face with her hands. "Sorry, it's so embarrassing."

"Awww, but we love Moe," Kelsey said.

Jenny West was the one who came up with the nickname at camp when they realized that the usually quiet, petite, polite May snored like an old fat man if she drank too much. *Shhh, Moe, you're snoring... Moe, roll over on your side.* And in the morning, she'd hear all the details about all of her gross Moe noises.

But this morning, May was less interested in whatever disgusting snorts and rumbles Moe had made last night than about her insistence on staying outside near the water. She remembered now. She had been dreaming about Marnie Mann and the night she drowned.

11

It was the summer after May graduated and went back to Wildwood, where counselors had to work the entire camp term except for two designated "Off-Campus Nights." Of course May and Kelsey had scheduled their free nights to be together.

For the first, May's mother had "surprised" her by flying into Portland for the weekend. Instead of spending the night barhopping with Kelsey and a bunch of their Harvard and BC friends who had come up from Boston for the occasion, she had taken a sightseeing bus tour with her mother, followed by dinner at a Cantonese restaurant May had researched online, only to have her mom complain that it was "froufrou" and "overpriced."

When the second Off-Campus Night came around, May preempted any further visits by making clear to her mother she was going camping with her friends for the night. *You're taking a break from camping to go camping?* It was a twenty-minute argument that ended only after May lied and said there would be no boys, even though she was a grown woman who could sleep with whoever she wanted, but of course she didn't say that.

Nate had brought Ecstasy for the two of them, having heard from friends who had taken it at Tufts that it was the best high—and the best sex—they ever had. After two months of celibacy, May was more than game for the adventure. But they made the mistake of mixing it with alcohol. Instead of spending the night making out and feeling each other up as planned, Nate kept wandering around the woods, and May wound up blacking out at the tail end of the night. She was so wasted she didn't even remember crawling alone into their tent to crash. She was horrified the next day to realize Nate could barely sleep because of her snoring. It was the first time any man had witnessed Moe in action.

What made that Off-Campus Night traumatic to this day wasn't her failed drug-fueled sex experiment with Nate, though. It was Marnie's drowning. Her boyfriend had been at the campsite too. By the time May woke up the next morning, word had spread that he couldn't find her.

May was the one who insisted they needed to call 911. She had also called Lauren, who had notified the camp owners, who contacted Marnie's parents. By midafternoon, a full-blown search was underway. Marnie's body wasn't found in the lake until the following morning.

Until that night, May and Kelsey had never really had to deal with any serious responsibilities. As burdened as May often felt by expectations, the reality was that she was sheltered. School, piano lessons, camp. Scholarship and loan applications could be stressful, but they were normal kid things. Even once they were at camp as counselors, they were there to camp, too, while providing some gentle oversight to the kind of well-behaved kids who tended to go to art camps.

Marnie's death changed all that.

Until that final summer, May had despised Marnie. In hindsight, maybe the two of them were too similar, both of them pianists and A-plus students. Marnie was admittedly the more talented musician, but her smugness about that fact could be insufferable.

Only a few weeks before Off-Campus Night, Lauren had lectured May about needing to grow up and stop bickering with Marnie like warring schoolgirls. And so May had followed instructions, setting out to smother Marnie with kindness until she finally cracked. It actually worked. For once, Marnie actually stopped trying to prove that she could one-up everyone else at Wildwood. She told May she had a boyfriend working that summer in Hartford and asked if they could join the Off-Campus Night get-together she'd heard Kelsey was planning. She even confessed that she had always been a little jealous of May—the outsider girl on scholarship who had somehow won over the preternaturally cool girl Kelsey Ellis and seemed to hold a special place in her idol Lauren's heart.

Marnie told her all kinds of things.

When they first realized Marnie was missing, Kelsey had grilled May on what she and Marnie had been talking about the previous night. According to Kelsey, the two of them had been huddled together near the lakeshore. "Like a couple of little coconspirators."

May had tried so hard to remember the conversation, wondering if it held some clue as to where Marnie may have wandered off to. But she couldn't remember a single word. She could picture them next to each other, checking behind them from time to time to make sure no one else was listening. Or she might have made all of that up in the desperate process of trying to remember. For some reason, though, she had a terrible feeling that whatever they were talking about was something May hadn't wanted to know.

The reality is that Marnie Mann had been so unbelievably cruel to her when they were young, there were times that May had wished her dead. And then she was, and twenty-two-year-old May was still alive.

The campers were terrified when they found out why one of their counselors had not returned from her night off campus. They didn't understand how she could have drowned when she was such a strong swimmer. No matter how many times they were told that the coroner believed Marnie dove into the water and hit her head on a rock before drowning, several kids refused to go into the lake, certain that they would die too. Parents began to show up, insisting upon the return of their traumatized children and camp fees. *How could this have happened?* they demanded to know. There was talk of lawsuits.

May and Kelsey had abruptly been forced into adulthood. They shared a collective sense of guilt. Why hadn't they been watching out for this girl they'd known for years?

And then Lauren announced that it would be her final summer at

Wildwood—scapegoated for not monitoring the girls' conduct while they were off-site for the night. Someone at the camp had to take the fall. Who better than the camp's music director, the lone Black staff member, who obviously had enough talent and ambition to make a go of it elsewhere?

When they were younger, Lauren had seemed like the bad bitch babysitter in charge. But that summer, she had become more like a friend. With her quiet departure from her position, it felt like she had sacrificed herself for them; and in return, they owed it to her to grow the fuck up.

They never talked about Marnie after the funeral, as if that entire chapter of their lives could be buried along with her corpse, wearing Marnie's favorite recital dress: a navy blue gown with a jeweled scoop neck.

May remembered now that she had been dreaming about the search for Marnie as she fell asleep by the fire the previous night. How helpless she had felt, yelling to everyone that they needed to search the water, when May herself could barely manage a dog paddle. It had been fifteen years since Marnie's death, but May still found herself thinking about her at the least predictable moments.

"Yoo-hoo, anyone home?" Kelsey smiled at her expectantly.

"Sorry"—that was apology number four so far, by May's count—"I'm really out of it."

"Well, let's get you some coffee to start with," Kelsey said, "and I'll make the eggs."

"I thought I heard you on the phone when I went up to bed last night," May said. "You sounded upset. Was everything okay?"

The pause that followed as Kelsey turned on the gas beneath the skillet on the stovetop felt long. "Me? No, I crashed as soon as I hit the sheets."

"And did anyone hear a car engine really late?" May asked.

"How could we hear anything with Moe in the house?" Lauren said, handing her a mug of coffee, black the way she liked it. "Go get your bathing suit on and stop worrying. We've got everything under control here."

Before she knew it, it would be time to go back to Josh and their apartment and routines. Maybe for one short weekend, she'd try to be more like Kelsey. Not her prior idea of Kelsey, sophisticated and confident with the perfect life laid out in front of her. The new Kelsey, who found a way to seem light and fun even though her life had been turned upside down to the point that she still cried alone in bed at night.

Fake it 'til you make it, as they said. That's how she'd gotten by at the DA's Office at first, pretending to be a bulldozer of a trial attorney who could hang with the cops and bend a jury to her whim, until she actually began to see herself that way.

"And then I'll take a Bloody Mary when we're ready," May added.

12

She had spent much of the past three weeks anticipating this weekend, and now it was already over. As much as she didn't like the idea of leaving, the truth was that May was exhausted, deep into her bones, physically, emotionally, and cognitively, after only three days. She used to be the kind of person who could work all day in a crowded office and then go out and socialize into the night—rinse and repeat, seven days a week, fifty-two weeks a year—but that was before.

Back then, she thought of her mother's life as so sad. Outside of work, Coral believed in only doing "one big thing" per day, and the "thing" could be as simple as going to the grocery store or meeting a friend for lunch. She used to scold May for being so busy, insisting that her daughter was going to "run herself into the ground" or give herself "burnout." Now May found herself satisfied with a schedule like her mother's. One thing a day was pretty much all she wanted to handle.

May had even taken one of those online Myers-Briggs tests to confirm that her personality had indeed changed. She used to be an ENFJ—extroverted, intuitive, feeling, and judging—meaning that she found energy in being with other people, focused on ideas and concepts rather than facts and details, made decisions based on feelings and values, and opted for plans and organization over spontaneity and flexibility.

But after the last few years? According to the test results, she was now an INFJ. And that change from E to I wasn't subtle: she was 98 percent I. Granted, she was previously only 58 percent E—not the kind of extrovert who jumped in as a team leader at work or held court at the center of a party. But she used to thrive in the company of other people. She might not have led the conversations, but she loved being part of them, always believing that she learned something new simply by listening.

Curious about whether other people had gone through the same kind of personality shift, she came upon a published study where the researchers found that, early in the pandemic, there was a counterintuitive decrease in neurotic tendencies that contribute to stress. But in the second and third years after the initial onset, the researchers found significant increases in neuroticism and declines in the characteristics that help people to successfully navigate social situations. May felt validated by the findings until she got to the part that noted the personality changes were most pronounced in young people.

The researchers speculated that younger people displayed more significant personality changes because their personalities were still in development and were therefore less fixed. Did May not have a fixed personality? She thought about the code-switching she had come to master so well. Conscientious daughter around her mother and her friends from church and school. Docile, hardworking student, whether studying academics or the piano. Confident, in-on-the-joke wing-woman to her friends, even when one of them would make a throwaway comment about how May wasn't "really a minority" because she was half white. The prosecutor who, in the words of the cops who worked with her, "was like a dog with a bone."

May wondered if perhaps all her efforts to be the type of person who could fit in anywhere and find a way to please anyone had made her so malleable that her personality had never fully formed. Regardless of the reasons, May had somehow gone from being a person who found energy in the company of others to one who *needed* downtime, who found energy in solitude. And while she had enjoyed her time at the beach house, she knew that she needed to get back to her work, her life, her routine, her isolation. Would she ever revert to her former disposition? It seemed like everyone else had just gone back to normal, but May felt broken in ways she was still discovering.

Downstairs, Kelsey was changing the sheets in the bedroom, soon to be occupied by Nate. "Oh, I wish you were staying," Kelsey said, looking up from her current task of stuffing a pillowcase.

"I wish I could stay longer too," May replied. "But I have a lot of work to do, and I need to get back to it."

"Isn't that one of the perks of being a law professor?" Kelsey said. "Time off, like when we were back in school? Summer camp for life?"

"Unfortunately, no. I've been warned by the senior faculty that summer can vanish in the blink of an eye if you're not careful. I'm trying to keep myself on a writing schedule. With all the class prep from teaching last year, I didn't finish an article in time to submit it to the law reviews. I want to make sure I have a solid draft by August. I'm up for contract renewal next year and need it to be a slam dunk." In year six, she'd be up for tenure—the golden ticket for a legal scholar, a guarantee of lifetime employment.

"You put so much pressure on yourself. I have no doubt that you'll sail through with flying colors. You always do!" Kelsey tugged playfully on the sleeve of May's T-shirt, and May turned her head so Kelsey couldn't read her expression. She had never told anyone, not even her mother or Josh, that her departure from the law firm wasn't exactly voluntary.

She took a seat at the foot of the bed and gestured for Kelsey to sit beside her, wrapping one arm around her shoulders. "Hey, you never brought it up again, but if you ever want to talk about the decision whether to go ahead with the baby, I want you to know I'm here for you—even if you just need a sounding board."

Kelsey placed a hand on May's knee. "Thank you so much. That really does mean a lot to me."

"It's been like old times being here together. I still feel so guilty for not reaching out after Luke—"

Kelsey shushed her. "That's ancient history. And, for what it's worth, I still have a lot to mull over before I decide to go forward. I assume Luke told his parents that we fertilized my eggs. The clinic said it was the best way to maximize our chances of it working. And if I get pregnant and they find out, they'll stop at nothing until they know whether he's the father. I really don't want to have anything to do with them after they wouldn't defend me when he died."

"Do they really think you had something to do with it? The police even said you're not a suspect." Kelsey had mentioned that much in conversation, but May already knew from following the investigation.

"I'm not a suspect, but I am pretty sure my father pulled some strings to get them to put out a statement to that effect. You know how he gets in the middle of everything when it comes to me. They wouldn't usually clear someone publicly if the case is still open, right?"

"No, probably not," May said quietly.

"So I don't think Luke's parents were ever willing to close the door on the possibility that my father's influence may have gone further than that. I've always had this lingering fear they'll even try to stop me from using the fertilized eggs, even though it's clear they don't have that power. But if I actually get pregnant? Maybe they'll try to have a relationship with my kids, and who knows what they might say about me behind my back."

May arched a brow. "Kids, huh. Multiple?"

"Yeah," Kelsey said, smiling. "If I still have time."

The idea of getting pregnant by a dead man who would have eventually been your ex-husband struck May as surreal. Yet she understood Kelsey's willingness—it was her only option if she wanted a biological connection to her children. And May knew how much Kelsey yearned to be a good mother after losing both her own mom and then the stepmother who finished raising her. When Kelsey's father had divorced Nate's mom, Jeanie, she initially made some token efforts to stay in touch with Kelsey—the occasional card, a Christmas gift—but within a few years, even those ceased. May could still remember how upset Kelsey was when her former mom-slash-stepmom no-showed at her college graduation after Kelsey told her how much she wanted her to be there.

"I can research the law on that if you want. I don't think they'd have any kind of rights to visitation."

"Thanks, but I've got someone in Boston working on it. I wish I could build a time machine. I'd go back and have the babies before my surgery. We talked about it, but we had just gotten married and Luke was trying to get the restaurant going. We thought we had so much time. Maybe if we'd had the kids, he wouldn't have left me. Maybe he wouldn't have even been in the car that night."

May took Kelsey's hand in hers. "Honey, don't do that to yourself, okay? There are no time machines, and you still have the eggs. You have choices."

"I know. It just might be a really dumb idea. It would be better if I could get remarried first. I'd even be willing to use an egg donor and surrogate if that was important to him. You know, to leave Luke out of it. Would that be crazy?"

"Nope, not at all. And whatever you decide, anything you need—really, I'm here."

"Live-in, full-time nanny?"

"Yeah, no."

The moment was interrupted by the sound of the front door opening. They walked out of the bedroom to find Lauren entering the kitchen, a grease-smudged paper bag in hand. "You guys, the farm stand down the road had cinnamon rolls the size of my head. I couldn't resist."

After sliding a gigantic pastry onto a plate, Lauren pulled a crumpled piece of paper from her purse. There was a tear at the top of the page where she'd pulled it down, but the two words filling the top line of text were clear: MISSING PERSON.

"So . . . weird question, but does this guy look familiar?"

Square jaw. Blond hair tousled with plenty of product. Good teeth. May glanced at the picture and shook her head. "I mean, he kind of just looks like a generic white guy. Even his name is generic. David Smith?"

Kelsey said nothing, staring at the picture with a furrowed brow.

"Take a closer look," Lauren encouraged.

May did as instructed, but every time she thought maybe something about the man's general appearance might be familiar, she lost it, and he became a total stranger again. Even the name rang a distant bell, but she had likely encountered a David Smith or two at some point in life. "What are we missing?"

"Am I losing my mind, or is that the guy from the rental car? On Friday. The asshole in the white car who stole our parking spot."

May felt her breath catch in her throat as she realized that Lauren was right. The man in the picture looked an awful lot like the guy they had seen in Sag Harbor. "I'm ninety percent sure that's him. We should call the police. There's a number here."

"Call them and say what?" Lauren asked, sounding wholly unconcerned as she reached for another pinch of cinnamon roll. "We don't even know his name—except it's on this flyer. We saw him on the street for like ten seconds."

"We at least know he was in Sag Harbor at around five p.m. on Friday. They're probably putting together a timeline of his whereabouts. You never know with a missing-person case what detail is going to crack the investigation wide open."

"I've got to be honest," Lauren said, "and no offense, I know you had your reasons for being a prosecutor, but I'm not in the habit of calling the police voluntarily."

"My *reasons*?" May said. "I wasn't aware you thought my job was something I needed to justify." She couldn't remember ever speaking so sharply to Lauren.

"You may be used to getting the benefit of the doubt when you're talking to cops, but let's just say that's not everyone's experience. I grew up with a father and brothers. When I see police heading in my direction, I assume the worst."

"Seriously? If we have information that might help—"

"The way I see it, it's not my job to help some random dude. That man could be some Ponzi-scheming crook who ran off with his clients' money for all we know. Or a drug dealer going through something with his supplier. No one asked us to get involved. Why do you assume he needs our help? Maybe you should ask yourself, after everything that happened, why and when you feel it so necessary to call the police."

May felt like she'd been slapped across the face. The comment was an obvious reference to her phone call to police on the subway platform, the moment that had been captured in that awful video.

Kelsey cleared her throat. "You guys, this is getting a little intense. Can we—"

"Someone is looking for this guy," May said. Her hand was trembling as she struggled to enter the number from the flyer into her cell phone. "I'm calling."

"You know they're going to run our names if you do that," Lauren said.

"I don't care," May said. "We'll tell them what we know. They'll add his whereabouts with that woman in whatever timeline they're putting together. Who we are is irrelevant."

"You have no way of knowing that," Lauren said. "If nothing else, some thirsty clerk at the police station could take to Twitter talking all about the three canceled friends holed up in a beach house together. DA Karen, the sidepiece symphony director, and the rich girl who hired a hit man."

May was about to enter the final digit when Kelsey grabbed the phone from her hand. "You can't call!"

"I will leave your names out of it if you want. It's just one piece of information."

"It's not," Kelsey said in a low voice. Her face was flushed.

"Are you worried because they'll realize who you are?" May said. "This has nothing to do with Luke or his case."

"It's not that," Kelsey said. She placed May's phone on the kitchen island but kept her hand on top of it. "Do you remember those notes you wrote on the cocktail napkins? When we were in Sag Harbor?"

Lauren and May were silent. Of course they remembered.

"I left the note under their windshield wiper."

"You what?" Lauren said.

"It was stupid."

"Which note?" Lauren asked, her voice stern.

Kelsey avoided Lauren's gaze and May could barely make out her response. "Yours."

She meant Lauren's.

He's cheating. He always does.

PART TWO

OUR DAVID SMITH

13

East Hampton detective Carter Decker was hunched at his desk over a sandwich and a set of phone records, more excited about the former than the latter. The sandwich was stuffed with layers of prosciutto, salami, ham, and provolone on focaccia that could have come from the heavens, but was actually from his beloved Luigi's. The phone records were for a suspect in a recent smash-and-grab robbery at a high-end national chain store in the village. It had happened in the rush of summer, and now the upper-crust part-timers who came east to escape the stench and chaos of a New York City summer were exchanging whispers about their irrational fears of being robbed on the street or in their homes.

The mayor wanted an arrest made yesterday, but Carter knew he'd need the case locked and loaded for the prosecutor's office to make the charges stick in the long run, and having a surefire timeline for the suspect's whereabouts at the time of the robbery took . . . well, time. A small part of Carter wouldn't mind if a delay in an arrest drove down tourism for the summer. Sometimes he looked around the town where he was born and bred and couldn't believe it was the same place.

He tried to focus on the records, but found himself closing his eyes as he savored another giant bite of his sandwich. Phone records were tedious work, and the strain was kicking in. Just as he was about to take a break, his cell rang. He recognized the number from two earlier phone calls that he had neither answered nor returned. Rhode Island area code. It was the lawyer for Tinsley Smith, who had also been calling him incessantly.

Carter was used to family members of missing people "lawyering up" when they became suspects, but this was the first time he'd seen a family hire a lawyer when it wasn't even clear a crime had been committed. He let the call go to voicemail and allowed himself the luxury of finishing his lunch in peace before checking the message.

"Detective Decker, this is Anthony Walker calling again on behalf of my client, Tinsley Smith. I know you've already spoken to Mrs. Smith about the disappearance of her son, David. She's deeply worried about his well-being and is concerned that the department isn't treating her fears seriously. We've hired some local people in the area to print up and distribute missing-person flyers, but we could use a more thorough response from law enforcement and hope you can help us. Please give me a call back as soon as possible to see how I can facilitate."

Carter pushed the phone records aside and reached for his laptop. He entered *Anthony Walker lawyer Rhode Island* into the search bar and hit enter. Former prosecutor, now a plaintiff's lawyer. Boston College Law School, cum laude, a few multimillion-dollar jury verdicts to tout on his website.

Carter eyed the stack of paper he'd stashed on the corner of his desk—more copies of the flyers the family had somehow already managed to blanket the East End with, describing missing David Smith as a thirty-six-year-old man, six-foot-two with a medium build, last seen Saturday at Gurney's hotel, where he had been staying, in a gray T-shirt, jeans, and white Gucci sneakers.

David Smith's photograph stared back at Carter from the flyer. Carter had no problem recognizing good looks in another man, and this guy was objectively handsome, plain and simple. Chiseled jawline, deep-set eyes, a mop of blond hair. Not quite Brad Pitt, but not exactly unlike him either. Preppier, without the edge. Even if Carter hadn't looked into the Smith family's background—even without cues like Gurney's resort and the Gucci kicks—Carter would have known David Smith was from money. Just from the look. He was the heir to a publishing fortune built when print media could still make a family rich for generations to come.

The call was going to have to be made sooner or later. He pulled up Walker's number from his last voicemail message and hit enter. The lawyer answered on the second ring.

"Detective Decker, thank you for getting back to me so quickly."

It hadn't been quick at all, but Carter appreciated the lawyer's attempt to start out in a cordial place.

"Happy to stay in touch as we gather more information, but, as I explained to Mrs. Smith, we really don't have any evidence to suggest that her son is in any danger. He's an adult on vacation—and according to the staff at Gurney's, seemed very affectionate with the woman he checked in with at the hotel. It wouldn't be unusual under the circumstances for him not to be in contact with his mother for a couple of days."

The night-shift manager at Gurney's had called David's plus-one a "real box of chocolates," which sounded to Carter like a good reason for a single man not to call his mommy for the weekend.

"Except his mother has been calling and texting him, and he hasn't responded, which she insists is extremely unusual. Look, it's not how I deal with my mom, to be sure, but Mrs. Smith sent me some screenshots of their ongoing text conversation. Two days of silence appears to be unprecedented. And the hotel housekeeping staff tells me that the room appeared unused both yesterday morning and today. Bed still made. Towels still folded. A duffel bag filled with David's clothes."

"But his rental car isn't at the hotel, and I didn't see a second bag for his female companion. It's not unusual out here for people with the means to do so to make day trips to other locations without checking out of their hotel. He could have gone to Shelter Island or the North Fork for the weekend, or decided to spend a couple days in the city."

"I understand your skepticism, Detective, but that's not what's going on here. Calls to his phone are going straight to voicemail, suggesting his phone's either off or dead. And David's been using his corporate card on his trip out here. Charges for the hotel, Wölffer Estate

Vineyard, the Surf Lodge in Montauk, something called Page in Sag Harbor on Friday night, two p.m. Saturday at Topping Rose." Carter estimated the two-day tab to be more than what he made in a month. "No charges since, coinciding with his phone going dark."

"People do still use cash, or David's date might have picked up a check or two."

"Between me and you, Detective, I get the distinct impression that David doesn't date women who ever picked up a check."

Carter pressed his fingertips against his eyelids. Ninety-nine percent odds this kid was off living a rock-star lifestyle with his weekend box of chocolates, but there was always the other percent.

"If David and his mom are so close, how does she not know who her son's traveling with?" he asked.

"You think most single men tell their mothers about every woman they spend time with?" Walker said. "I've got some calls out to David's friends. Hoping one of them knows who she is so we can see if anyone's heard from her either. His mom said his car's in the shop getting some work done. I found a Hertz charge for a rental car picked up in Providence Friday morning, due back Wednesday. They don't have trackers on their rentals, but maybe you can put out a BOLO or something. I've got a Florida plate number for you."

Carter could already tell this lawyer was more than tough talk. He knew his stuff.

"I can do that. And I'll put out a request to check airports and train stations. Any chance David's cell is a company phone like his credit card?"

"I'm not sure," Walker said, "but I can check."

"If it is, you'll be able to get the records faster than I can. If not, I'll subpoena them on my end. And do me a favor and shoot me a copy of those credit card charges with dates and times." He spelled out his department email address for the lawyer. Carter wasn't quite ready to jump into a full-blown search for David Smith, but he would check the phone records for any obvious avenues of investigation. And he could enlist some of the high school students volunteering with the department for the summer to retrace Smith's steps through the receipts to see if anything unusual happened along the route.

He found Sergeant Debra McFadden in the break room, feeding a dollar bill into the vending machine. "What's happening, D-Mac?"

"I'm about to say a very loud fuck-you to this stupid keto thing I've been doing. What do you think, Skittles or a Milky Way?"

"You love Skittles."

"I really do. *C. 8.*" She pressed the machine buttons with emphasis.

"And you shouldn't diet. It's stupid. Especially for you."

"I don't know how you managed to make that sound like a compliment, but thank you." She tore open the snack bag and offered him first dibs, which he declined.

"You working with the Explorers again this summer?" he asked.

"Yup," she said, her eyes briefly closing with pleasure as she chewed her tart candy. "They're good kids. And it's easy OT."

They'd had three dates before Debra asked Carter if kids were in his future. He answered honestly, and that was that. He handed her a copy of the David Smith flyer. "You've seen these around town yet?"

"No, but I heard Kelly say something about finding her future husband on a missing poster. Now I see why."

"Think you can send some of your kids out to follow his steps? I'm getting a list of all of his credit card charges. Sounds like he was making the rounds to the usual hotspots. Maybe someone noticed an argument or something? I can walk the kids through what to look for, the questions to ask or whatever. Just need you to tee me up for that."

"Sure. I'll round them up now. You hook up anyone for the smash-and-grab yet?"

"Nope. Still working it."

"Damn if part of me isn't sort of rooting for them. They took twelve-thousand-dollar handbags, Carter. Twelve thousand dollars. For a handbag. Think about that."

She held out her candy bag again, and this time he extended his palm to accept the offer.

"You trying to make me hate people even more than I already do? Let me try to think about this missing dude instead."

14

"Oh, Kelsey," Lauren said, pushing the cinnamon roll plate away as she stepped back from the kitchen island. "What did you do? What did you go and do?"

"It was just a joke."

"A joke?" Lauren was glaring at Kelsey as if she had kicked a kitten.

"I mean, we all cracked up when you wrote it. You said yourself you'd do anything to make someone laugh."

"Oh, don't you even think about putting this on me," Lauren said. "I wrote that for two sets of eyes only—yours and May's. You told us you were going to put them in a scrapbook. Were you lying?"

Kelsey raised her palms in the air. "No, I swear. I promise. It was spur-of-the-moment after you guys left for the bookstore. I walked out and their car was still there. Imagine coming back to your car and finding a note like that. They deserved it after the stunt they pulled."

Lauren rubbed her temples. "Jesus, they may not have even seen us waiting."

"You guys said she was gloating with a big smirk on her face."

"I only said that because May did."

May was replaying the moment in her head. Is it possible she had jumped to conclusions again? "Now I'm not sure . . ."

"Well, you sounded sure at the time. I thought it would be funny and a little bit of karmic justice."

"If it was so damn hilarious to wonder what would happen when they got back to the car, how come you didn't tell us?" Lauren's voice was ice-cold.

Kelsey was blinking back tears. "Lauren, I'm sorry. It was a stupid, impulsive thing, and I was in my cups."

"No, no, no. Don't blame it on drinking. You're the one who swore up and down you were fine to drive. You didn't tell us because you knew we'd be pissed. You walk around practically disguised to avoid being recognized, but then you do something stupid like that."

May had been silent, relieved on some level to have Lauren's ire aimed at Kelsey instead of her. But the full import of Kelsey's admission was sinking in. May had learned years ago how an anonymous note could spiral into unintended consequences. They had to do something.

"Don't you see, now we really do have to call the police. We can't just do nothing." May's tone was more scolding than she had intended. "Think about it, Kelsey. You said it was fun to wonder what would happen when they found the note. What exactly were you imagining?" When she did not respond, May answered her own question. "The whole reason the note was perfect was because it sounded so authoritative. Not only is he cheating, but he *always does.* The voice of someone who knows with certainty. How could he just explain that away? It was sure to start an argument. We have to tell the police."

"We don't know that for certain," Lauren said, slapping her palms against the countertop. "If they did see us, they probably figured out right away it was us trying to fuck with them."

"Or they got into a fight that escalated," May said, "and now his body's at the bottom of the Long Island Sound. Or he got mad at her for not believing him, and her body's in the Sound, and he's on the run."

"This is getting ridiculous," Kelsey said, her voice shaking. "No one's body is in the Sound. Maybe they got into a fight and he stormed off, and now she reported him missing because he's ghosting her."

"Or more likely," Lauren said, looking directly at May, "it has nothing to do with that stupid note."

"There's two numbers here," May said. "The East Hampton police department and this other number with a 401 area code. It's probably for the family. We can call them instead."

"And they'll immediately give that information to the police," Lauren said. "And then that many more people will know about the immature stupid shit we pulled."

May's gut was telling her the note and David Smith's disappearance had to be connected. She tried a different tack. "We could make an anonymous phone call saying we saw the couple bickering near their car in Sag Harbor on Friday."

"And how are you going to make an anonymous call to the police?" Lauren asked. "They can trace everything these days."

"I don't know. I can find a pay phone."

"Where?" Kelsey asked. "In 1997? That's not going to happen, May."

"You don't have to insult me, Kelsey. You're the one who did this."

Lauren shook her head emphatically. "I know you think you're doing the right thing," she said, crossing her arms in front of her. "But Kelsey and I are right. We don't actually know anything that would help the police. And calling them is just going to put us in the spotlight all over again. Think about how embarrassing that will be—three grown women starting some Crank Yankers bullshit with a couple of strangers over a parking spot. You want your students and your fellow faculty members thinking of you as petty like that?"

May could feel her head beginning to prevail over her instincts. The reality was that they had no proof that this David Smith was in danger or that his current whereabouts were related to the note Kelsey had left on the car. They had all been through so much, and the last thing they needed was to be in the public eye again. She had dodged the bullet once, when Fordham decided not to revoke her offer at the law school after the subway incident.

Something like this would surely derail her when she came up for contract renewal next year. Not to mention the repercussions to Lauren, who had written the note, and to Kelsey, who had left it.

Kelsey literally jumped when a chirp sounded from her cell phone. She picked it up from the kitchen island and looked at the screen.

"Shit. It's Nate. His train is almost here. I need to go get him from the station." She grabbed her keys and walked out the front door, taking May's phone and car keys with her.

15

May had her laptop open on the kitchen island, staring at the screen in frustration. She had been searching for information about the missing man since Kelsey had driven off, but to no avail. Even with the benefit of the area code from the flyer, which covered the entire state of Rhode Island, the name was simply too common, and every online search she tried seemed to bring up a hundred different David Smiths.

"Total waste of time," May said as she sat back on her stool and crossed her arms.

Lauren was picking at the cinnamon roll, shaking her head with disapproval. "Will you please just give this up? You are not going to find that man in a sea of a million people with the same name, and even if you did, what exactly do you expect to learn? You're going to play Sherlock Holmes from a computer and figure out where he is? He obviously has someone looking for him. And if he's wearing Gucci sneakers, they probably have the resources to find him without your help, May. This isn't your job."

May typed in another search: *David Smith Rhode Island wealthy*. Among the hits were a quote from someone named David Smith who said that "art isn't made for the wealthy," a statement from a Rhode Island state senator that the wealthy needed to pay their fair share, and a wealth manager named David Smith. She clicked on the wealth management firm's website, but the picture wasn't a match. "Not our David Smith," she reported.

"He is most definitely not *ours,* May. You're letting that crime-obsessed imagination of yours go wild. The note was just a joke. I'm sure they laughed it off and threw it away. Think about it."

"But what if you were actually right? What if he really was cheating, and that note made his girlfriend check his phone or whatever? That's exactly the kind of fight that can set off domestic violence."

"Okay, I'll give you that." Lauren sighed, wiping her fingertips on a paper napkin. "But think, May. If he *wasn't* cheating, there's no way an anonymous note is going to lead to a fight like the kind you're talking about. He'd show her his phone or do whatever he needed to convince her the note was a prank. Will you give me that?"

May nodded reluctantly.

"And if he *was* actually cheating, the police who are looking for this man will find that out. They'll read his texts. All his emails. Check out his dating profiles or whatever. It always comes out once the police start to look. Aren't I right about that?"

May conceded that point as well.

"And they're also going to find out where this man was going. They'll ping his phone or whatever voodoo they do. He's probably paying for stuff on a credit card. Isn't that what the police will do?"

May had to admit that everything Lauren was saying was true and led to an inevitable conclusion. "Yes," she conceded, "which means that we really can't tell them anything they won't find out on their own."

Lauren had been nodding along as she spoke. "So we're good now?" Her face fell when May hesitated.

"There could be cameras on Main Street, though. What if they see Kelsey leaving that note there? And if there's footage of us getting back into the car, it's Josh's license plate."

"Then they'll trace the plate, Kelsey will have to tell them about her little prank, and you won't have anything to do with it. But there's no need to call attention to it for now." When May said nothing more, Lauren walked around the island and gave her a quick hug. "We're on the same page?"

"Yeah," May said, nodding in agreement.

"And I'm sorry for what I said about you being a DA and the police and all of that. It was a lot."

"No, I appreciate when you share those things with me. It's important."

They were interrupted by the sound of the front door opening. "We're here!" There wasn't a hint of tension in Kelsey's voice, let alone any indication that she had run off with May's keys and cell phone.

It had been almost eight years since May had last seen Nate, and she hadn't been sure what to expect. As he stepped through the door, backpack slung over one shoulder, she noted the spray of gray at his temples and a few fine lines around his eyes, but those eyes were still dark and intense, and he had a jawline that could cut glass.

Now that she was seeing him again in person, the stark differences between Josh and Nate were even more obvious. The dark hair and medium build were about the only similarities. Where Josh's energy was laid-back and goofy, Nate had always been a bit edgier—an adult version of the boy you'd cut class for to smoke cigarettes behind the gas station.

"You look good, Hanover." She felt a tingle at the nape of her neck as he pulled her into a hug, and hoped no one could see the flush of her skin. *Damn it.* What was wrong with her? "So what have you birds been up to so far?"

May was quiet as Kelsey and Lauren walked Nate through their weekend. Friday-night dinner in Montauk. Saturday at Main Beach, followed by takeout from La Fondita. Sunday-morning shopping, pool day, then 1770 House. The weekend had gone so fast.

While Lauren was asking Nate about the train ride, Kelsey pulled May into the living room. "I'm sorry I ran out like that, but—"

May held up a hand to stop her. "I already talked to Lauren. You guys were right. Let's just let it go, okay?"

"Oh my god, thank you, May. Thank you, thank you, thank you. And I really am sorry for taking your stuff. I totally panicked."

"Yeah, that was pretty bitchy."

"Love you?" Kelsey said, wrinkling her nose.

"Love you too."

"And I saw the way you and Nate were looking at each other. You sure there's not something still there?"

"I'm happily engaged, Kelsey." She held up her left hand, ring forward, for emphasis.

"I believe that's what the lawyers would call nonresponsive."

"Stop being a shit-stirrer."

"Well, that's no fun. For what it's worth, I think he was flirting with you."

As May led the way back to the kitchen, she realized she was smiling.

She sent a quick text to Josh before starting the engine. *Heading out now. ETA 5:17.*

Drive fast. The apartment's quiet without you.

Any hope of driving quickly was dashed when she reached 27 and found it stacked with an endless line of cars whose drivers had the same idea of waiting until Monday to make the trip back to the city. During the stops of all the stop-and-go traffic, she scrolled through her list of podcasts and eventually settled on the latest episode of a true-crime series about the unsolved murder of a Chinese American lawyer in Washington, DC. May had been obsessed with the case for years.

She realized she already knew all the facts being presented in the episode, and found her thoughts wandering. It had been so hard to say goodbye when they all walked her out to her car. She gave them each one last hug, holding on tight to Kelsey and Lauren as they agreed they had to find a way to see each other again soon. The hug with Nate had been quick, and she had avoided looking at him afterward.

She would never cheat on Josh—not now. The lockdown had locked her down as well, first with the move-in and then with the engagement. But she never told Josh there was a possibility she'd be seeing an ex-boyfriend today. And then her own body betrayed her when he gave her that initial hug. *You look good, Hanover.* After all these years. One throwaway compliment and her head was already wrecked, thinking about how things used to be.

May was forbidden by her mother from dating in high school—boys were a distraction from schoolwork and the piano, she insisted, and May didn't have the judgment or (ironically) the experience to keep them from taking advantage of her. May suspected that her father's decision to leave her mother when she got pregnant might have had something to do with her mother's views, but a prohibition was a prohibition.

As a result, Kelsey was always at least one step ahead of her when it came to boys. She had already let her seventh-grade boyfriend under her bra while May was still trying to figure out tongue kissing. May remembered feeling scared but excited when Kelsey demonstrated how the feeling of a boy's fingertips tickling her rib cage while his arm was wrapped around her waist was enough to make her tingle "down there." *Matt Lenox is the one who did that. I got so out of my mind, I let him grind on top of me until he . . . well, you know. But he's way too stupid to be my first. So now I know I can just lead a guy's hand to that spot and let him figure out how much I like it.* She was a one-girl sex advice column for teenagers.

Nate and May had known each other since she was twelve years old, but it wasn't until her junior year in college that he suddenly kissed her after a night out drinking with Kelsey and their fake IDs. By then, May's virginity existed only in her mother's imagination. At May's insistence, they kept their hookups a secret. Sleeping with your best friend's brother felt like a violation of the sister code, she said. The truth was that her privacy about sex wasn't limited to Nate. Maybe it was all those lectures from her mother that had made boys all sound so mean and dangerous, but once she finally went there, she wanted to keep that part of herself strictly to herself—and the guys she chose to share it with.

Even though May thought she knew a thing or two about guys by then, being with Nate felt like graduating from the bunny slopes directly to a Black Diamond. Good-looking, cool, confident, and—from what she could tell—very experienced.

After a few carefully planted questions to Kelsey, May began to worry about what she had gotten herself into. According to his own sister, Nate was a "babe magnet" who tended to get bored easily and move on—the same approach he had shown both to school and life in general. "I love him, but as a boyfriend? I wouldn't wish him on my worst enemy."

May was determined not to get hurt, telling herself that the two of them were just having fun. It was all going according to plan until May's senior year when Kelsey showed up at Harvard unannounced, a DVD of *Working Girl* in her purse, hoping for a break from her BC roommate and an impromptu slumber party in May's single. Her brother was already there. After a split second of surprise, the explanation became obvious, and May prepared herself for the onslaught. *How could you sleep with my little brother? How could you lie to me?*

But Kelsey wasn't mad. Quite the opposite; she was ecstatic. She literally clapped her hands like a kid getting a present. Kelsey was the founding member of Team "Mayonate," as she quickly dubbed them. Once the secret was out, May no longer had an excuse to keep her relationship with Nate covert, which meant it became a "relationship," whether it had been one before or not.

If Nate was rattled by the small yet sudden shift in their status, he didn't show it. Their illicit one-on-ones were replaced by group hangs where Kelsey was usually around too, and that changed the dynamic in subtle and not-so-subtle ways.

Perhaps it was inevitable in every trio that someone would end up feeling odd-man-out at any given moment—how many times in the past few days had she wondered whether Lauren and Kelsey were the real friends, while she was just an add-on?

When May was dating Nate, any one of them could occasionally feel like the third wheel in different contexts. Sometimes Nate was the dude crashing the gal-pal lovefest. Sometimes it was Kelsey who needed to take a hint that her friend and brother wanted to be alone. And May still recalled the sear of the bizarre sense of jealousy she sometimes felt around them. Jealous of the brother who seemed to know her best friend's every secret even before she did. Jealous of the friend who was always going to be her boyfriend's closest confidante, the one who promised she'd never abandon him the way their father had.

But usually? The three of them just clicked. As time passed, May found herself thinking about a future with Nate and how gorgeous their children would be. She and Kelsey would literally be family. Their children would be cousins. How perfect would that be? Kelsey often egged on the fantasy, talking about the day they might all share a house on the Cape.

But whenever May allowed herself to believe it might actually happen, she'd remember Kelsey's warning: *I wouldn't wish him on my worst enemy.* Kelsey knew Nate better than anyone. She had said that for a reason. What had been hot hookups with a hot guy had become another thing for May to worry about.

She was almost relieved when she got dinged by Harvard Law, meaning she'd move to New York to attend Columbia. She'd be the one to pull the plug before he got around to dumping her. But then he began talking about moving to New York after graduation, and she suddenly found herself in a long-distance relationship with a guy who was supposedly constitutionally unfit for any relationship at all.

She became determined to make it work. She'd find a way to keep Nate interested until he made the move to the city and figured out what he was going to do with himself. May had always been the girl who needed to excel at whatever she tried, and keeping things hot with Nathan Thorne became almost an obsession. She started reading those stupid women's magazines that promised to teach you the ten ways to make his thighs quiver. She watched porn to learn how to give the best oral. *Pull my hair. Do it harder. I'll let you do anything.* One day in class, her torts professor called on her and she was unprepared because she'd spent the previous night messing with her iPhone to figure out the best angles for a homemade sex video.

And then, on spring break, she forewent the opportunity to travel with the moot court team to Stanford and visited Nate instead. Years later, she still tried to block out how ridiculous she had been. The lingerie. High heels. Handcuffs. A stand to hold her phone as a makeshift amateur camera. Oh my god, the stupid plastic phone stand. It cost $4.99 at the CVS and kept tipping over, and Nate would have to be the one to fumble with it because May was incapacitated by the handcuffs. When it was over, she grabbed her phone and said she was deleting the video because it would be more slapstick than hot and steamy.

But when she was alone on the train at the end of the weekend, she put in her headphones and watched. She had wanted to seem confident and bold, but she looked so nervous. Small. Ashamed. In a society that sexualized and fetishized women who looked like her, she had cast herself in a demeaning role of her own making. And why? Just to hold on to Nate? Nate, whose own sister said he wasn't serious enough for a relationship. Nate, who had only chosen a major after Kelsey and May convinced him that poli-sci wasn't that much harder than the blow-off subjects he was considering and would keep his employment doors open after graduation. Nate, who had been cut off financially from his stepfather but nevertheless seemed to assume he'd someday see a piece of the Ellis empire. She shouldn't compromise herself for any man, but especially not for one who wasn't a serious person.

She never told him why she was breaking things off, or even that she had made a final decision—not initially. She just stopped visiting, and when he offered to come to New York, she begged off, claiming she had too much schoolwork. He kept pushing, calling to ask her where she was and what she was doing. He went from being the guy who was her incentive to get a term paper finished early so she could sneak in a night in his room, to the guy whose name on the phone flooded her with guilt. He eventually asked her point-blank whether they were still a couple. Her reply was unnecessarily cold. "I'm not sure we ever were."

Kelsey had called her, begging to know what was going on. Instead of admitting her own insecurities, May reminded Kelsey of what she had once said about Nate. Kelsey initially insisted she was only kidding, but eventually conceded that Nate had a lot of growing up to do while May had a huge career waiting in front of her. Mayonate was over.

Four years later, she saw on Nate's Facebook page that he was leaving his marketing job behind and moving to New York to get more serious about his acting. Kelsey was the one to arrange a reunion between the two of them, jokingly referring to it as a "play date." It was immediately clear that Nate was nowhere close to becoming a working actor. He searched ads in *Backstage* everyday but didn't even have an agent. He was bartending in Hell's Kitchen. When he asked to walk her to her building, she'd been tempted. He was still cool, funny, sexy Nate. But she politely declined, listening to her head instead of the parts that wanted to take him home. And she'd been telling herself that she had made the right decision ever since.

Over the years, she'd find herself thinking about Nate on occasion, but it wasn't until Josh made it clear that he was serious about her that she began comparing the two of them. Josh was safe: smart, serious, and well employed. He was also fun to be with and completely devoted to her. He had all the traits she had been ingrained to look for if she were ever going to take the leap. Even May's mother approved. He did not, however, make her feel the way Nate used to. But weren't those feelings precisely the ones she had decided to avoid when she ended things with him? Of course she had made the right decision.

The blast of a horn made her realize that she was half a block behind the next car. She also realized she had taken the single memory of saying goodbye at the house and turned it into a way to rethink her entire relationship with Nate. Why was she like that? Because maybe that was one part of May's personality that hadn't changed. When May was anxious, her fears ate at her until she found a reason—a concrete, rational reason—to put them away, hopefully for good.

Before she realized exactly what she was doing, her turn signal was on. She'd make one quick stop in Sag Harbor. Just to put her mind at ease about David Smith and that note on the windshield, and then she'd never think about it again.

16

It had been two days since May had been back in the city, and with each passing hour, it seemed possible she would never have to think about David Smith or the whole parking space incident ever again.

But when Joe, the swing-shift doorman, called up to say that two police officers were in the lobby for her, that cocktail napkin left on a windshield was the first thing she thought of.

"Did they say what it's about?"

"Nah, I don't ask questions, you know?" Joe said. "Especially when it comes to the NYPD. Figured they're working on one of your cases. Want me to ask?"

Joe obviously assumed she was still at the District Attorney's Office. It's not as if she sent out a memo to the entire building about the change in her résumé.

"No, it's all good, Joe. Send them up."

She had already pulled her Smashing Pumpkins T-shirt over her head and was slipping on a bra when Josh followed her into the bedroom, trailed by Gomez. "Are we having people over? I didn't see anything on the calendar."

"Nothing scheduled." They had begun sharing their calendars with each other after the official engagement. She was still getting used to the idea that he was aware of how she spent each minute of her time, even when they were apart. "I guess the police are here to see me about something."

She headed for the roller bag, open on the upholstered bench at the foot of the bed, still unpacked. Pre-2020 May would have had the empty suitcase tucked neatly away within fifteen minutes of coming home. She pulled out her black shirt-dress while she untied the drawstring of her running shorts with her free hand.

"What about?" Josh asked.

"No clue," she said, fumbling with the buttons of the dress. She paused in front of the full-length mirror next to the closet door and smoothed her hair into place. *But I do have a clue,* she thought. *I have a terrible feeling that I know exactly what this is about.*

"You don't have to snap at me. What has been going on with you lately? You said that trip would help you get back to normal, but you've been high-strung ever since you got home."

She looked at him with an arched brow. Sometimes she wondered if Josh even knew her.

"Very poor word choice," he conceded.

"Indeed."

The doorbell rang. They were here.

When Joe had first called up about police, she'd feared the worst: uniforms from East Hampton. But these two were plainclothes. Detectives. Detective Danny Brennan, specifically, with a second detective in tow. As far as she knew, Danny was still assigned as an investigator to the Manhattan DA's Office. That was good, she was hoping.

"Hanover!" Danny's voice was husky as he drew out the syllables of her last name playfully. "How have you been, lady? You look good. Rested. Getting out of the game has served you well."

I am definitely not rested. "Not totally out of the game. More of a coach now."

"As they say, those who can . . . do. Those who can't—"

"How *dare* you?" she said with feigned outrage. "You know firsthand that's not true when it comes to me."

Danny Brennan had been her principal law enforcement witness in her last major trial—an attempted rape and murder case where the defendant was caught crawling through the window of a ground-level apartment, gloved and ski-masked, armed with a hunting knife, zip ties, and condoms. He claimed his only plan had been to steal anything valuable from the apartment, but May had been able to use two prior sex-offense convictions and a plethora of violent pornography found on his computer to persuade a jury he had more terrifying intentions.

Danny's shoulders shook a bit as he chuckled quietly. "No question about that. Not too many ADAs charge as hard as you did. And, oh, say hi to Clark here. New to detectives. Trailing me today."

"Hi, Clark." One name only, but she was sure it was his last name. Even when she and Danny had gotten close enough that she moved to a first-name basis, she had always remained Hanover to him.

The trainee raised a sheepish hand. "Hey."

"Have a couple quick questions," Danny said. "Could've called but figured it'd be good to get the new guy outside for a bit since we had the time."

"Sure, of course. Come in. Um, this is Josh." Josh looked up from the pasta pot he was filling with water and gave an awkward wave.

"Yeah, I'm just gonna wait in the bedroom while you guys talk, okay?"

Gomez waddled behind him, almost like he knew trouble was coming.

"So what's going on?" she asked once they were alone. Realizing how aggressive she sounded, she softened her tone. "Or are you just here to butter me up into going back to the DA's Office?" It was the kind of harmless flirtation that women learned as a coping skill to avoid tension.

"I'd give it a shot, Hanover, if I thought it would work," Danny said with a wink. "Clark, why don't you lay it out?"

"Sure." The new detective cleared his throat with a nervous cough.

"So we got a phone call from a detective in Suffolk County. East Hampton, to be exact. They've got a missing-person case out there and are looking for possible witnesses. They got your name from a—"

Clark was cut off by the *wrong answer* sound of a game-show buzzer. *Aangh.* May was happy for the interruption. So they *were* here about East Hampton.

"See, Clark, this is why I brought you here to get some training on safe ground with Hanover. You gave up way too much information. You owe zero explanations, and you ask the questions, not them. Leave them wondering what you do or don't know. Scare them, they might walk into a trap. Like this: So, Hanover—sorry, Professor Hanover—where were you last Friday, July twenty-first?"

She was relieved when he turned to Clark and said, "See, with a real interview, you got to do it more like that, you see?"

The younger detective was nodding eagerly. "Yeah, I got it."

Thanks to loose-lipped Clark, she knew that the East Hampton police already had her name. But how?

"I was in East Hampton," she said.

"With anyone or alone?"

"With two friends visiting from out of town."

"Did you happen to have any interactions with this guy?" In the photograph Danny pulled from his blazer pocket, David Smith was wearing a suit and tie, his light, wavy hair combed neatly into place. It looked like a corporate headshot, but wasn't familiar from any of the online searches she had done for David Smiths who lived in Rhode Island. "Last Friday, he might have looked more like this."

It was a second photograph of the same man, this time on a beach, hair windblown, a slim-fit floral-patterned shirt left unbuttoned over his swim trunks. It was the picture that had been on the missing-person flyer that Lauren had brought home from the farm stand. Side by side, the competing images reminded her of the social media meme—me on LinkedIn versus me on Instagram. Two completely different portraits of the same person, but neither one entirely authentic. "His name's David Smith. He may have been with a girl—a young woman, I mean."

She shook her head. Wouldn't the people who were looking for him know who his girlfriend was? "I don't know the guy in the first picture, but assuming he's the same guy in this one, there were missing-person flyers around the Hamptons with that same photo. Why? What's up?"

"Not real sure, but if they care enough to ask for a courtesy interview from another jurisdiction just because you were born a little Miss Nancy Drew, I gotta think the kid's family has some suck."

Danny had been the one to give her the nickname, based on her habit of asking the DA investigators for extra work on her cases. Even if she had all she needed to get a conviction, her curiosity often led to nagging questions that she could not leave unanswered. The investigators probably would have started boycotting her requests if they didn't occasionally pay off in big ways. May, in short, had been a kick-ass prosecutor.

She was wondering why Danny would be using the nickname in this context when she realized what must have brought her to the attention of the police. Her curiosity. Her inability to accept questions without answers. Her refusal to mind her own fucking business.

It was the detour to Sag Harbor on the way home.

She hadn't left her name with the restaurant, and had made it a point to park four blocks away. Even if someone managed to write down her license plate after she asked a few questions, it would have traced back to Josh, not her. How did the police find out who she was? And why did they send an investigator from her former office to question her?

"I do love a good mystery, but I'm not sure what you mean, Danny."

"According to the detective out east—name's Carter Decker, by the way—they're retracing the missing guy's steps to see if he might have gotten into some kind of jam. Guess he had dinner at someplace called Page on Main Street in Sag Harbor. They canvassed the local area. A few people remembered seeing him with a girl. Young woman. The waiter said they seemed fine and normal. Nothing of interest. Then, when the police went to the American Hotel, no one recognized the guy, but the hostess told them an Asian woman had come in Monday asking whether anyone had seen the guy on Main Street. She thought maybe the couple might have been arguing outside. So now this Carter Decker wants to know why you were asking around."

She had only gone back to the restaurant to check if anyone had seen Kelsey leave the note on Smith's car. She learned that no one at the American Hotel remembered seeing David Smith at all. When May mentioned the possibility of surveillance cameras outside, the hostess kindly volunteered that they didn't have any, and that from what she'd heard from surrounding businesses, no one had found any footage of the missing man.

If this Detective Decker had known to call the DA's Office for a courtesy visit, it meant that he knew not only May's name but also that she had formerly worked at the prosecutor's office.

"One of my friends saw the flyer at a farm stand. I thought it was possible I spotted him in Sag Harbor when we went there for drinks Friday, but I really wasn't sure." The easiest way to maintain consistency with a lie was to imbue it with as much of the truth as possible. So far, so good. "On my way home, I decided it wouldn't hurt to go back and see if anyone at the restaurant recognized him. They didn't, so there was really nothing for me to call in to the tip line." All entirely true.

"But you suggested they might have been arguing. Is there a reason you thought that was the case?"

Danny asked the question breezily enough, but it was good follow-up work. This was it. She either told the truth or she didn't. She pictured herself telling him about the note. Then she'd have to tell Josh, too, and he would not approve. Josh liked Nice May, not Snarky, Bitchy May. And Danny would tell Carter Decker. And the note was mean. Really, really mean. That's why it had been funny. People would keep talking about it. Someone would post it online. It would go viral. If she tried to explain that Lauren had been the one to write it, and Kelsey was the one who left it on the car, she'd lose both of them as friends. And the law school could even treat a second round of negative attention as grounds for not renewing her contract.

She was determined to make sure no one ever found out about that horrible note.

"The couple I saw on the street was sort of snipping at each other." She remembered the two of them, his arm comfortably draped across her shoulders, hers wrapped around his waist. "But, like I said, I have no idea if it was even the same guy. I think I let my imagination get a little carried away from me. Nancy Drew and all."

"Yeah, when I talked to Decker, I told him it was probably something like that. You know there's a podcast now about that Washington, DC, case you were so obsessed with?"

"Of course I know. I was listening to it on the drive back from East Hampton. Come to think of it, I wonder if that's what made me itchy for something to amateur-sleuth for a little while."

"Weird way to spend your vacation, Hanover. I'll relay all this to Decker, but he might want to talk to you himself."

"No problem. Let me give you my cell." She jotted the number down on a notepad they kept on the kitchen island and handed it to him. "How'd he know where to find me?" She tried to keep her tone light.

"Turns out you're not the only girl detective running around Sag Harbor. The hostess you talked to described you to the servers who were working over the weekend, and one of them remembered you and your friends. They said one of your friends can pound the booze, by the way."

"How embarrassing."

"They also said you tipped very generously, so there's that. Anyway, they found the credit card charges for your table. Lauren Berry split the check with you? That sound right?"

"Yeah, one of my girlfriends." Great. They had Lauren's name, too.

"Guess Decker googled you, found your profile, called the law school, and got a message that email was a better way to contact you during the summer. Sweet gig, Hanover."

She smiled politely and nodded. "Oh great, he googled me. Total shitshow, right?"

"Yeah, that. I almost reached out when that all went down, but, you know . . ." She knew, all right. "To be honest, my guess is he felt a little hinky about you, so called the DA's Office to check you out. I didn't have your cell number so offered to track you down myself, and he took me up on it. Figured Clark and I could make a house call."

"Makes sense," she said. "Well, it's good to see you."

"Yeah, you too. Can I get phone numbers for those friends of yours too? I get the impression this Decker cat's got absolutely nothing. Trying to find anyone who might have noticed the smallest thing. That's how cases break sometimes, right?"

She tried to think of any excuse not to provide their contact information, but came up empty. "Of course." While she pulled up the contacts on her phone, he handed her back the slip of paper containing her own number and she added Lauren's and Kelsey's information.

"I forgot how perfect your handwriting is. So which one's the wino?"

She laughed. "My guess is the waitress was talking about Kelsey."

"I'll pass this on to the folks on the East End." He folded the sheet of paper and tucked it into his pocket with the photographs of David Smith. One slip of paper. A simple little note—but the potential for so much damage.

"I don't even think they noticed the couple I was thinking of," she said, leading the way to the apartment door. "I eavesdrop more than the average bear."

"I can only imagine. But maybe they'll have noticed something that you missed."

"It's possible." She hoped her voice didn't betray the simmering anxiety that was about to boil over.

In the hallway, Danny paused and turned around. His voice was low as he sought out May's gaze. "And hey, Hanover? That video. I know you. I can see what happened, but I also know you probably still beat yourself up over it."

She looked down at the floor. "That's not *not* correct."

"You're good people, lady. Don't forget it."

"Yeah, thanks," this time returning his gaze.

"And your op-ed? I read it. It was smart. And badass. Like you."

17

@NYTOPINION—JUNE 19

GUEST OPINION Who Will March For Us? After experiencing a racially motivated assault, former New York County prosecutor May Hanover wonders where are the allies for Asian Americans after the recent increase in anti-Asian hate crimes.

...

@NYTOPINION—JUNE 19

"Three months ago, a man tried to attack me on a subway platform. 'Go back where you came from, Chink bitch.' I imagined falling to the tracks. I could have died, another tragic story for the front page of the *Post*. I found myself thinking, but wait, I'm from Indiana.

...

@NYTOPINION—JUNE 19

"Hate crimes against Asian Americans have surged and no one seems to care. In 2020, anti-Asian hate crimes in 16 of the country's largest cities increased almost 150% over the previous year, even as the overall number of hate crimes reported to police declined.

...

@NYTOPINION—JUNE 19

"Scores of Asian American elders have been senselessly assaulted by random strangers on the street. These are painful statistics and stories—especially when it feels like no one cares.

...

@NYTOPINION—JUNE 19

"It's clearly no coincidence that the surge in anti-Asian crimes has occurred in the context of the Covid-19 pandemic, when politicians unapologetically invoked terms like China-virus and kung-flu. But the bridge from anti-China sentiment to attacks against Asian AMERICANS . . .

...

@NYTOPINION—JUNE 19

". . . is a manifestation of the xenophobic 'perpetual foreigner' stereotype, in which even native-born citizens are viewed as unassimilated outsiders.

...

@NYTOPINION—JUNE 19

"And xenophobia and misogyny often intersect. To my assailant, I wasn't just a Chink or a bitch, but the most despised combination of all: an Asian American woman.

...

@NYTOPINION—JUNE 19

"With every casual 'me love you long time' or 'happy ending' joke, our culture hypersexualizes and dehumanizes Asian American women.

...

@NYTOPINION—JUNE 19

"Having marched in my share of streets, I am left asking, who will march for us?" Read the full opinion at GUEST OPINION Who Will March For Us?

@AABAOFNY—JUNE 19

GUEST OPINION Who Will March For Us? So sorry this happened to our board member. Thank you @mayhanover for finding your voice to tell your story and ours.

@UNAPOLOGETICALLYOPINIONATED—JUNE 19

GUEST OPINION Who Will March For Us? TERRIFIC op-ed by hate-crime victim about rise in anti-Asian violence. We are all allies!

@NOTABOT—JUNE 19

GUEST OPINION Who Will March For Us? Who will march? I will! Anyone else?

@EATINPIZZALIKEABOSS—JUNE 20

You guys, this *GUEST OPINION Who Will March For Us?* is by May HANOVER? Married name maybe, but snarky question: Are we sure she's even Asian?

@BRADPITTSNEXTWIFE—JUNE 21

@Eatinpizzalikeaboss And she's a former prosecutor, putting black and brown people in prison, claiming she has "marched in her fair share of streets"? I smell BS.

@AMATEURSLEUTH—JUNE 21

Okay @eatinpizzalikeaboss @bradpittsnextwife, y'all sent me down the rabbit hole. Found her LinkedIn. Looks Asian in her profile pic, but probably mixed (explains last name). Fancy private summer camp for the arts, Harvard undergrad, Columbia Law, DA. Marching in streets-LMFAO.

@PIXIESTICKS—JUNE 23

@Amateursleuth I also sussed out her LinkedIn. Says she starting as Associate Professor Fordham Law this year.

@LAVIDADAVINA—JUNE 27

Ok wait for it. Pretty sure this woman *GUEST OPINION Who Will March For Us?* is the same crazy woman I filmed cuz she was bugging out. Subway platform in March, so timing lines up. Looks like her. Context matters?

@LAVIDADAVINA—JUNE 29

Wow! Guess that video blew up. For those asking, I started recording cuz she scolded every maskless person she saw. Man made the mistake of trying to win her over. Look at her screaming her ass off like the black man's murdering her while giving the white racist a pass. Lol.

@LAVIDADAVINA—JUNE 30

Oh lord, y'all are NOT calling her Asian DA Karen. I'm dead. #AsianDAKaren

@JAYDENSMOM—JULY 1

@LaVidaDavina. That does look like the op-ed author. Not to make excuses for her, but is it possible she yelled at the wrong person? Maybe she thought the other guy was the one who said it?

@LAVIDADAVINA—JULY 1

@JaydensMom. Except that's exactly what you just did—make up an excuse. And gee . . . I wonder why she'd just assume that of all the dudes on the platform, HE was the one she should scream at and sic the police on? 🤷‍♀️

@PIXIESTICKS—JULY 2

Wonder if @Fordham knows its new law prof @MayHanover is #AsianDAKaren.

@PIXIESTICKS—JULY 3

Oh, interesting, everyone. Look what you find when you pull up the profile for #AsianDAKaren:

> @mayhanover THIS ACCOUNT DOES NOT EXIST

The first two days after the publication of May's guest op-ed felt heady. She was glued to her devices, soaking in the adoration from the atta-girl texts and emails pouring into her phone, retweets by former law professors she had worshipped, and an invitation from *The Washington Post* to contribute any other essays she had in mind about the Asian American or mixed-race experiences.

But as she had learned during her first year of teaching, there's a reason some professors never read their evaluations. Seventy-eight students might love you, but it's the words of the two critics that sting. Despite all the positive responses to her op-ed, she was offended that total strangers began to question her motives based only on her non-Asian last name, mixed-race appearance, and the fact that she had been a prosecutor. Josh had to talk her out of replying to each individual troll.

It wasn't until the account called LaVidaDavina posted a video from the subway platform that things really got out of control, though. The clip showed what had happened to May from a completely different point of view. It made it look like she had instigated the entire confrontation with the African American man she had described as her assailant. It made her look absolutely unhinged and insane. And worse than anything, it made it clear she had accused the wrong man.

It had been May's first time riding the subway since the shutdown. All she did was ask a few people to put their masks on. The subway mandate was still in place.

Aw, you're too fine to be wearing that mask anyway, girl . . . What, I'm not your type? That's good. It's cool . . . Why you looking at me like that?

Please, just stay away from me.

Seriously? You're gonna act scared because I dared to speak to you?

Yes, you're scaring me. Step back.

I didn't step front. *You're tripping.*

Stop, go away.

Oh lord, this is one crazy bitch.

She turned her back to him, began walking away—quickly. Despite the distance she was trying to put between them, she heard his next words clearly. *Go back to where you came from, Chink bitch.*

With those words, she pictured him charging her from behind, pushing her to the tracks, like those other Asian victims she had been reading about in the news. She was next. This was how she was going to die, all because she took the subway. She realized she was screaming, her fists clenched at her sides, yelling as loudly as she could.

HELP, SOMEBODY, PLEASE HELP!

When she turned, bracing for the incoming blow, he wasn't as close as she had feared.

Are you really acting like I'm threatening you right now? You're gonna panic like that? He stepped toward her. She had replayed it so many times in her head. She was sure of it. He definitely moved in her direction. That was the only reason she would have reached for her phone.

STOP! I'M CALLING THE POLICE.

Okay, of course you are. You know how that ends for me? Are you serious? She began to scream that awful scream—the one that got snipped and clipped and replayed and memed.

It wasn't until May saw the video that she realized the voice she had heard behind her as she tried to put distance between herself and Darren Foster, the words she still had nightmares about—*Go back to you where you came from, Chink bitch*—didn't belong to Foster. That vile command had come out of the maskless mouth of a white man with his knees spread wide on the bench beneath the poster reminding passengers that masks were still required within the transit system.

But the video made it clear that May leapt to the conclusion that Foster was the culprit. She became yet another woman to weaponize her power as a woman to sic the police on an African American man. She had issued a statement of apology that the *Times* published, and had tried to reach Foster personally to explain, but the video was more powerful than any words she could offer. The fact remained that May was the one lecturing strangers about masks and then screaming like a murder victim when no one was actually hurting her. And she had topped it all off by writing an op-ed claiming to have been the victim of a hate crime.

The hashtag #AsianDAKaren was a top Twitter trend for nearly a week.

May knew the video must have reached a tipping point in the zeitgeist when even her tech-phobic mother found out about it thanks to some blabbermouth at her church. The frequency of her already frequent phone calls tripled overnight. She said she was "worried" about May to the point where May had to talk her out of flying to New York, but more than anything, she seemed disappointed.

It's just not like you to be like that.

You need to explain to everyone you weren't yourself.

What got into you? As if an invasive entity had taken over her brain, voice, and body, because it was so unthinkable that May might lose her temper, or make a mistake, or lash out in a moment of rage.

Josh was more supportive. He made it possible for her to hunker down in the privacy of their apartment, handling the dog walks, running all their errands, and becoming her conduit to the outside world. He even offered to max out his credit cards to hire a publicity consultant specializing in crisis management.

And the retweets continued. She became the latest example of what she learned the internet called a Milkshake Duck—a person lauded online for some admirable characteristic who turns out to be horrible in real life. The guy with the hilarious Twitter thread about a piece of shrimp in his cereal gets called out for being an abuser. The "hot cop" who went viral while helping storm victims resigns when his anti-Semitic Facebook posts are discovered. The camper who jumped into the rapids to rescue a drowning dog is revealed to be a deadbeat dad.

The idea behind the meme is that the whole internet might fall in love with something fabulous like an adorable baby duck who loves to drink milkshakes, but then once the milkshake-loving duck comes under scrutiny, it turns out the duck's just another piece of crap.

May thought of the meme itself as a duck/rabbit, that famously ambiguous image that can be seen as either a duck or a rabbit. The philosopher Ludwig Wittgenstein used it to describe two kinds of "seeing." From one perspective, the Milkshake Duck was a misanthropic trope: Don't meet your heroes, as they say. Even the delightful duck might be awful, because you can't vouch for anyone in this world.

But from May's perspective, it could also be seen as an observation about the current culture, fueled by social media. Put yourself out there on the internet, and the mob will find a reason to take you down, even if you're just a sweet baby duck trying to eat some ice cream.

May's phone had rung in her hand almost immediately after she hit the final button to confirm that, yes, she really did want to delete her Twitter account. She was terrified it would be the dean of the law school, calling to revoke her job offer. Instead, it was Lauren, who gave her exactly what she needed at that moment, asking if she was okay, promising her it would be all right. She, too, knew what it was like to be judged and vilified by total strangers.

Those strangers don't know your truth. Only you do.

Unlike her mom and Josh, Lauren didn't judge, and she didn't try to solve May's problems. She was the one to convince May that Twitter wasn't the real world, going so far as to send her the statistics to back it up. May didn't need her 780 SAT math score to realize that only a fraction of the population had heard anything about either her op-ed or the unwanted attention that had fallen upon her in the aftermath.

And then Lauren had reached out to Kelsey, and May had both of them to remind her that life does move on. By the time the law school semester started, even her students didn't seem to care that the brand-new professor was the same woman some of them must have heard about over the summer. From what May could tell, they had their hands full adjusting to classes after two years of virtual education and were only interested in material that would be on their final, although they did seem fascinated whenever she shared an edgy story from trial practice. If she had to guess, they didn't expect anything about Professor Hanover to be edgy.

The entire subway incident, all things considered, was behind her. But it wouldn't remain that way—not if it all happened again, this time because she couldn't leave a man alone for stealing a parking spot.

18

Carter Decker wasn't sure he wanted to trust the instincts of some Manhattan DA investigator he didn't know from Adam.

According to the investigator he'd just spoken to, Hanover was a busybody by nature. In his words, "like a dog with a bone when she can't get an answer about something nagging her." Maybe that's exactly the kind of person who might go looking for a missing person on her own, just because he may or may not have been one half of a couple she saw bickering on the street, but the whole thing felt off to Carter.

He'd seen the video when he initially googled her. It was the first hit in the search results, before her bio on the Fordham Law School website, before the op-ed that she had published about the subway incident. The woman seemed very tightly wound, but he couldn't see any connection to David Smith's disappearance, if he was even willing to call it that yet. The fact that Smith's cell phone last pinged on Saturday definitely had him worried, but he could also imagine a guy overloaded with work calls and a prying mother letting his battery go conveniently dead for a few days.

His thoughts were interrupted by the buzz of his own phone. Another 401 area code. He was beginning to think that David Smith's mother had sent his number to the entire state of Rhode Island. "Decker."

The caller said his name was Simon Bowlby, asked if Decker was the detective working on the David Smith case, and then explained that an attorney named Anthony Walker had suggested he call about his friend David. "I haven't talked to Dave since Thursday night. We got beers after work and watched the Red Sox game. He was planning to leave the next morning for the Hamptons with Christine."

He finally had a name for the plus-one. Walker had confirmed that Smith's phone was company-issued but was still working on getting the call records. "You have a last name for Christine? A contact number?"

"No. I've only met her a few times when we've hung out in groups. She's in marketing or something like that. Pretty sure she went to Colby, but I don't know how I know that. Oh, she was wearing a Colby baseball cap at the brewery and I asked her. So yeah, Colby."

"So is she Dave's girlfriend or what?" Carter asked.

"I mean, sort of? Like he sees her pretty regularly, but it's not exclusive."

"Does she know that?"

"Um . . . knowing Dave? Maybe not explicitly."

"His mom didn't seem to know anything about her."

"If your mom is Tinsley Smith, you don't introduce her to a girlfriend unless you're ready to get married."

"Because?"

"She's, I don't know . . . clingy. Dave's dad was already geriatric when he was born, and Tinsley really leans into the idea that it's up to Dave to keep the legacy going, or whatever. She wants Dave to be locked down with kids already, but she also doesn't really approve of anyone. Like no one would be good enough for Dave unless they were the equivalent of the royal family. She thinks the kind of girls Dave dates are twit gold diggers."

"And are they?" Carter asked.

"Sometimes, but he doesn't always see it if they hide it well enough."

"How about Christine?"

"Definitely not a twit, but she's definitely got a side to her that falls within Dave's blind spot."

"Such as?"

"Honestly? I get the impression she's almost playing the part of someone you'd want to marry. A super-fun girl around the guys, super-doting toward Dave. Almost too good to be true. But she's the kind of person who yells at the waiter when she thinks no one's listening. Does that make sense?"

"Definitely paints a picture, yeah. You said it wasn't exclusive. Was he still dating around? If he was using any dating apps, we could get into his accounts—"

"No, man. Apps are lame. Just say hey to a girl in her DMs. It's, like, less formal that way."

Carter had just been swiping—more left than right—that morning. "And these women he'd talk to online, were they friends? Acquaintances? Strangers?"

"A little of all of that, I guess. Like mutual follows, or people you met a long time ago and reconnect with. I don't know how old you are, but probably how Facebook used to be."

Carter was only forty-two, not much older than Dave Smith, but this guy was one step away from calling him a boomer.

"And you think Christine didn't know about these contacts with other women?"

"I seriously doubt it. Here's the thing: Dave was originally going on this Hamptons trip with another girl. I never met her, but I got the impression he was really into her. We'd be out for drinks and he'd be all distracted, texting with her constantly. He said it sucked that she lived like an hour or two away—maybe he said Hartford? So they couldn't see each other that often. I think that's what was keeping him from breaking things off entirely with Christine, but it seemed like he was thinking about it. He'd let things go cold with her for weeks, telling her he was slammed with projects or had work trips, when it was really because of this other woman. And then, like, three weeks ago, he tells me she turned out to be a total crackpot, and that was the end of that."

"A crackpot how?"

"I don't know. He said he didn't want to talk about it, but I got the impression he was pretty hurt about the whole situation. Like he might have really loved her and was disappointed when it didn't work out."

"And you don't know anything else about this woman?"

"Nope."

"But you're sure the woman here with him this weekend was Christine?" Once he got access to Smith's Instagram, he would presumably find a connection to an account for someone named Christine who attended Colby.

"Yeah, at least as of Thursday night. I don't have her number, but I sent out a text blast to a bunch of people hoping word gets to her. Hopefully one of them can call home base and Tinsley can stop calling everyone under the sun about Dave."

"You don't sound especially worried about your friend."

"I mean, not really. Maybe because I don't want to be worried?"

"You're close?"

"Yeah, man. Real close. I've known him since sixth grade." Simon's voice had softened. Gone was the *bro*-vado. "I don't even want to think that anything . . . yeah, no. He's just out there partying, is my guess. Lost his phone or something. That's got to be it."

Carter had heard this kind of wishful thinking from witnesses before, trying to convince themselves that the worst case couldn't possibly be the truth. "And what does partying involve for Dave?" he asked.

"What do you mean?"

"Drugs, for example?"

"I mean, weed, yeah. That's like legal now."

"Nothing else?"

"Some coke on occasion, but very rarely. Back when we were in our twenties? Yeah, that was pretty regular, and he did go on a bit of a binge after college when he was going through a rough time. So if I'm telling you all this, it means I'm being honest. These days, it would only be if it's going around at a party or something. So if you're thinking this a drug thing, it's not."

The local market for recreational cocaine was relatively well mannered, but Carter knew that summer could bring in some rougher dealers from out of the area, drawn to visitors who didn't have access to a regular supplier.

Another call was coming in to Carter's phone. A 401 area code again. Not the mom, not her lawyer. He thanked Simon for the information and switched to the incoming call.

"Is this the East Hampton police department?" The woman was slightly out of breath. Tentative and nervous.

"Yes. Detective Carter Decker. This is my cell."

"You've been looking for Dave Smith?"

"Yes. His mother has reported him missing."

"Then I think you've been looking for me. My name's Christine Harper. I just saw him Saturday."

"And you're not with him now?" Carter asked.

"No. I'm in New York City. Or at least I was. I'm on the train now."

"Going where?"

"I was planning to go back home to Providence until my phone blew up with people looking for me. I managed to get on the Long Island Railroad right before they closed the doors."

"So you're coming back out here?"

"Yes."

"And I'm sorry, are you meeting Dave? Where is he?" He felt like he was one step behind during this entire conversation.

"No, I'm meeting you. Or someone else from your department. I assume you have questions."

"I do, and I've been trying to ask them."

"I promise you, I have no idea where he is. But I'd prefer to talk to you in person. That's why I almost face-planted down the stairs running for this train. If I sound weird, it's because I'm still catching my breath."

"I'm not sure that's even necessary, Christine."

"It is, Detective. Because it sounds like I'm the last person who saw Dave, he would never ignore his mother for two days because he's scared shitless of her, and if you haven't already done so, you're going to go to our hotel room and find a shattered statue of a bird that I threw at him the last time I saw him. So, yes, I think you need to see me in person."

19

Lauren Berry was twenty-six years old, three years into her work at Wildwood, when she first noticed that Thomas Welliver was flirting with her. He was fifty at the time, but had the voice of a much younger man.

That's how she first flirted back, telling him he had a good voice: *You could make a fortune in voiceover work.*

I already made a fortune doing something much easier.

"I miss you." Even twenty years later, he still had his timbre.

"No, you don't," Lauren teased. She had come inside to pour herself a glass of water. Kelsey was deep into a novel on her chaise longue, and Nate was swimming laps. She decided to put together some tortilla chips and guacamole, but was dawdling to have time inside with Thomas and some air-conditioning. "That's not how we do."

They talked most days, but not all. And they saw each other regularly, but for them, that meant at most once a week, and only when they were in the same city. At first, she told herself that was enough. She was an artist. She moved—a lot. She traveled. She toured. She composed. She had no interest in having children. She had no need for a traditional, glued-at-the-hip relationship.

But then friends started getting married. They sent out holiday cards with happy photographs in front of vacation beaches and Christmas trees. She convinced herself she deserved the same things. But, *oof,* the expectations of the men with whom she tried to make a go of it were absolutely suffocating. It turned out that someone to talk to and spend a night with once a week or so suited her just about right. And besides, no one else loved her, looked at her, admired her, smiled at her, flat-out adored her like Thomas Welliver. He said he had no idea what happiness was until he met her.

Well before Lauren was in the picture, he and Jessica were so unhappy that they agreed to separate, but while the divorce papers were being drafted, Jessica decided that she didn't want to lose all the perks of being Mrs. Thomas Welliver.

The Welliver marriage endured for the sole purpose of continuing Jessica's role as one half of a Texas Power Couple. Thomas believed he owed her that much since she had made the decision not to have children in large part because that was his preference. So the marriage and accompanying philanthropic efforts continued, while they each had quiet relationships with other people.

Thomas had offered to leave Jessica many times over the years. More than offered. Almost like he asked permission. But if that happened, Lauren might be expected to act like a Mrs. Thomas Welliver. It wasn't for her.

"You can't even let me sweet-talk you," he said.

When she had been the one to insist on tendering her voluntary resignation from Wildwood after the drowning, she had assumed it would also be the end of their relationship. She was always a little out of sync with the camp parents' expectations. But she had talent—something the kids recognized because they didn't respond to résumés or networking allegiances. They could feel at a cellular level that she loved music and was able to bring out the best in them.

In another world, it's possible she would have eventually set aside her career as a working musician—composing, performing, conducting, producing—to settle into a year-round job teaching children how to do all the things she had wanted to do for as long as she could remember. But then Marnie Mann drowned.

By that time, it was her ninth summer at the camp. She would have expected to be treated as part of the mourning family, like everyone else. But she was the youngest, by far, of any adult with responsibility at the camp. She was the one who acted as the bridge between the elders and the kids. And she didn't look like everyone else.

Apparently, if something really bad happens in an idyllic place, all eyes move to the person who's not quite like the others. And the rumors about her and Thomas certainly didn't help.

She was tempted at first to fight for her position. She even called her mentor at the Louisiana Philharmonic for advice, who put her in touch with the president of Tulane, who contacted their very successful alumnus Thomas Welliver, who owned the camp. And that was, well, ironic.

Lauren was only thirty-one years old at the time, but she wasn't stupid. She had never been stupid in her whole life. She knew how the world worked. Marnie's death was terrible, but it was also an accident, and all those parents knew that. But they also knew they couldn't continue to send their beloved kids to Wildwood to get them out of their hair without finding someone to blame. As long as they had someone to blame, they could add more adult managers, institute new rules about monitoring the activities of counselors off-camp, blah blah blah.

In short, it would be easier for the camp to survive the scandal if someone at Lauren's level appeared to be getting the ax. The truth was that she already knew her viable days at Wildwood were numbered when Marnie had walked in on her and Thomas in Lauren's cottage, Thomas's hand not moving quickly enough from beneath Lauren's dress.

She'd known Marnie since she was thirteen years old, and Marnie was constitutionally incapable of keeping a secret. Even so, the anonymous note slipped in the middle of the night beneath the door to the administrative offices seemed out of character. She would have predicted that Marnie, always vying for popularity she never managed to find, would use her newfound secret as currency among the other counselors and campers.

Once Lauren began to hear rumors that the camp owner's hand had gone up her skirt, she knew she could not remain an effective den mother. When Marnie died, the answer seemed clear. It was time for her to go. Two potential scandals killed with one resignation.

But despite all her assumptions, it had not been the end of her relationship with Thomas.

He must not have been exaggerating about missing her, because he had called her every day since she'd been in the Hamptons. "I am looking forward to being back in my own house," she said.

"I've got your flight information. Can I be your ride?"

"Can't wait." She couldn't think of anything more romantic than someone as busy as he was picking her up from the airport. "I love these women, but lord, I forgot how the two of them together can be a whole situation."

She had been so excited for the Crew to reunite. But Kelsey and May both wanted so much from her that after only three days it was exhausting. There was a reason she didn't have either a husband or children, and the combination of the two women could still feel like parenting.

Even the other night, when May went on about instantly knowing Josh was the one, Lauren suspected she'd been putting on some kind of act for Kelsey's benefit, maybe to make sure that Kelsey wasn't still disappointed that May and Nate had not become a permanent item. Lauren knew damn well that when May clicked with a guy from day one, it said more about the nights that might follow than any long-term plans for the future. Until three years ago, Lauren would have bet hard cash that May was going to join Lauren in the never-marry club. Every time anything started to get serious with a guy, she'd make certain it didn't stay that way by finding someone else to hook up with—someone who didn't see her as a perfect little nice girl. After Lauren's first two encounters with Josh, she figured he was on borrowed time. But when faced with the choice of being locked alone in her studio apartment for the foreseeable future or hunkering down with Josh, May made the move, with the engagement to follow.

May had confided in Lauren that since she began therapy after the subway incident, she was talking openly about issues beyond her anxiety. Apparently her shrink thought May had something like a female version of the Madonna-Whore complex, dividing potential partners into two camps—the fun ones and the "good" ones. It sounded like a lot of psychobabble bullshit to Lauren. Maybe May just liked a certain kind of relationship with a certain kind of man. Or maybe Lauren was, as the therapists called it, "projecting." But sometimes Lauren worried that May had agreed to get married so she wouldn't have to admit to anyone—especially herself—that she'd only moved in with Josh because she feared being lonely. And if lying to Kelsey about being in love at first sight was part of the cover, so be it.

When Lauren had first asked Kelsey to contact May because she needed a friend, Kelsey said she wasn't sure she could ever forgive her for not reaching out to her after Luke was murdered. As hard as she knew the two of them had worked to be there for each other the past year, it was clear Lauren was still their common connection. She had always been the kind of person who, once she made a friend—a real friend—was a friend for life. Found family, is how she thought of it. As good, if not better, than blood. As different as she was from her family of origin, she still loved them unconditionally, even if they didn't understand the choices she had made since she started out on her journey as a young teenager. She was lucky because not all families were connected like that. Some of the parents at Wildwood were so psyched to dump off their kids that they literally high-fived each other as they walked back to their luxury SUVs on drop-off day. And then there were kids like May or Kelsey, who had either lost a parent or never knew them to begin with.

It was only natural that some of them looked to the camp's adults to be their family, if only temporarily. Kelsey, as much as she tried to act all grown, had always struck Lauren as a kid searching for love. She was an okay flutist and a fairly gifted vocalist—more poppy than classical—but musical training was never her passion. The camp was special to her because it felt like home.

Had Marnie lived, they probably would have remained close professionally. Marnie had said so many times, "I want to be you when I grow up," and Lauren had been encouraging her to keep working on her original compositions. But when Marnie died, May and Kelsey were the ones who were there—no longer children but not quite Lauren's peers either—and their mutual need to connect had nothing to do with music. And after all these years, she had come to see Kelsey and May not like children or sisters precisely, but also not merely friends. She knew they felt the same way about her. She just wished they'd feel that way about each other again, too.

Kelsey especially needed the support of found family. Of all the overly doting and protective parents Lauren had dealt with at Wildwood, Bill Ellis arguably outdid them all, especially after the divorce from Nate's mother. Even now that Kelsey was a grown woman helping him run his real estate empire, he treated her like a child. If she didn't answer her phone on a Friday night, he'd want to know not only where she was but who she was with. When she wanted to buy her first apartment in Roslindale, he gave her an extra three hundred and fifty thousand dollars so she could buy in what he called a "safer" neighborhood that also happened to be closer to him. And though he paid her a meaningful salary, it was clear to Lauren that he was never going to pay her enough to be able to turn down Daddy's help when he offered it.

Kelsey even joked that she owed her alibi at the time of Luke's murder to her father's overbearing ways. The night he was robbed, she was supposed to be on a date with a guy she met on OkCupid, but her father insisted that it would be embarrassing for him to receive an honor at the International Achievement Summit without her at his side. Her would-be date ghosted her after news of the murder got out. Kelsey had tried masking her despair with humor, saying that she never got a third date, but did get filet mignon and an alibi.

No matter how many years passed, Kelsey's father was never going to stop treating Kelsey like a child. But if she did go forward with her decision to have a baby alone, that might be a way to bring her fractured family back together, which Lauren knew was what her friend wanted most in this world. Nate would definitely be a rock-solid uncle. And if Nate was helping Kelsey, it would be hard for Kelsey's father not to accept him. Perhaps even Nate's mother, Jeanie—despite the memory loss—would understand at some primal level that the baby was a part of her family.

Lauren told Thomas she'd call him tomorrow and made her way

to the backyard, where Nate was still swimming laps. She and Kelsey were halfway through the chips and guac when Lauren's cell rang. The ringtone was "Maggie May" by Rod Stewart. She answered on speaker.

"Hey there, woman. We were just saying we miss you."

"Yes, we miss you!" Kelsey managed to say with a chip in her mouth. "Come back here right now. It's boring without you."

"You're clearly having a miserable time," May said dryly. She paused, and Lauren could picture her pulling at the ends of her hair, the way she always did when she felt anxious. "Absolutely suffering. I don't even know how to say this, but the police are probably going to call you. Both of you."

"What? How would they even know about us?"

"They came to my apartment. They asked who I was with. I didn't have a choice. They have your names. And your phone numbers."

"How?" Lauren asked. "Were there cameras or something?"

"No, it was because of me. I'm so sorry."

"We talked about this," Lauren said. "I thought we all agreed."

"I know, and we did. But I messed up. I'm so sorry."

"So you called them?" Lauren asked. "Without telling us? After you promised we were on the same page?"

"No, I didn't call anyone. But I went back to the American Hotel."

"You did what now?" Lauren said.

"On my way home. I only wanted to see if there might have been surveillance cameras that got Kelsey on video. I didn't tell them anything except that I'd seen the missing-person flyer and thought it was possible I saw him in front of the restaurant. I asked if anyone else recognized him, but no one did. Then I asked if maybe it was on camera, but they said there weren't any. But then the police were canvassing the neighborhood and the staff at the American Hotel mentioned I had been in. They found my name from our bill."

Next to her, Kelsey was shaking her head, mouthing silently, *Un-fucking-believable.*

This was just like May, or at least just like the annoying goody-two-shoes part of her. Granted, back at Wildwood, Lauren would have taken a hundred nerds like May over the entitled brats who would disobey all the counselors, confident that their rich parents would never allow them to be disciplined. But she also recognized that May was in sore need of a bad-influence friend like Kelsey. May helped Kelsey make better decisions and to be a little more aware of her privilege, while Kelsey taught May to lighten up and have a little fun.

May's connection to confident, vivacious Kelsey—with the good clothes and rich father—helped earnest, provincial May fit in without having to conform by pretending she was someone other than her earnest, provincial self. But as much as Lauren joked with May about being the rule-following sheriff, she knew that part of May resented the responsibility.

She remembered May breaking down that summer after college graduation when she had to work as a counselor, seeking out Lauren in her cabin after check-in one night. As they sat together on the floor, leaning against Lauren's bed, May admitted between sobs that she had applied to law school just so she wouldn't have to take a crappy job or stay unemployed while waiting for the economy to bounce back. Lauren had hugged her, promising that everyone her age was in the same boat. She should only go to law school if she wanted to, Lauren said, and there was nothing to be ashamed of if it took a while to find a good job. Her assurances only made May cry harder. Lauren still remembered her exact words as she rolled herself into a ball on Lauren's lap like a cat.

"You don't understand. It's my mother. Her culture. Her whole reason for having a daughter in America. All the sacrifices she made—I'm the outcome. I can't be bad. I can't fail. I can't just be average. It's not fucking fair." In that moment, May didn't sound sad or insecure or worried. She sounded angry. She sounded *pissed.*

It was a familiar feeling that Lauren had been ingrained to hide from an early age. She hadn't gotten to where she was by showing her anger. And there was no question in Lauren's mind that May's anger had always been there, simmering beneath the perfect, polite surface. If she had to follow the rules, so should everyone else.

"So the police just showed up at your apartment?" Lauren asked.

"They didn't have my number. I guess they googled me and realized someone at the DA's Office would be able to reach me. They sent an investigator I know."

Kelsey sobered up quickly. "So they must know about the note, right? Otherwise, they wouldn't send someone to your fricking house?"

"No, I really don't think so. I told them I saw a couple arguing in Sag Harbor, but that I wasn't sure if it was the same guy or not. And I said I didn't even know whether either of you had noticed. We just have to make sure we don't contradict each other."

Lauren resisted the urge to remind her that one way for them to be completely consistent would have been not to draw the attention of the police in the first place. "Okay, he hasn't called us yet, so Kelsey and I will figure out what to say and make sure we stick to that story."

"I think I should come back," May said. "If something did happen to this David Smith guy, the police might find the note in his car. They could check the nearby restaurants and figure out the American Hotel uses those kinds of napkins. I should be there, just to make sure we're all on the same page. But I know Nate's there and there's no extra room now."

Lauren knew exactly what was actually going on. May wanted to be here to have some sense of control over the situation, because May could not handle uncertainty of any kind. But May was also a really good lawyer. If everything did go to shit, she should be here. "We'll figure it out when you get here," Lauren said.

"Of course," Kelsey added. "We never wanted you to leave in the first place."

"Okay, I'll tell Josh I've got major FOMO and want to go back."

Lauren was relieved to hear that May hadn't told Josh anything. She'd only met the guy a couple of times, but if she had to guess, he'd disapprove of their behavior and try to convince May to blame it all on her friends. "If the police call in the meantime, just make sure to tell the truth about where we were. Pretty much the only way we could end up screwed is if we get caught in a lie. And stay calm if they call, okay? You're tourists who don't recognize the guy and don't remember seeing a couple argue."

As far as Lauren was concerned, it was the truth. Lauren had years of practice picking a story and sticking with it.

20

HOUSTON WEEKLY

NOVEMBER 2, 2019

A SYMPHONY SCANDAL PRIMER:
WHY IT'S MORE THAN TABLOID FODDER

The recent scandal at the Houston Symphony initially seemed like little more than deliciously juicy tabloid fodder: a pissed-off high-society wife who decided to go nuclear on her wealthy husband when she discovered his decades-long affair with a younger woman. But a story that could have ended as tantalizing water-cooler gossip has burst open multilayered and nuanced discussions about the intersections among race, gender, sex, wealth, and power. If you haven't been following the story that won't quite go away—and the reasons why it has resonated—here's what you need to know.

Who Are Thomas and Jessica Welliver?

Thomas Welliver's estimated net worth is $890 million, although *Fortune* speculated only two years ago that the notoriously private Welliver may invest money in ways that deflate public estimates of his worth. He made the bulk of his millions (billions?) as the President and Founder of TMW Engineering, Inc., a company that provides seismic data to the lucrative oil and gas industries. The 66-year-old Thomas has been married since 1984 to Jessica Welliver (née Carrington), a graduate of SMU and former high school history teacher prior to her marriage. She is reported to have a passion and talent for architecture and design and has overseen the construction and resale of several multimillion-dollar estates. Last year, the *Houston Chronicle* listed the Wellivers as number nine on its annual list of Houston's most philanthropic families. The Thomas and Jessica Welliver Foundation supports education, cultural arts, health care, and public service. Thomas and Jessica Welliver are also the founders of the Wildwood Camp for Youth Arts in Moultonborough, New Hampshire, which Jessica Welliver has said was created to join her interests in supporting education, children, and the arts. Jessica has specifically identified Wildwood as a way to be involved with children after regretting the couple's decision not to have their own.

Who Is Lauren Berry?

Lauren Berry is probably best known to Texans as the first African American Music Director of the Houston Symphony. Born in Lafayette, Louisiana, she was considered a piano prodigy, playing at Carnegie Hall when she was fifteen years old. She attended Tulane on a music scholarship and became a member and then first-chair violinist of the Louisiana Philharmonic Orchestra, while also playing her own compositions and other works with orchestras and ensembles in North America and Europe. After serving from 2000–2008 as the Music Director for the Wellivers' Wildwood camp, she lived in California, working as both a session musician and a composer, primarily for film scores. Her score for the animated film *What Lions Know* was nominated for an Academy Award in 2014.

The Connection Between the Wellivers and Lauren Berry

On April 16, Jessica Welliver sent an email to Roberta "Bunny" Atkins, a member of the symphony's governing board of directors. Published photographs from various regional social events suggest that Jessica Welliver and Atkins are at least friendly, as does the tone of the full email

("Dear Bunny, Sorry to drag you into this, but I'm desperate to save my marriage with Tommy, even if it means blowing things up for a while"). According to the email, which has not yet been independently verified, Thomas Welliver exercised his clout as a donor and former board member to influence the symphony's decision to select Berry as its next Music Director.

Also according to Mrs. Welliver, but not independently verified, Ms. Berry first "ensnared" Mr. Welliver when they both attended a music-focused fundraiser in New Orleans for Tulane, their mutual alma mater. That "unwelcome entanglement" led to Ms. Berry's hiring as the Music Director at Wildwood, a decision that Mrs. Welliver approved, unaware of the "true nature of this woman's interest in my husband."

According to Mrs. Welliver, she first became aware of her husband's supposed affair with Ms. Berry when she received an anonymous letter in July 2008 from someone purporting to be a Wildwood camper who discovered Ms. Berry and Mr. Welliver together in a compromising position. Ms. Berry departed from her position at the end of the summer session of 2008, and, according to Mrs. Welliver, she believed that the affair had ended and her marriage remained intact.

In her email to Ms. Atkins, Mrs. Welliver claimed to have "ironclad" evidence that Ms. Berry continued to pursue Mr. Welliver for years, using their prior affair as "leverage" to gain both direct financial support and behind-the-scenes assistance with her career, including the appointment to her current position at the Houston Symphony, where she was now, for the first time ever, in geographic proximity to the Wellivers. Mrs. Welliver pleaded for Ms. Atkins's assistance reaching a severance agreement with Ms. Berry since her employment was gained under "false pretenses." In a foreboding conclusion that some have likened to blackmail, Mrs. Welliver warned that she didn't "want to air these unseemly facts publicly, but will do whatever is necessary to get this predatory woman out of our lives."

Rather than help Mrs. Welliver behind the scenes, Ms. Atkins shared the email with the rest of the board and the symphony's legal counsel in what she called her fiduciary obligations as a board member. A copy of the email was leaked anonymously to the *Chronicle*.

The Ugly Media Aftermath

The revelation of what is purported to have been a longstanding, though perhaps not continuous, affair between a wealthy, powerful white man and a younger, talented, African American woman has given rise to various interpretations. One approach to the story is through a gendered lens, raising questions about the power dynamics between the parties (if the affair did in fact happen). Mrs. Welliver clearly depicted Berry as the sexual aggressor, the woman who wore down her husband's resistance and then refused to go away when he tried to salvage his marriage. From this point of view, she is Glenn Close's bunny-boiling home wrecker from *Fatal Attraction,* and Thomas Welliver is the man paying decades later for succumbing to a moment of weakness.

But we know more about the power dynamics of workplace sexual relationships now, post Harvey Weinstein and #MeToo, than we did—or Thomas Welliver and Lauren Berry likely did—whenever their purported affair commenced. While a relationship between a camp's director and its owner may have been viewed as consensual at the time, the inherent power differential between the parties makes the notion of "consent" murkier than it once was—especially when the person with more power is married, leaving the relationship shrouded in secrecy and the less powerful party less able to seek counsel from friends or family.

There is also no question that the scandal has been used to invoke racial "dog whistles" and to criticize a so-called "woke mob" looking to increase diversity, equality, and inclusion within elite, historically white-dominated spaces. What began as fodder for local society columns went national when some media outlets seized upon the salacious story to question Berry's qualifications for her position and to suggest that she was appointed by the symphony only for the sake of having a first African American Music Director. By framing Berry's appointment as a product of tokenism rather than a reflection of her talent, hard work, and qualifications, these outlets injected the story into a larger culture war.

And finally, the story presents yet another example of the ways that private wealth can influence public and quasi-public institutions. If Mrs. Welliver is to be believed, Ms. Berry might not have been offered her current position, however well qualified she might be for it, without a wealthy-insider benefactor. And the fact that Mrs. Welliver turned to her private access to a member of the symphony's governing board in an attempt to fire her husband's alleged lover demonstrates the power that she appears comfortable wielding behind the scenes.

Berry's success as the first African American Music Director of the Houston Symphony is a milestone worth celebrating, reflecting progress in an artistic sector that has historically lacked diversity. It is unfortunate that tawdry tabloid fodder has cast a shadow over her important accomplishments, but it also presents an opportunity to critically examine the way the story has been framed. Only Mr. Welliver and Ms. Berry truly understand the power dynamics between them and whether they were affected by differences in race, gender, wealth, and power. But as we have learned in recent years, sometimes not even the two parties to the relationship necessarily agree.

Note: As of the writing of this article, each of the Wellivers has declined to reply to inquiries. The Houston Symphony issued a statement supporting Ms. Berry's appointment, saying they "remain thrilled to have been able to recruit such an accomplished and talented person to lead our institution." Ms. Berry neither confirmed nor denied Mrs. Welliver's allegations and issued a statement that she was proud of the symphony's work and committed to its continued excellence. A search of court records shows no filings for separation or divorce involving the Wellivers. Board member Atkins stated by email, "It was with great pain that I shared the relevant information with the board, and I trust everyone involved to refrain from further distracting from the symphony's important work."

21

Lauren tried unsuccessfully again to link her phone to Kelsey's car stereo. She finally gave up and scanned terrestrial radio until she landed on a Fleetwood Mac song. Stevie's dreams were unwinding and love was just a state of mind by the time she spotted the train pulling into the East Hampton station.

She scanned the cars lining both sides of the street, people poised to greet their arriving guests. No one looked remotely like her except for one woman who exited the train platform, giving Lauren a friendly nod as she passed in front of her idling car to cross the street. Lauren returned the gesture.

Her phone buzzed in the console's cupholder. It was a text from Thomas. *Can I call?*

He always did that even though she told him it wasn't necessary. She assumed it was his way of showing respect for the fact that she had her own life.

I'm picking up May from the train station and she's due any time.

I thought she left.

Girl had FOMO and came back.

Ha ha. You called it. Will try again later. Just had something weird to tell you.

Can you text it?

Remember that woman Tinsley Smith?

The name felt vaguely familiar, but she couldn't bring it into focus. She typed three question marks and hit enter.

Big donor to Wildwood. Owns newspapers around the NE. Lives in Rhode Island.

She felt a surge of panic. Rhode Island. May had looked up the area code on that missing-person flyer. It was Rhode Island. What had May said when she first saw the flyer? "Even his name is generic." David Smith.

Oh yeah . . .

She stared at her phone, willing the blinking dots to turn into words. Please, please, please. Please let it be a coincidence. Don't let it be him.

Her son is apparently missing . . . from the Hamptons.

What? For how long? She was about to hit enter and realized her mistake. May had already told the police they had seen the flyer, so that had to become part of the lie. She erased and started over. *OMG, I saw a flyer about someone missing. I never would have made the connection.* It was actually the truth. She hit enter, then immediately sent a new message: *How'd you hear?*

Tinsley called Jessica, who described her as quote apoplectic. I think she's calling everyone she knows.

Lauren had grown used to how effortlessly Thomas mentioned Jessica in their conversations. Now that she was trying to remember Tinsley Smith, she recalled that she'd gotten involved as a camp supporter because she had been in the same sorority as Jessica at SMU.

As she composed a reply, she tried to pretend she didn't know the things she knew. *That's scary. Hopefully he's okay.* Enter.

Keep your eyes peeled. How ironic would it be if you found him?

I'm sure Jessica would be thrilled for me to be the hero of the story. After she hit send, she realized it sounded cattier than she had intended.

She saw moving dots but no new message, and then spotted May heading in her direction from the far end of the platform. *May's here. Gotta run!*

Have fun.

May reached out her arms for a hug, but Lauren grabbed her bag, tossed it in the open hatchback, and rushed May into the passenger seat. Thomas had said it would be "ironic" if Lauren found David Smith because it had been his mother, Tinsley, who called her sorority sister, Jessica Welliver, to warn her that Marnie Mann's family was talking about suing Wildwood and the Wellivers.

"Did you just rob a bank or something?"

She was already pulling away from the curb onto Cooper Lane when she responded. "We have a problem. That missing guy? That's the kid who was dating Marnie Mann when she died."

PART THREE

WILDWOOD

22

Carter had no problem spotting Christine Harper standing alone on Railroad Avenue. As she had described over the phone, she had shoulder-length strawberry blond hair and was wearing a purple T-shirt and white shorts. One hand shielded her eyes as she searched from one end of the street to the other. Carter approached cautiously. "Christine Harper?" he asked.

Christine's eyes met his, and relief washed over her face. "Oh good, you're here. Just you?" She shifted her hot-pink roller bag to make way on the sidewalk for other train passengers searching for their rides.

Carter had been irritated when Christine insisted on meeting him in person to tell him what she knew. She was probably one of those people who binged crime shows where the worn and weary detective magically discerns the truth about a witness's character by searching their souls with a look in the eyes. "Were you expecting a cavalry?"

"I didn't know what to expect. My head's reeling. I still can't believe this is happening. There was some part of me afraid that Dave's mother would have pulled all her strings to have me rounded up and water-boarded. From what I've heard, she's calling everyone Dave has ever met—or at least the ones she knows about. Someone told her I was the one here with him and that I was still in New York, and she was talking about having me arrested. My mother was asking if I needed a lawyer and is freaking out."

"Well, let's start by finding somewhere a little more private." He led the way to his Dodge Charger and opened the passenger door. "Front seat, not the back. You're not in custody, to be clear. And you don't need to come with me, in fact. If you'd prefer to talk in a coffee shop, or not talk at all, this is all completely voluntary. You understand that?"

She looked at the open car door and then to him. "But is it actually voluntary? Or is this like on TV shows where the police tell the guy he's not under arrest and is free to go, but then arrest him anyway when he tries to leave?"

He smiled. He'd been right about the television thing. "It's voluntary-voluntary. If you want to test it, you can wave that cabbie over right now. His name's Al. I promise I won't stop you."

"I know I sounded confident and everything on the phone, but that's how I get when I'm overcompensating. I'm legit scared right now."

"I get it." He pointed to the handle of her roller bag. "Can I take this now?"

Once they were on Newtown Lane, he told her that instead of him asking a bunch of questions, he'd like to hear from her about the trip with David.

"Starting from when?"

"Whenever you think you should start."

"Well, we came down Friday morning from Providence. We drove onto a ferry and then I think another two short ferries. Got here midafternoon. Had lunch at the hotel. Um, I kept calling it 'Gansevoort,' but it's not that. You probably know already."

"Gurney's, I think?"

He saw her nod in his periphery. "That's it. Then we drove out to Montauk village and walked around. Looked at a few shops. I bought a T-shirt for my niece. Then we went back to the hotel. We both had work emails to deal with since we'd been offline all day, so we sat out on the deck, enjoying the view of the ocean."

"And David seemed normal during all of this? No reason to be upset or nervous about anything?"

She shook her head. "No, it was all fine. Then we went to a different town called Sag Harbor. I've never been to the Hamptons and had read that there are a lot of nice little shops in that area, and I knew our dinner reservation was there—at a place called Page. And all of that was fine, too. But then after dinner, we came back to our car and there was something on the windshield. At first, David thought it was a parking ticket and got really annoyed because we hadn't seen a meter or anything. But as we got closer, I realized it looked more like a napkin tucked under the wiper. It was on my side of the car, so I was the one who removed it. It was a handwritten note."

"And what did it say?" Carter asked, hitting mute to silence his dash-top radio.

Christine hesitated a beat before answering. "It said 'He's cheating. He always does.' "

He could see why she had paused. A scorned woman who had already admitted having a heated argument with her missing boyfriend the last time she saw him makes for a pretty good primary suspect. "And then?" he prompted.

"I walked back over to his side of the car and just held it up so he could read it too. He kind of squinted at first like he didn't even get it and then he started laughing and grabbed the note and balled it up. He seemed surprised when I didn't find it so funny. So I said, 'Well?' And he kind of scoffed, so I said, 'Are you?' He totally denied it, saying I couldn't possibly think someone would tell me he was cheating with an anonymous note. I wanted to believe him, but honestly, why would someone make that up? Which is what I said to Dave. He said it was probably some stupid TikTok thing. People messing with strangers to start fights and record them. I wasn't sure what to believe, but I figured it was best either way not to make a public scene on the sidewalk. People record everything nowadays for spectacle."

"What happened to the napkin?"

She pursed her lips, trying to remember. "He tossed it in a trash can down the street."

"So then what happened?"

Christine looked down, her fingers nervously fiddling with the cell phone in her lap. "I pretended to let the issue drop. We had a couple of drinks at the hotel bar. We went back to the room. We had . . . like I said, I pretended everything was normal."

"I assume you mean sex."

"Yes. And afterward, I fell asleep. By the time I woke up on Saturday, he was already awake and at the hotel gym. I tried to get into his phone while he was in the shower, but it was locked. Then we went to brunch . . . I don't know what it was called. It was at an inn that looked like a big house. It was really nice."

"There was a charge on his card for Topping Rose?"

"Yes, that's the place. The whole time we were there, I was looking at him, trying to tell myself it was all in my head. I pictured some bored teenagers leaving notes on cars, trying to stir people up for shits and giggles. My mom told me when she worked at the mall in the eighties, she and her friends would superglue quarters to the tile floor and then hide behind the cashier's desk to watch people bend over and then freak out because they knew they'd been punked. I really, really wanted him to be telling me the truth," she said, sounding genuinely hurt. "But my suspicions kept eating at me."

Whether she intended to or not, Christine was dragging out the details of what happened. Maybe she was trying to win his favor by coming across as likable. Or maybe she was replaying her thoughts because part of her regretted whatever she might have really done to her boyfriend.

"And you didn't let it drop," he said.

"No. When he dozed off for a nap in the hotel after we went to the beach, I held up his phone to his face. I wasn't sure it would work since his eyes were closed, but it did."

"It depends on the settings," Carter said. He had changed his own after growing tired of his phone refusing to unlock if he was wearing sunglasses.

"I looked at his texts first. Then his photographs. No suspicious messages. No nudes. I scrolled through his apps. No Tinder, Bumble, OkCupid, or whatever. I really was ready to stop worrying. And then I opened his Instagram. I don't do much social media for myself because I think of it as work, so I never noticed how many women he was following. Lots of flirty messages going back months. Women he met at bars. In airports. Old classmates from high school. Seemed like a third of them were married. And it was clear from the direct messages that he was doing more than following some of these women. There were messages about meeting up for drinks, had fun last night, that kind of thing. My guess is he may also have been texting these women too, but then deleting the messages so I wouldn't see them."

So far, everything Christine had told him was consistent with what he'd heard about David from his friend Simon.

"So what did you do after you discovered all the Instagram activity?"

"I woke his ass up and confronted him," Christine replied, anger creeping into her voice. "He denied any actual cheating, but it was too obvious from the messages. He was totally gaslighting me. Calling me crazy and paranoid," Christine said, the pitch of her voice rising. "Then when he finally admitted it, he told me he thought he had a 'love addiction.' His college girlfriend died the summer after graduation at some camp, and he started blaming that. I didn't really see the connection. I told him he was just making excuses. Then he made it sound like he was somehow the victim, complaining that someone catfished him."

David's friend Simon had told Carter that David had fallen hard for someone who turned out to be a "crackpot." "David told you he was catfished?" he asked.

"He didn't use that word, but he said some woman used a fake name to dupe him into falling in love with her, as if I was supposed to feel sorry for him. I said he was looking for sympathy when the truth is he was a giant narcissist who thrived on female attention. He lashed out and told me I was a monster—like *I* was the bad guy. I was so fucking mad. Sorry, language. I grabbed a little figurine from the hotel dresser—it was a bird—and threw it. I wasn't aiming at him, I promise. I was just pissed. I mean, we had just slept together the previous night and he was lying right to my face, saying I was ridiculous not to believe him. It hit the wall and shattered. He started calling me crazy, so I packed up my stuff as fast as I could and got out of there. I took an Uber to the Amagansett train station and got on the next train to the city to stay with my friend."

"And have you spoken to David since then?"

"No."

"He didn't call or text you? Try to convince you to come back?"

She shook her head. "Oh, I think we both made it pretty clear there would be no going back."

Carter had not found anything disrupted in the hotel room when he initially searched it, and the hotel staff only realized the bird figurine was missing when Carter specifically asked them about it after Christine's call. Apparently the housekeepers didn't take an inventory of missing or damaged items until checkout. Was it possible Christine cleaned up the scene after the fight and was only telling the truth now because the hotel would notice the bird was missing? Or had David Smith cleaned it up himself after Christine left on her own, just as she was saying she did?

Carter nodded. "Let me shift direction for a second. Is there anything else unusual that came up during your trip?"

She was biting her lip as she shook her head.

"Did David say anything about maybe purchasing drugs or any other kind of meetup that might have taken a bad turn?"

She shook her head again, this time a bit less emphatically. "I mean . . . unless he decided to try to find another woman to spend the rest of the weekend with, but obviously I wouldn't know that."

"What about any phone calls that seemed unusual?"

She shrugged. "We were both on the phone a lot. Work never ends, you know? But nothing that seemed to be bothering him."

He flipped his sun visor down and handed her the list of weekend calls from David's phone that he had stashed there. He watched as her eyes scanned the pages. It seemed to line up with the times she recalled him on the phone, she said, but she couldn't add to the information. He called specific attention to an incoming call late Friday night from a Rhode Island number that Carter had not been able to lock down yet.

"I was already asleep by then, and that number doesn't look familiar. Sorry."

He only had one question left by the time he pulled into the station parking lot. "How long had the trip here been in the works? Did you two plan it together?"

Christine sighed. "I have no idea. I found out by accident. He opened the Resy app for us to look at dinner options in Providence, and I noticed that the location that popped up was the Hamptons. When I asked him if he was planning a trip, he told me it was supposed to be a surprise."

"And when exactly was that?"

"I don't know . . . two weeks ago? It was a Friday night, so I guess two and a half weeks ago."

According to Simon, Smith was originally planning to bring a different woman to East Hampton, but Christine didn't seem to know that yet. Smith's hotel reservation was booked the morning after Christine had seen the Hamptons restaurant search on his phone. Carter's best guess was that Smith felt locked into taking Christine after she saw that he'd been looking at restaurants in the Hamptons.

The lies, the other women, a shattered clay bird—none of this painted a picture of a happy couple, but the fact that Christine was being so forthright about the ugly details suggested to Carter that she might be telling something close to the truth. He'd call her friend to confirm she really had been in the city since last Saturday, but if so, that did not bode well for David Smith. It was looking increasingly unlikely that Smith was just off having fun, as Carter had originally hoped. Maybe he went looking for a party and found the wrong drug dealer. Accidental fentanyl deaths were spiking again. Or maybe his goal had been a new hotel companion, and he ran afoul of the wrong boyfriend or husband.

In the police lot, Carter pulled Christine's bag from his trunk and led the way to the station. "I'll get a more formal statement from you in writing if that's okay, and then we can get you on your way."

They were greeted inside the lobby by a loud, imperious voice. "I'm only asking you one simple question. Have you received any new information about my son's disappearance or not?" The voice's owner placed her handbag on the reception counter. She had a silver-gray bob and wore a bright blue linen blazer with a black skirt.

"As I told you before, ma'am, let me find a place for you to wait until I can reach the detective in charge." Tim Keene, the on-duty desk sergeant, sounded harried. Clearly this exchange had been going on for some time.

"His last name is Decker. I have his number." She pulled a cell phone from her purse.

Carter asked Christine to take a seat on a bench in the foyer, then approached the front desk. "I'm here. I'm Carter Decker."

She looked him up and down, not bothering to mask her displeasure. "I'm David's mother, Tinsley Smith."

23

Lauren unlocked the front door of the beach house to find an empty kitchen, the sounds of a Bob Marley song audible from the back of the house. As she and May walked toward the sliding screen door leading to the pool deck, she could make out Nate's voice.

"It's not like my acting career's exactly red hot right now. I want to help you. I'll move back to Boston. Maybe I can get a job with the company."

May stopped in her tracks, gesturing for Lauren to do the same. Lauren hesitated, torn between her eagerness to tell Kelsey what she'd learned about David Smith and her reluctance to interrupt what seemed like an intense conversation about Kelsey's decision to have a baby.

Lauren couldn't hear Kelsey's response, but she saw her friend drop her head into her hands and run her fingers through her hair. May looked to Lauren with a furrowed brow. They both recognized the worry in Kelsey's body language. This was Kelsey undecided. Overwhelmed. At peak stress. Was this about the baby, the possibility that the police might call about David Smith, or something else entirely?

As Nate continued speaking, May slid next to Lauren and nudged her toward the staircase, out of sight of the deck. Lauren managed to make out the words "You keep saying that, Kelsey, but it's not true. It's never been true. How do I convince you of that?"

"But it's unnatural. It's not only a question of biology."

So they were talking about the baby. For Kelsey to have a biological child, half of its genes would come from Luke. What would she tell her children about their father? Lauren couldn't possibly imagine making that choice for herself, but as she'd told Kelsey repeatedly, she'd love whatever decision made Kelsey happiest.

Lauren flinched at the sudden sound of a ringtone. May yanked her phone from the back pocket of her shorts and silenced it.

"Hey!" Lauren called out, nodding at May to follow her lead. "We're back." She opened the screen door onto the deck, where Kelsey and Nate sat at the dining table, damp-haired and wrapped in beach towels.

"I couldn't stay away," May said, dropping a kiss on the top of Kelsey's head before taking a seat in the chair beside her.

"Welcome back, Hanover. Get your suit on." The way Nate was squinting at May against the sun, that smile inviting her into the water. That's not the way Nate ever spoke to Lauren. She could see a flush in May's cheeks. There was something still there.

"That might have to wait," May said. "Kelsey, can we maybe talk in private?"

"No time like the present," Nate said. "Like I told Kelsey, you can get some sun and some Bob Marley whether the police call you about the note or not."

May stared at Kelsey.

"Wait, am I not supposed to know?" Nate asked. "Oh shit, I'm so sorry."

"It's not a big deal," Kelsey muttered.

It was clear to Lauren from May's face that she disagreed. "Really? If it was no big deal, we should have told the police everything from the very beginning."

"Look, May." Nate pressed his hands together in a prayer gesture. "I didn't mean to add to the stress level. It's not like I would ever tell anyone. You know me. If someone tells me to keep a secret, it's mums-ville. I'm a vault, baby."

From what Lauren knew about Nate, it was true. She remembered May joking one time that Nate could make it through Guantánamo based on the number of times she had pressed him futilely for information he didn't want to provide—his first time, his exes, how many people, and so on.

Lauren was a little annoyed that Kelsey hadn't consulted them before talking to her brother, but May was clearly livid. "You're the one who told us we couldn't call the tip line or everyone would think we were terrible," she said, "and now I've basically lied to the police because of you."

"I was talking about strangers who would judge us," Kelsey said. "Nate actually thought it was funny."

"Missing people are funny?" May snapped.

Lauren was beginning to wonder if May was especially mad that the person Kelsey had chosen to confide in happened to be Nate. Lauren had always suspected that their breakup had been awkward.

"May, that's not what she meant," Nate said. "The note. Sorry, but the note was funny."

"Leaving it on the car was not funny," May said.

"Yes, it actually kind of was," Nate said. "They sound like a couple of douchebags. It's not like she could have predicted the guy would go missing."

Lauren clapped her hands twice, demanding their full attention. "It's not just about the note anymore." She shared what Thomas had relayed to her, attributing the phone call she had received to a "Wildwood donor." "That was the guy Marnie Mann was dating her last two years of college."

Kelsey looked confused as she shook her head. "I remember she had a boyfriend, but there's no way I'd remember his name. Are you sure?"

"I'm positive. I knew his mother, Tinsley. She was a major donor." Lauren wasn't surprised that neither May nor Kelsey remembered Marnie's boyfriend. To them, Marnie was the competitive girl who tried to boss around the other campers when they had been students. She was also a truly gifted pianist—not as talented as Lauren had been at her age, but almost enough to warrant the term *prodigy* that parents tossed around so loosely. The only reason May had returned to camp as an adult was because the economy tanked and she needed a job for the summer. And Kelsey had taken the summer gig only because May would be there, one final summer of music and fun before slotting into the track her father had created for her at his company.

But Marnie? Marnie had spent at least part of every summer during college at Wildwood to learn from Lauren, determined to be a working musician. She could be an insufferable brat, but when Marnie ended up dating the son of a generous camp benefactor, of course Lauren had heard about it.

That final summer, Kelsey and May were no longer teenaged girls. They were college graduates delaying adulthood for a few months. Lauren had grown tired of hearing May complain about Marnie treating her like a "second-class citizen." Yes, with a single mother on a teacher's salary, May wasn't raised with the kind of money that the Marnies and the Kelseys of the world enjoyed, but that didn't mean she went without privilege. It was clear her mother sacrificed so May could have the best education possible. As a result, May spent her summers with fancy kids doing fancy things, and then graduated from a college that immediately opened doors at the highest echelons of wealth and power. And as far as May's complaints about the pressures of being a "model minority"? She had no idea what it was like to be the other kind.

Lauren remembered snapping at her that "no one likes a tattletale, especially when she's a grown woman with a degree from Harvard still pretending that she's part of the downtrodden. Go take care of it." It was the last time May ever came to her complaining about Marnie or any other counselor.

She had been so pleased to learn that May, Kelsey, and Marnie were all going to the same camping party on their big Off-Campus Night away from Wildwood. And then Marnie never came back. And now, fifteen years later, her boyfriend was missing.

24

Carter led Tinsley Smith through a dimly lit hallway of the police station, her square-toed pumps clapping against the tile floors. "I couldn't stand being at home any longer without answers. I was in my car, on my way to his apartment, just to be there in case he returned, and the next thing I knew, I was on the highway. I need to know that you're doing everything possible to find him. I don't know how to convince you that something is desperately wrong."

He reached for the doorknob of the interview room that was their intended destination. As he escorted Tinsley inside, he found himself newly irritated by a flashing fluorescent light that should have been changed weeks ago. Until now, whatever fears this woman carried about her son were formed back in Rhode Island, where he presumed she had a beautiful home and could surround herself with comforting friends. This was different. She had driven hours to the place her son was last seen. She was in a police station. It was real now. And if his growing fears about David Smith turned out to be correct, she would at some point go back and replay every detail of her time in this police station, including this room. Its smallness. The sterility. The chip in the wood on one corner of the table. And this fritzy fucking light.

She smoothed the back of her skirt as she took a seat, insisting again that her son always responded promptly to texts and calls and would never turn his phone off for such a long period of time.

"We do have a new development that's significant," he said. "We located the woman who came here with your son."

She brushed a wisp of hair from her face as she relaxed back into her chair. "Oh, thank god, that's wonderful. And she's all right?"

He nodded. "Yes. In fact, that was the woman I walked into the precinct with."

"With the pink bag?"

"Yes. She's the one."

"And does she know where David is?"

"I'm afraid not. By all appearances, she left the Hamptons for the city on Saturday—alone."

Mrs. Smith winced as she realized the implications of the timing.

"Are you certain of that? How do you know she's not involved in whatever's happened?"

"I have some details to follow up on, but she returned immediately when she learned your son was missing and has been cooperative. I'll be double-checking her timeline, to be sure, but it looks for now like it all squares up. But since you're here, I'd like to ask you some questions that might be helpful to the investigation."

"Anything, of course." She shifted her handbag from her lap to the edge of the table.

"Does your son have any enemies?"

"No," she said, shaking her head vigorously. "He has a tight group of friends he's known since childhood. He's well liked at work. Trust me, I have been racking my brain trying to figure out what could have possibly happened. When I was looking online about crimes committed out here, I saw some articles about robberies. Is that common? Is it possible someone targeted him to rob him?"

"Anything is possible, but let's not get ahead of ourselves. Let's operate on the assumption that David is fine. We just need to find him."

Mrs. Smith nodded slowly. "Yes, of course. Stay positive. Besides, David would never resist a robbery attempt. He was mugged in San

Francisco about five years ago, in fact. They pulled out a knife and he handed over everything as calmly as he could possibly muster."

Carter also doubted it was a random robbery. In a world rife with twelve-thousand-dollar handbags on display, it was plain dumb to shoot someone over a car or some spare cash.

"I've spoken to his friends. Your son was seeing the woman who was here with him fairly regularly but was dating other people as well. Is it possible he ran into a jealous husband or boyfriend?"

"That's something I wouldn't know. We talk about many things, but not that. I've always figured he'll tell me when and if someone will be around for the long term." She pressed the chipped spot on the table corner with her index finger.

"Your lawyer was able to get an itemized list of your son's phone records. One number has been frequent for the last six months but then stopped suddenly a few weeks ago." He recited a number with a 959 area code. "The area code covers Hartford, Connecticut. David's friend Simon told me that your son had been seeing a woman who lived in Hartford. In fact, he originally planned to come here with *her*, but there's evidence that she may have lied to him about her identity. The number's disconnected now." If David really had been catfished, Carter suspected the number had come from a burner. If the catfisher bought a throwaway phone, he'd never know who was actually on the other end of the line. If, on the other hand, someone had used their own phone, but simply used an app to mask their real number, he'd be able to unveil the account holder. He had already drafted subpoenas to the major burner-app companies. "Did your son mention anything about this person?"

"No, I know nothing about any of that." Mrs. Smith's tone had turned frosty.

"The woman your son was here with—her name's Christine. She said David described himself as having a love addiction."

She placed her hands on the table. "I'm sorry, I don't like the road this conversation is taking. It sounds like you're blaming David for whatever is going on."

"Not at all, Mrs. Smith. I'm just trying to learn more about your son and anyone he may have had contact with." The truth was that one type of addiction often correlated with others. Carter did not find drugs in David's hotel room, but he could have gotten bad dope or made a deal that went wrong. "David apparently told Christine that he attributed his need for female attention to the death of a college girlfriend."

"The only girl David has ever brought home to meet me, still to this day. It was tragic. She drowned the summer after college graduation. She was a perfect match for him—from an excellent family and full of spunk. David was visiting her that weekend in Maine. Some of the camp counselors had the night off. They were all drinking. I sent him for therapy so he'd know it wasn't his fault, but David always blamed himself. The kids at the camp composed an original song for her funeral—it was a music camp. That's how she and David first met. A college friend of mine founded the camp, and I was a big supporter." Carter could tell that talking about her missing son was providing comfort, so he allowed her to continue reminiscing. "I had to drag David there for the annual donors' concert, but then he met Marnie, and I could tell he was smitten. The camp was very competitive, and, even so, Marnie stood out as the star. She was an extraordinary talent. When he called me to say her body was found in the lake, he just broke down. He wasn't even like that when his father passed away—I suppose because his death was long expected and maybe even something of a blessing. But Marnie? Yes, I suspect it did affect his future dating relationships, but I guess it's not something he would share with his mother."

When Christine had mentioned the college girlfriend's death, she said it took place at a camp. Now that Tinsley Smith was talking about a competitive music camp, something was tugging at the corner of Carter's brain. He'd seen a reference to a music camp recently, reminding him of his own childhood dreams of being able to afford sleepaway camp. The closest he ever got was the three-week half-day sports camp at the local Y.

"What was the name of the camp?" he asked.

"Wildwood."

Ooh, baby, baby, it's a wildwood. The same reaction he'd had when he first saw the camp name on May Hanover's LinkedIn profile.

He assured Mrs. Smith he'd continue to keep her up-to-date on the investigation and offered to help her find a hotel if she was planning to stay in the area.

"I'm going to stay with a friend in Wainscott, but thank you so much, Detective. And I'm sorry if I've sounded pushy in my voicemail messages and at the front desk. Now that I've met you, I can see that you are working diligently. I'm just so scared."

"I understand."

He was surprised when she gave him a brief hug at the police station door.

Back at his desk, he scrolled through his text messages and found the photograph of the neatly handwritten note that the DA investigator in Manhattan had sent him. It had come from May Hanover. Her cell phone number, followed by numbers for two other names: Lauren Berry and Kelsey Ellis. He opened the browser on his laptop and searched for Lauren Berry first.

He was entering Kelsey Ellis's name when Debra McFadden appeared, a bag of Skittles dangling from one hand. "A call just came in about a suspicious vehicle parked on Old Stone Highway. You better get out there."

25

Lauren leaned forward to get a better look at May's laptop screen. May was hunched over her keyboard at the dining table on the deck, with Kelsey tucked in the chair beside her. On the other side of the table, Nate was conducting his own searches on his phone. The house's wireless speaker was still streaming, and a Jimmy Cliff song about a wonderful world with beautiful people made a ridiculous juxtaposition with the tension that had settled over the four of them.

They had all been trying to dig up as much information as they could about David Smith—or "THAT David Smith," as they now referred to him.

"I think I vaguely remember talking to him on Off-Campus Night," May said. "I had been going out of my way to make peace with Marnie after you told me to stop feuding with her. And she told me about her boyfriend, and then he was there. It must have been him, but there's no way I would have recognized him after all this time. I remember he let the name of his prep school drop, and I was jealous because I had been desperate to go there for high school but didn't get a scholarship. It was Phillips Exeter!" She was already typing a new search into Google.

"Yep, here it is," she announced. "He's mentioned in an article in *The Exeter Bulletin* about his ten-year-reunion. Don't all those prep-school kids kind of know each other?" May's eyes searched Nate's and Kelsey's for answers. They had also attended private schools in the Northeast.

"Not a hundred percent," Nate said, "but yeah, maybe. Like Boston kids from those circles will meet up at home during Christmas break. The New York kids do the same. That kind of thing."

"Check and see if you have any mutual friends. Maybe we can find out more about David through them," May suggested.

Nate was scrolling through his phone, but Kelsey reminded May that she didn't have any social media accounts.

"Not even a private one with a fake name?" May asked.

"Nope," Kelsey said. "I'm now a blissful Luddite. No social media means no trolls."

May's phone rang on the table beside her laptop. "I better get this."

"Wait, is it the police?" Lauren asked. As much as she had been opposed to calling the police voluntarily, she still wasn't prepared to lie to them. There had to be a way for them to thread the needle.

"No, it's Josh. I'll be right back."

Lauren noticed Kelsey watching May as she walked away. As soon as May pulled the screen door closed behind her, Kelsey said in a lowered voice, "Should we really be cyberstalking this guy and his friends? I thought the whole reason she came back was to get our stories straight in case the police called, but now we're all getting pulled into the Scooby gang."

Nate snickered. "I can't wait until David Smith reappears after trying to embezzle half a billion dollars to the Cayman Islands—*And I would have gotten away with it if it weren't for those meddling kids.* May!" he called out, a theatrical singsong flair in his voice. "Can you come back here? We need to talk to you!"

Kelsey shushed her brother, gently swatting at his arm, as Lauren took May's chair. One of the open tabs on her laptop was for David Smith's Instagram account. He had 412 followers. She clicked on the list. "See if you guys recognize any of these people," she said, turning the screen toward Kelsey as Nate stood to look over her shoulder.

Lauren thought May looked stressed when she returned, but before she could ask if everything was all right, May was asking if they had found any mutual contacts yet. Kelsey had spotted three familiar names.

"So let's DM them," May said. "Or I can, since you don't have an account."

"I'm sorry," Kelsey said, "but why are we even doing this?"

"To find out who David was here with."

"But why?" Kelsey pressed.

"She'll either know what happened to him, or is with him, or killed him. Or he could have killed her and is on the run. But we need to know who she is."

"No, we actually don't," Kelsey said. "We're like one step away from those true crime fanatics who obsessed over every detail of my life after Luke died. Let the police find that woman. This is none of our business."

Lauren could feel Kelsey's skepticism stoking her own doubts. "It's true, May. The police will find her on their own before we do. You already talked to one cop. I think we need to focus on what Kelsey and I should say if they contact us. We can just say we didn't notice whatever couple you were talking about. Right? Keep it simple?"

Nate was nodding in agreement. "May, that sounds—"

"Speaking of none of your business." May put her hands on her hips. Yep, Nate's presence was definitely getting on her nerves.

The awkward silence was cut short by the sound of May's phone ringing. Her expression morphed into confusion as she glanced at the screen, then held up a finger to silence them.

Lauren could tell it was a man's voice on the other end of the line but couldn't make out any of his words.

"I'm actually in East Hampton . . . Yeah, I did a boomerang to the city, but I'm back here again . . . Um, sure. I can meet you somewhere. Oh . . . Um, yeah, in fact, they're both here with me." Lauren shook her head so hard her earrings clinked, signaling her opposition to whatever May was about to agree to. "Yeah, that's fine."

May was reciting the address of the rental house.

"That was the detective looking for David Smith," she said. As she set her phone down on the table, her hands were shaking. "He wants to speak to all three of us."

26

After May's first year of law school, her constitutional law professor invited her to claim a guaranteed spot in what was usually a by-application-only seminar on jurisprudence. He was one of the school's most esteemed scholars, and his mentorship reportedly was a golden ticket to a federal appellate clerkship and the professional success that typically followed. The wrinkle was that it met on Friday afternoons and May had promised Kelsey she'd get a four-day schedule once she could choose her own classes as a 2L, so they could visit each other more often. They were even talking about surprising Lauren with a Los Angeles visit. When she politely declined the professor's invitation, she asked whether he ever taught the class at a different time. His disappointed and dismissive sigh still burned in her memory. She applied each remaining semester and was rejected every time.

May had always struggled to maintain boundaries when it came to her close friendships, but since last year, her connection to Lauren and Kelsey had become a defining aspect of her own identity. Not calling the tip line was already out of character for her, but lying to the police was another level entirely. Meanwhile, it was becoming clear that they were all keeping secrets. Would Kelsey have even told them that she'd confided in her brother if Nate hadn't slipped and said something? And Lauren attributed the information about David Smith to some anonymous "camp donor," but her source was obviously Thomas Welliver. Did she really think May of all people didn't notice the name at the top of her screen while she'd been texting this weekend?

She was starting to regret her decision to return to East Hampton, and the detective wasn't even at the house yet. And it didn't help that Nate was here being his best kind of Nate. That look he gave her when she walked out onto the deck made her momentarily forget about David Smith and the police.

And the way he had tried to beckon her back to the deck when she'd gone inside to talk to Josh? Yes, she had walked away from the middle of their conversation, but the call, immediately on the heels of that interaction with Nate, had felt like a sign. She was an emotional cheat who owed it to her fiancé to pick up.

When Josh overheard Nate's voice in the background and asked who it was, she answered truthfully. She didn't want to add any more lies. Josh didn't bother to hide how upset he was. More than upset, he was angry—and jealous. When she told him it wasn't "a good look," he said it didn't exactly look good that she had returned to East Hampton without telling him that her ex-boyfriend would be there. "You told me there were only three bedrooms. Where's everyone staying?" Then she said he couldn't be serious.

She had come so close to telling him the truth about everything. If Kelsey could tell her brother, she should be able to tell her fiancé, right? But she knew Josh. She knew how desperately he wanted her to avoid any kind of public attention—for her sake, as he always emphasized. He would not be happy about the note.

Lauren was right. They just needed to get through this conversation with the detective and then they could move on. Nate had offered to stick around in case he could help, but May decided the fewer people the better. He was going for a walk until they texted him to come back.

Now Lauren was asking for the third time whether lying to the police was an actual crime. May had told her it was complicated, but Lauren wanted the complete explanation. "Lying itself isn't necessarily a crime if you're not under oath. But if you file a written statement, it is, and they can even prosecute you if you say something that winds up going into a written police report. Or for filing a false report."

"Well, that sounds to me like they'd throw us in jail."

"You could both just refuse to talk to him," May said. "An interview's entirely voluntary. He can't force you."

"I like the sound of that," Kelsey said. "We can tell him to kick rocks and then go back to our vacation."

"Nothing personal," Lauren said, "but I think you're a lot more likely to draw negative attention to yourself for refusing to talk to police in a criminal investigation than if they find out you left some juvenile note on a car. By the time the true crime crazies got done with you, they'd be calling you a serial killer—Luke, this David Smith guy and his girlfriend, probably Marnie too. Maybe we should just tell the cops the truth about the note at this point and get it over with."

"You guys can do that if you want," May said, "but then he'll know I was lying. I don't think I crossed the line into an actual crime, but he'll tell the DA's Office, and they'd probably feel obligated to notify the bar. I could lose my license and my job."

"So we're not doing that," Lauren said, reaching over and squeezing May's hand. "I'm really sorry, May. We should have let you call on Monday the way you wanted to."

How many times today had May thought the same thing? It was too late now, but it still felt good to hear.

"As long as we don't contradict each other, we'll be fine," May said. "I saw a couple bickering on the sidewalk in Sag Harbor and thought it might be the missing guy from the flyers. Neither of you noticed. End of story."

They were nodding along in agreement. "And if they bring up the note?" Lauren asked.

"We don't know anything about it," May said.

"And what if they know about David's connection to Wildwood?" Kelsey asked.

"We can tell the truth about that," Lauren said. "We didn't make the connection between a kid we met a few times fifteen years ago and the David Smith on the flyers until I got a phone call today from a camp donor."

"And then you told the two of us," Kelsey added.

"You know what?" May said. "We should actually tell him about the Wildwood connection on our own when he gets here. It'll show we're trying to be helpful and not hiding anything."

Because they had nothing to hide, right?

27

Carter double-checked that the number on the modern-style farmhouse matched the one May Hanover had given him. He squinted against the late-afternoon sun as he stepped from the car, remembering the last time he'd been on this block, more than two years earlier.

His mother's best friend, Sharon, had lived two doors down. She inherited the house from her parents in the '90s, along with a small grocery store they owned in Springs with an adjacent deli. Sharon had promised her mother she'd never let go of the modest house because of its unencumbered view of Gardiners Bay.

For years, as ice cream shops and bakeries were steadily replaced by designer boutiques and galleries, Sharon had resisted the temptation to cash in on the potential for windfall profits. She sold good, simple food that real people needed at an affordable price.

Four years ago, Carter would have sworn that the town where he was born and bred could not become any less affordable for the average person. Even on a good law enforcement salary, he had adopted the increasingly common practice among locals of renting out his own home for July and August while he moved to the studio apartment above his garage.

But the shutdown had blown this place up in a way he had never imagined. Families desperate to escape the confinement of their city apartments—now full-time virtual Zoom offices combined with home schooling—fled to the exurbs, creating bidding wars for available houses, sight unseen, all cash, above asking price. Carter had twice turned away realtors knocking door-to-door in search of someone willing to name a price to relocate.

And Sharon decided she had a price. The combination store-deli was now a gourmet health-conscious "nutrition boutique" selling bullshit like kombucha, oxymoronic no-dairy cheese, and thirty-dollar quarts of bone broth. Sharon lived in Florida. And the porch swing where she and Carter's mother would sit side by side to sneak an occasional cigarette after dinner had been replaced by an industrial-looking stone bench that probably cost what Carter made in a week.

He knew for a fact that Sharon had gotten two-point-seven million for her house, even though it was a small fixer-upper by a newcomer's standards. If he had to guess, these women were paying at least ten grand a week for their vacation rental—all for the honor of having to explain exactly what they knew about David Smith.

When May Hanover opened the door, he recognized her from the headshot on both her LinkedIn and Fordham Law School faculty profiles. Her face had been fuller in the photograph and her hair longer. She looked thinner now and had cut her hair above her shoulders.

She greeted him with a surprisingly firm handshake. "Detective, I'm May Hanover. We spoke on the phone. And I believe you already got some information from me through my former colleague at the DA's Office, Danny Brennan."

"Seemed like good people, a straight shooter."

"The best," she said, opening the door wider to let him in.

She led the way into the kitchen, where two other women stood near stools positioned around the center island.

"Detective Decker," May said, "these are my friends, Lauren Berry and Kelsey Ellis."

In photographs he had seen online, Kelsey Ellis had been a stunner, with shiny blond waves and a full face of makeup. She was still undoubtedly attractive, but had a more reserved, natural look, her ashy hair bundled in a loose bun. Lauren Berry, on the other hand, had come across online as intense and professional, almost aloof. But in person, she gave off a radiant energy, confident in a long, bright orange dress and hoop earrings the size of coffee coasters.

It was another reminder that an online persona could be a total fiction.

Kelsey greeted him with a smile that immediately struck him as forced. Smiling at a detective who has come to ask you questions was an unnatural response under any circumstance. He wondered if she was the type of beautiful woman who always assumed she could curry favor with a man.

"Can I get you anything?" May offered. "A bottle of water or a soda?"

"No, I'm good, thanks. Hey, when May originally gave that investigator in the city your names and numbers, I noticed your phone numbers are all from different states. How do y'all know each other, if you don't mind me asking."

It was a test to see if they'd try to hide their common connection to David Smith.

May Hanover jumped in first. "Kelsey and I were campers at a camp where Lauren was the director. We stayed in touch over the years."

Carter widened his eyes as if in surprise. "Whoa. That's a long time to stay in touch with people you only saw in the summer."

"We went every year, and then Kelsey and I went to college in the same city. Then we became counselors for a summer after graduation."

"It was a whole thing," Kelsey added. "All still besties to this day."

He wondered how it came to pass that three besties all happened to have individual scandals attached to their names, but he couldn't ask without making it clear that he was far more interested in them than he wanted to appear.

He was about to explain that their names had come up in the course of his investigation, but the woman named Lauren surprised him by speaking up.

"It's funny that you asked how we know each other. When you called May, we were actually talking about the weirdest thing I just learned. That man who's missing? We were apparently one degree of separation from him back when he was in college—and it was through the camp."

Carter nodded slowly, his expression neutral. "Is that so?"

"That's what I'm told, at least. So the camp May mentioned is called Wildwood. It's an arts camp. I was its music director when May and Kelsey were students and later counselors."

"And David Smith went there as well?" Carter asked. He wouldn't normally interrupt an interviewee who was being so forthcoming, but it was a way to mislead them into thinking he knew less than he really did.

She shook her head. "No, his mother was close friends with one of the owners of Wildwood, so she was a very generous donor and supporter."

"But that's the mother, not the son. Did any of you ever meet David Smith—either back then or on this trip?"

"Certainly not on this trip," Lauren said. "Well, unless he was the guy May thought she may have seen in Sag Harbor." She looked to May with a quizzical expression. "Does he know about that yet?"

"I think so," May said. "I told the guy in the city."

"We'll get to that again later," Carter said. "But back at the camp?"

"Yes, that's what we were all just talking about. I learned today that the David Smith who's been reported missing here was the college boyfriend of one of the regular campers."

"And how did you learn of that connection?"

"One of the camp's owners told me. His name's Thomas Welliver. His wife is the one who's friends with David's mother. Thomas and I have stayed in touch even after I left the camp."

She had surprised him again by being so open about her current connection to the married oilman. He'd read about the affair and the brouhaha that had followed at the Houston Symphony.

May crossed her arms and shook her head. "It's eerie," she said. "I couldn't drop this nagging sense after he was reported missing that he might have been that guy I saw bickering with his girlfriend on the street, but then it turns out he's someone we all sort of knew fifteen years ago. I never would have made the connection until Lauren told us."

"That's another detail I'll add to the big picture we're fleshing out. Is there anything else related to the camp you think I should know?" he asked. He gazed directly at Kelsey, who had been letting her friends do most of the talking, but she remained silent.

"I have no idea whether you need to know it or not," May said, "but the girl he was dating? She drowned the summer after her college graduation—when she, Kelsey, and I were all counselors at the camp. Her name was Marnie Mann."

He pulled a notebook from his back pocket and jotted down the name even though he already had it.

"Now, I know you're eager to enjoy your vacation," he said, his tone empathetic, "but your names have come up in our investigation. I'm sure it's something we can clear up with just a few questions, all on a voluntary basis, of course."

They all immediately agreed. *Absolutely*—May. *No problem*—Lauren. *Anything you need*—Kelsey. First the smile, then the cutesy "bestie" comment, now anything he needed? Was this woman trying to work him? Was she . . . flirting? Or was he the one reading something into the situation, given what he'd learned about her husband's murder?

"And if it's okay with you, I'd like to talk to each of you individually. It's fairly routine. May, you were a prosecutor. You're welcome to explain all that if you want."

"Thank you, but I don't think it's necessary. I'm sure we're all fine with that. I'll go first? Kelsey and Lauren, do you want to wait in your bedrooms until we're done—just to assure Detective Decker we're not sharing information?"

Her sarcasm was apparent, but the friends shrugged and began heading up the stairs. May led the way to the back deck and closed the sliding door behind them. The view of Gardiners Bay from this angle reminded him of barbecue parties at Sharon's old house. As he watched the sunlight flicker against the water, he thought about the twenty-two-year-old concert pianist who had drowned in that lake in Maine. He had no idea what Marnie Mann's death had to do with David Smith, but he was certain these three women did.

28

May wasn't generally a sweaty person, but she had an undeniable tendency to pit up under pressure. At the DA's Office, she had always worn black suit jackets over her silk blouses during trial, no matter how high the temperature soared in a courtroom. It had been only twenty minutes, but a constant stream of lies, straight to a detective's face, had left a beaded ring of perspiration around the base of her neck. She felt chills as she stepped from the pool deck into the air-conditioned house.

She walked up the stairs to the bedroom that was now Kelsey's and reached out to knock, but Detective Decker appeared beside her and called out instead. "Ms. Ellis? I'm ready to speak to you when you're all set."

He flashed a smile that was probably polite but felt a little condescending. He kept his eyes on her as Kelsey stepped past them and began heading down the stairs. "Thanks again for your time," he said, before leaving her alone on the landing.

May had been hoping to have a one-second face-to-face with Kelsey. Time to mouth just two words. *The note.*

He had known about the note.

She had stuck to the plan, denying knowing anything about it.

You said this couple you saw was bickering. Did it have anything to do with a note?

I have no idea. I couldn't actually hear what they were saying. It was just clear they were arguing. And they were pretty far away. That's why I can't be sure it was even the same guy.

Did you see a white car with a note on the windshield?

No.

Did you leave a note on anyone's car windshield?

Of course not.

Instead of having time to warn Kelsey, she watched helplessly as her friend stepped onto the back deck with the detective.

In the kitchen, she replayed the interview in her head. Much of it had been a rehash of what she had already told Danny Brennan at her apartment—the couple arguing, the missing-person flyer, the pit stop at the American Hotel to see if anyone else had noticed.

Even though the interview had remained informal and non-confrontational, there had been a bizarre, almost schizophrenic tone to it as the detective lurched between chitchat (how long had the trip been planned, who found the house, what rental agency had they used), extremely narrow questions (whether she recognized a specific telephone number), and repeated questions about Marnie Mann and whether May knew that Kelsey's husband had been murdered, the case still unsolved.

At least he hadn't pressed her when she said she knew nothing about the note left on Smith's car. He didn't seem to know the note was written on the type of napkin used at the American Hotel. He also didn't indicate he knew what the note said. But how had he known about it at all?

She was continuing her search of David Smith's social media accounts when her phone buzzed on the kitchen counter. It was Josh. She answered with an abrupt "Hey."

"Hey."

As whole seconds passed in silence, she thought maybe she shouldn't have even answered.

"Are you mad at me?" he finally asked.

Was she? Was she mad? No. Just disappointed. Disappointed in herself for being in this situation. Disappointed in him for being jealous of Nate. Disappointed in herself for giving him a reason to be suspicious of her. Disappointed in *them* for not being the kind of couple where she immediately told him what was going on when Danny had shown up at the apartment asking questions—or even when she first found out that Kelsey had left the note.

"He's Kelsey's brother," she said. "That's all."

"And also your ex-boyfriend."

"From fifteen years ago. Sorry, but you sound ridiculous, Josh." *Sorry.* Always saying *sorry*. A word he hadn't uttered yet.

"When we first met and did the whole so-what's-your-history thing, I was the one who said that none of that should matter. That nothing good comes from thinking of the person you're with as having been in love with someone else. You're the one who pressed the subject. You were the one who was curious, who said it was part of getting to know each other better. But whenever it came to that one particular dude, you didn't want to talk about it. You clammed up, locked down like Fort Knox. He's obviously a sore spot for some reason, like he's still in your head—so yeah, I guess I'm jealous. I'm sorry."

"That wasn't the kind of sorry I was hoping to hear."

"Okay, you're right. I'm actually sorry. I acted like a Neanderthal. Is that better?"

"A little bit."

"Me caveman. Me big dumb jealous caveman. Me fucked up. Me so sorry."

"Okay, that's better."

"But will you admit you get weird when the subject of Kelsey's brother comes up?"

"Why do you care?"

"Because we're getting married. I care about all of it."

"Yeah, I get it."

"Just promise me he's not the reason you suddenly decided to go back to East Hampton?"

"I swear." At least that part really was true.

"Are you guys having fun? No more FOMO?"

"No more FOMO," she said, trying to mask the sadness from her voice. Keeping so many secrets made her feel so distant from him.

She hit the button to refresh the comments on Dave Smith's most recent Instagram post, a selfie in which he was holding up a margarita, captioned "beach week, bitches." She had been monitoring the replies posted as news of his disappearance must have spread among his friends.

The muscles in her jaw tensed as she stared at the two most recent comments. "Josh, I'm sorry, but I have to go."

"Are you okay—"

"Yeah, it's fine. Um, it sounds like they dropped something downstairs and are yelling for me." Yet another lie. "I've got to go."

Before shutting her laptop, she cleared the browser history to be safe, then slid open the back door.

"We're not quite done here," the detective said.

"I think you are," she said.

Kelsey looked at her with a wrinkled brow. "It's fine, May. Everything's good."

"He hasn't been honest with us, have you, Detective? Out of an abundance of caution, I don't think any of us should talk to you right now. You've obviously come here with some kind of agenda and used deception to get us to speak with you."

He scratched at the thin layer of stubble on his jaw. "Funny you should mention deception. Your friend here just admitted she wrote that note I asked you about, which means she hasn't been honest with *you*—and I for one would like to know why."

She felt her eyes begin to water as she locked her gaze with Kelsey's. Kelsey pressed her lips together and gave her the slightest nod.

She could see immediately what Kelsey had done. When Lauren suggested they could just tell the detective about the note, May had been the one to point out that she had already lied to the police and could be disbarred for it.

Kelsey must have admitted to writing and leaving the note on her own. And she hadn't told them she was planning to throw herself under the bus because they would have tried to stop her—or at least she had believed they would. Would they have? May wasn't so sure. Kelsey was the one who had gotten them into this entire mess. Maybe she was making the right call. It was a stand-up move. But it was also incredibly stupid given what May had just learned.

She swallowed and shifted her focus to Detective Carter. "Kelsey, don't say another word!"

Carter placed both palms on the table, staring at Kelsey intently. "Make your own decision here, Kelsey. It really doesn't look good if you can't answer a few questions about how you happened to guess that a total stranger who stole your parking spot was cheating on his girlfriend. Sounds like you knew him a lot better than you are saying, and now that man has gone missing. Add to that the whole mystery of your husband's death, and, well, that's a lot of coincidences with you as the connection."

"Don't reply to that, Kelsey." May reached for Kelsey's hand. If she had to pull her out of that chair to get her inside and away from this detective, so be it.

"What's going on down here?" Lauren asked, opening the back slider. "I could hear you all the way upstairs."

"He's been lying to us," May said. "She's not speaking to you any further, Detective."

"She can't mess this up for all of you. Think about your own situations. Your own *reputations.* This doesn't look good."

Lauren folded her arms. "That sounds like you're threatening us with retaliation if we exercise our constitutional rights, which is why I definitely won't be exchanging further words with you."

Carter addressed Kelsey as he rose from his seat. "It would help to get your side of the story—"

"I'm going to listen to my lawyer friend for now," she said quietly, her gaze glued to her lap. "I can't believe you brought up Luke."

They were a united front.

The detective paused as he reached the door and turned to face them, clicking his tongue twice. "The three of you just got a lot more interesting to me."

After they heard the sound of his car engine, Lauren spoke first. "What the fuck was that?"

"I told him I wrote the note," Kelsey blurted. "Because of the parking spot. That I wrote it myself and left it there after you guys went to the bookstore and that you didn't know anything about it."

"Oh, Kelsey." Lauren closed her eyes.

"That's not the biggest problem," May said. "I stopped the interview because David Smith is dead, and if that detective didn't tell us that, he thinks we're involved somehow."

The sun-kissed pink drained from Kelsey's face. "He's . . . dead?" Her breath sounded uneven.

"I'm pretty sure," May said. "A couple friends posted RIP notes on his Instagram." She retrieved her laptop from the kitchen and turned the screen to face them.

Just heard the news. I can't believe you're gone. Sending love to you, Mrs. Smith. Someone named Megan Levy.

I'm broken. Best friend a guy could ask for. RIP, my brother. Simon Bowlby.

The scream that came from Kelsey's throat was visceral. It brought back memories of that horrible sound that had come out of May on the subway platform, a noise she didn't even know she was capable of making until she saw the video. Kelsey moved to the outdoor sofa and grabbed a throw pillow, holding it to her face as she yelled into it.

Lauren stood behind Kelsey and rubbed her back. "Honey, calm down. It's going to be okay."

Kelsey's shoulders were shaking as she sobbed into the pillow.

"Lauren's right," May offered. "It'll be all right. It was just a stupid note. A practical joke. It's not a crime. And you told the truth. That cop can't do anything to you."

Kelsey sniffed, trying to catch her breath as she wiped at her eyes with the backs of her hands. "None of that matters. Oh my god, my life is over."

Lauren looked to May. She seemed as confused as May felt.

"Why would you say that?" Lauren said. "What are you afraid of?"

The question made Kelsey begin crying again. "Talk to us," May said. "We're here for you. Is there something we don't know?"

Kelsey dropped her head into her palms. "Don't you see? What he said about Luke? And now David Smith is dead too? How could this happen? They're going to say I killed them both. I can't go through it all over again."

29

May had come inside to use the bathroom but found herself delaying her return to the deck. She needed some quiet time to herself. And she needed to put distance between her and Nate. He wasn't actually flirting with her, she now realized. He was just being himself—his cool, confident, gorgeous self—and she hated the effect it was having on her. When Nate first returned to the house after Decker's departure, Kelsey immediately walked him through everything that had transpired in his absence. May had taken the opportunity to pull Lauren aside to unpack Kelsey's meltdown.

"You didn't see how bad it was when Luke was killed. She said those same words—that her life was over." Lauren's eyes darted to the deck. "That everyone thought she was behind it. I was seriously worried she'd harm herself. She still doesn't know, but I called Nate and her father to make sure they were keeping an eye on her. The last thing she needs is the two of us judging her emotions. She needs our support."

May nodded, hoping the surprise didn't register on her face. She couldn't do anything now about not being there for Kelsey when her husband died, but May *had* supported Kelsey today. She supported her by running outside the second she realized David Smith was dead and ending the police interview. But that hadn't stopped her from feeling terribly sad that a man's life had ended. A man they had met before so many years ago. A man who used to be the boy who had refused to leave the lake until his girlfriend was found. The boy who had wept openly at Marnie's funeral.

He was gone now, and Kelsey's immediate reaction was to think about total strangers who might judge her for leaving some stupid petty note over a stolen parking spot. A man was dead, and Kelsey was making it all about Kelsey. How could Lauren not see that?

May wasn't ready to go back outside yet. She poured herself a glass of water, giving herself a few more minutes to be alone with her thoughts.

May knew from Danny Brennan that Carter wasn't some grunt cop chasing down loose ends unlikely to lead anywhere. He was the detective in charge. The fact that he'd spent valuable time trying to interview the three of them so soon after learning that Smith was dead meant that he had expected to find important information here.

She kept replaying Carter's questions in her head, trying to figure out what he'd been after.

He'd asked about the note, of course. It was possible it had been found along with Smith's body, but then he probably would have accepted her invitation of a bottle of water or a soda to get a fingerprint for comparison. Another possibility was that they had found Smith's girlfriend and she told him about the note, which would mean she was still alive.

He'd also asked whether she recognized that phone number he'd recited. She hadn't been able to commit the entire thing to memory, but she had googled the area code: 959. It covered northern Connecticut—another dead end.

And then there were the questions about the house rental. She had construed them at the time as icebreakers to get the conversation started on a friendly note, but that was before she knew the case had escalated into a murder investigation. And in retrospect, Decker's questions had been unusually specific for generic chitchat. Who found the house? How long had the trip been planned? What rental agency?

May had only known the rental website because she had looked up the house after Kelsey sent them photographs. She remembered thinking how lucky Kelsey had been to find it, since the house seemed to be booked solid for the summer. *How long have y'all been planning the trip?* Why had he wanted to know?

Did it really matter when Kelsey had booked the rental? It must, or Carter Decker wouldn't have asked.

She made her way over to the far end of the kitchen counter, where Kelsey had left the homeowner's detailed instructions after removing them from the refrigerator. She entered the number provided at the bottom into her phone.

Her pulse quickened with each ring. What was she doing? Why did she need to be like this? Why couldn't she bring herself to trust her own friends? She was about to hang up when a woman answered. "This is Arianna."

Kelsey had wondered if the number would lead to a handyman or property manager, but it was the owner. "Hi, Arianna. This is Kelsey Ellis. I'm renting your house in Springs."

"Is there a problem at the house?"

"No, it's absolutely lovely. Thank you. Sorry to bother you, but I'm trying to track down a receipt for the rental because it's tax-deductible for me, but I can't find it and I know I'll forget all about it once I'm home. Can you remind me when I put the deposit down?"

May waited in silence while the owner went to log into her account. *It doesn't matter,* she told herself. *Whether Kelsey rented this house three weeks ago when she said she found it, or six months ago, it doesn't matter. That cop has your imagination going wild.*

"I've got it right here. It was April 18. You paid in full. Do you want me to email it to you?"

"Oh no, please," May said. "You've done enough." Kelsey had rented the house more than two months before inviting them.

"Wait, you said your name's Kelsey? That's not what I have. Am I looking at the wrong records?"

May pictured Kelsey plucking the rental instructions letter from the refrigerator. *Who the fuck is Callie?*

"Oh right," May said, as if realizing something she should have known all along. "Duh, that's why I can't find the charge. My friend Callie's the one who booked it and then I Venmo'd her my part. Is it under a 959 area code?"

"Yep. Callie Martin. Mystery solved."

30

There you are." Lauren was standing over the Solo Stove on the back deck, poking at a wayward log until it fell into place, sending the flames a foot high. "We were just wondering whether we should check on you."

"What's wrong?" Kelsey asked. Even after years in the courtroom, May had never mastered her poker face. She realized she had practically been glaring at Kelsey.

"I need to talk to you." *Talk to you about how everything you've told us since you confessed about the note—no, ever since you invited us on this trip—has been bullshit.*

"Okay. You're kind of freaking me out right now."

Fuck it. Why should May have to confront her in private, adding yet another layer of secrecy to this entire trip? Lauren needed to know the truth, too.

"Who's Callie Martin?"

Kelsey opened her mouth, but no words came out.

"What is actually happening right now?" Lauren asked.

"That letter on the fridge from the homeowner? Addressed to Callie? Kelsey rented the house under a fake name. And she rented it three months ago."

"It's just a name I use," Kelsey said. "One Google search of Kelsey Ellis and up come all the articles about Luke's murder. It's just easier to use a fake name. Why does it matter?"

"It must or that detective wouldn't have been asking me all about the house and how long we'd been planning the trip. You didn't invite us until three weeks ago. And I reread the texts, Kelsey. After you floated the idea, I was saying we should stay at a hotel instead of a rental. You said you wanted the privacy of a house, then you said you had found one. You definitely didn't make it sound like it was already a done deal months earlier."

Nate held up a palm. "Whoa, you guys. I'm sure it's a misunderstanding."

"And you can stop acting like this involves you in any way," May snapped.

"Okay," Nate said, pressing his lips together. "I forgot how good you could be at telling me to shut up. Fair enough, but you guys are friends. Can we lower the temp a little?"

May's inner thermometer was only beginning to heat up. "Friends don't set you up to be grilled by the police two different times. Kelsey, first you didn't tell us you left that note. Then it turns out the guy was someone we used to know. And the way you reacted when you found out he was dead?"

New pieces of the puzzle were sliding into place with every sentence May spoke. Even when the white car had stolen their parking spot, Kelsey had been uncharacteristically patient, begging Lauren and May not to call any attention to them and insisting her good parking karma would save the day. Then, when they went for drinks, she had wanted the chair on the sidewalk facing away from the street. At the time, May thought Kelsey didn't want to be recognized, but she realized now that she hadn't wanted to be recognized by David Smith.

"You knew him, didn't you? Were you dating him? That's why you left the note, right? Not because of the parking spot. But because he was cheating on you with that woman he was with."

Kelsey's bottom lip started to quiver. "Please don't hate me. I'm so sorry."

"Oh my god," May said. "I can't fucking believe this."

"You," Lauren said, holding up a finger to May, "back off and let Kelsey talk. Kelsey, stop it with the lies and tell us what's going on. Everything."

For a second, May thought Kelsey was about to cry again, which would stretch her patience past its breaking point. But instead, she took a deep breath, as if steeling herself to finally come clean. "So you remember when that guy posted a link to my Tinder account on Twitter after I told him my real name? I stopped using dating apps after that, but once the shutdown was over, I was lonely. I wanted to try again. So I decided I just wouldn't use my real name, and I could tell them the truth if things ever got serious."

"Why the fake number?" May asked.

"Let her speak," Lauren admonished, "and then we can ask our questions."

"One guy actually traced my number and it came back to the company. He figured out who I was before I was ready to tell him. And dudes can be super creepy and I don't want some rando to have my real number forever because I texted him a few times. I could also use different area codes that way. I was contacting guys outside of Boston because I thought it was less likely they'd recognize me from news coverage of Luke's case. I also started an Instagram profile so that if anyone googled Callie Martin, they'd find a real person. I just don't post any shots of my face."

So many lies. All those complaints on their group text thread and Zoom cocktail parties about not being able to date until Luke's murder was solved, while Callie Martin was out there living her best life.

"Sometimes, late at night, all alone—usually with wine involved—I'd start thinking about people I used to know from high school and college, googling them and wondering what they're doing now."

"Nothing good ever comes from that," Nate said playfully. May shot him a look.

"Anyway, I wound up seeing David's comment on an Instagram post from a mutual friend from Choate. He was good-looking, so that caught my attention. Then I saw one of his own posts was a screenshot about the merger of two newspaper chains with various people congratulating him on the deal. So I googled him and liked what I found. Before I knew it, I was sending him a direct message."

"Marnie's ex-boyfriend?" May asked. "Seriously?"

"I swear, I had no idea. Not when I first reached out. Once we started texting and talking, I gave him a burner number with a Hartford area code and said I lived there, but we always met either in Rhode Island or on weekend trips. Once we started to get more serious, he told me about his college girlfriend who drowned on a weekend off from the arts camp where she was a counselor."

"You've got to be—"

"May—" Lauren was shaking her head.

"I swear on my life," Kelsey said. "I couldn't believe it either, but then I realized I picked him for a reason. He went to the same kinds of schools, came from a good family in the Northeast. It makes sense we'd have come from overlapping social circles. Anyway, by the time he told me, I was already wanting to drop the fake name and all the lies. We both had made it pretty clear we could see the potential for a serious relationship, and he was asking if I might consider moving to Rhode Island. And yes, I rented this house because we were planning to come here together."

Nate stood and poked at the fire nonchalantly. He already knew all of this. It was so obvious.

"After he told me about Marnie, I felt like if there was any possible way he would understand why I had been lying to him about my name, I had to tell him the truth right then and there. So I did. He listened. Like, really, really listened." Her voice softened at the memory, and May could tell that she was thinking more now about the loss of this man she cared for than whether May and Lauren would understand. She wiped away a tear forming in the corner of one eye before speaking again. "He said it was almost like a sign that we had both known Marnie. It just felt like this enormous weight falling from my shoulders and I could actually imagine a new life with this person who might really love me. He was even talking about introducing me to his mother and seeing if he could work from Boston. I was so fucking happy."

May pressed her lips together to keep herself from screaming. *And yet you didn't mention a single word about him to us.*

When Lauren stood and moved to the sofa, Kelsey rested her head on Lauren's shoulder.

"Oh sweetie," Lauren said. "Why didn't you tell us any of this?"

"I was embarrassed," she said, sitting up again. "I knew what I was doing was wrong, but it was also sort of exhilarating. Like I was out there in the world pretending to be fun as fuck without all my baggage. And then I met Dave. I think I didn't want to tell you about him too soon because you'd tell me it would never work out. I wanted to keep believing it might be real."

"I'm so sorry you lost him," Lauren said.

May suppressed an eye roll. She could not believe Lauren was buying any of this.

"When we were trying to figure out a time for me to come to Providence, he asked whether I wanted to have kids because that was important to him. I gave him all the details of my fertility situation, and that's when he dumped me," Kelsey continued, her voice cracking. "He said he should have broken it off the second I told him I'd been lying about the other things. I was devastated. The future I had pictured for us was suddenly gone, poof. I think I kept the rental in the hopes that maybe he'd somehow change his mind, but nope. He basically ghosted me. And I decided the silver lining was that I had a great place for us to finally see each other in person."

She offered May a sad smile, but May couldn't bring herself to return it.

"I had no idea he'd come here anyway with some other woman. I was so drunk by the time I went to bed that night. I called him to say I couldn't believe he used our vacation on someone new already. He called me out about the note, realizing it must have been me who left it. He told me we never promised each other monogamy while we were still long distance, which was true. But he had been meaning to end things completely with her because he wanted to be exclusive with me. Until the kid thing came up—that was a deal-breaker. He was his parents' only child and the 'bloodline,' as he called it, had to continue. His mother would never have it any other way, and she controlled all the family money. So I folded. I told him if that was really the only sticking point, I was willing to use an egg donor and a surrogate so he could be the biological parent."

"You called him?" May asked. "When?" This time, Lauren did not try to silence her.

"Friday night, after you crashed on the deck."

"I heard you when I came inside. You were crying. I asked you about it the next morning and you denied the whole thing."

"I'm so sorry," she said, placing her hands on her heart.

"So how'd you leave things with him?" Lauren asked.

"He said it was a lot to process and we should take some time and talk when we were back at home. And then you found that missing-person flyer when you went to the farm stand on Monday. I let myself believe that he had broken up with that other woman and was taking some time to himself to think about us."

"I'm sorry," May said. "No, I'm actually *not* sorry. You really expect us to believe that? You've been lying to us this entire time. And if you think the police won't find out about this, you're an idiot."

Nate held his hands in a T. "Maybe we can time-out here?"

"Shut up, Nate." She stood directly in front of Kelsey on the sofa, towering over her, not caring that she was infringing on her space. "You called him on Friday? They obviously have his cell records already. The cops know, Kelsey."

"I used a Providence burner number so he'd be more likely to pick up."

Providence. The 959 number that Carter Decker had asked about. "You just carry around a bag full of burner phones?"

"No, it's just an app, CellBurner."

"You sound like a full-fledged criminal right now," May said.

"That's not true," Lauren said. "A bunch of the women in the symphony use the same app when they book gigs or for online dating so people don't have their permanent number."

"I'm sorry," May said. "Jesus, no, why do I keep saying that? I am *not* fucking sorry."

"Please, May, will you just stop for one second?" Kelsey pleaded. "Calm down. I promise you, I'm telling you the truth."

"Don't you dare tell me to calm down after what I've done trying to help you. What I see here is a woman scorned, who left that note to try to stir up shit between the guy who dumped her and the woman he was on vacation with, a phone call where you tried to get him back, and now the guy's dead. And if I see that? You can be damn sure that cop sees it."

"I can't believe you're saying that," Kelsey said. "How could you possibly think—"

"Tell me: How does all that look to you? Of *course* the police suspect you."

"Well, it sounds like you do, too. Wait, is that why you never reached out to me after Luke died? Did you actually doubt me? Or, let me guess, you didn't actually doubt me, but didn't want my stench to tar your perfect little reputation? Tell me, May, when exactly is it that you think I killed Dave? I've been with you the entire time."

"That's not true. That Friday night, I thought I heard a car engine. And you left for Montauk the next morning to get Josh's car while we were still asleep, and neither of us even heard it. Until we find out when David was killed, there's really no way of knowing."

"You're being so mean right now," Kelsey said.

"Mean? *Mean?* We're not sixteen years old anymore, Kelsey."

"I screwed up, okay? I should have told you guys, but I was just so happy to have you back in my life again. And you can be so fucking judgmental, May. I thought maybe you changed after that video, but, nope, apparently you can make a mistake, but I can't."

"That's not anything like what you—"

May jumped at the *thwack* of the fire poker against the edge of the fire pit. Nate closed his eyes and shook his head. When he opened them, he looked directly at May. "Okay, that was a little extra. Sorry. Very loud. But for what it's worth, I know Kelsey's telling the truth. When you heard her crying on the phone Friday night? That was when she was talking to *me*. She told me exactly what she just said to you about the phone call to David. She was happy about the possibility of getting back together with him but really upset about the idea of not having her own children. She needed someone to talk to but didn't want to tell you guys about the note. She was worried you'd be mad at her and it would ruin your whole hive thing or whatever."

"Pretty ironic, isn't it?" Now Kelsey was the one glaring back at her.

"How so?" May asked.

"That you of all people would be mad at a friend for leaving an anonymous note."

May stepped away, as if Kelsey's words literally burned, nearly bumping into the fire stove. Kelsey raised her chin as her gaze shifted from May to Lauren.

Not now. Not after all these years.

"What exactly am I missing, you two?" Lauren asked. "What note?"

"Please, Kelsey, don't—" May heard the desperation in her own voice.

Kelsey looked over at May, lowering her chin with a nod. "Forget about it. It's stupid. I shouldn't have said anything."

May felt some of the tension release in her jaw.

"No," Lauren said, "I saw your reaction, May. What note?" Neither Kelsey nor May spoke. "What. Note." They both kept their eyes on the blaze of the fire. "That can't be it, right? All these years, I blamed Marnie. She walked in on us. I saw her. I went to her afterward and asked her—no, begged her—not to tell anyone. I thought maybe I could trust her after how much I had helped her. But then that letter showed up at the office, which I never would have expected from her. At worst, I expected her to show off her shiny new secret. And there you were, the girl trying to bury the hatchet, because I was the one who practically ordered you to. And you, May, you never fail at anything, do you? She told her new buddy what she knew about the grown-ups."

The note was never supposed to get Lauren fired. It was supposed to get Thomas Welliver in trouble for being a married lech taking advantage of a much younger woman whose employment he controlled. May had been trying to protect Lauren. She was trying to make Welliver pay for being a scumbag.

When she found out Lauren would be leaving Wildwood along

with them at the end of the summer, she thought she might die from the shame. Kelsey found her curled up under a piano bench. May had sworn her to secrecy and then confessed to the mess she had created.

Lauren was staring at her now through the smoke from the fire pit, waiting for May to deny it.

"Lauren, I didn't know—"

"That's the problem with you, May. You have never known what you *don't* know. You don't know how lucky you are. Or how easy you've had it. Or even which man is talking to you on a subway platform. But you're always so damn certain. You go off on Kelsey for keeping secrets, and yet here you are, after all these years? After all the chances you've had to tell me it was you?"

"I'm sorry, Lauren. It was so long ago."

When May looked to Kelsey for support, Lauren wagged a finger in the air. "Uh-uh, this is on me, not her. This is too much. You need to go home, May."

"Please, let me explain—"

"Leave. Now."

No one tried to stop her when she walked away.

31

May managed to hold herself together as she walked through her building lobby, waving hello to Joe behind the doorman's desk and wishing him a good night. When she opened the apartment door, Gomez was waiting for her. He always seemed to know if she was the one who'd stepped off the elevator.

"You're back?" Josh said, hitting pause on the Yankees game on the television. "I was just telling Gomez that it wasn't Momma in the hallway no matter what his nose was telling him."

"I got you, baby." She placed her purse on the cabinet beside the door and scooped the ecstatic pug into her arms before accepting a peck on the lips from Josh.

"What are you doing home?" he asked, rolling her bag toward the bedroom. "I thought you guys were having a good time."

She shook her head, not knowing where to begin.

"Tapped out? Can I remind you again that you did say in New Orleans that I was the only human being you could tolerate for more than two straight days?"

She wanted to laugh but was afraid she might burst into tears instead.

He stopped and turned to face her. "Hey, what's wrong? You look really upset. Was it something with Nate?"

She kept shaking her head. "It was something . . . with everyone. But it's Kelsey. She was lying, and I figured it out. But they turned it all around on me, and they all hate me now. I blew it."

Except for Nate trying to tell her that he was sure everything would work out in a few days, no one had even said goodbye to her as she carried her bag to the driveway, only to remember that she had taken the train to East Hampton. She bit the bullet and took an Uber back to the city so she could get home as quickly as possible.

She had spent the entire ride trying to decide whether she could bring herself to believe Kelsey's side of the story after all her lies. In the end, it wouldn't even matter. She knew Lauren would never forgive her.

Josh was reaching to give her a hug when her phone rang. She pulled away from him to get to her purse, letting Gomez jump to the floor. Maybe it was Lauren.

The 631 number was familiar. Detective Decker.

"This is May." She mouthed an *I'm sorry* to Josh, but he scoffed and shook his head, his eyes widening in astonishment that she'd cut him off so abruptly.

Decker didn't even bother with a greeting. "You left your friends awful suddenly. What's up?"

"You're watching the house?" she asked. "Wait, did you follow me home?"

"A white Toyota Camry with Florida plates was called in as suspicious this afternoon, parked there for nearly four days without moving. The responding patrol officer found the driver's-side seat fully reclined. Two gunshots, right in the face. So yeah, this is a homicide investigation now, May. You knew that when you convinced your friend Kelsey to clam up, didn't you? And now you're right in the middle of it."

"I told you before I'm not talking to you without a lawyer."

"No, you told me *Kelsey* wasn't talking to me. And then an hour later, you cut your trip short. The officer sitting on the house said it looked like you might have been crying while you waited alone for your Uber. That sounds to me like you may have gotten into an argument with your friends right after you kicked me out of the house, and then decided to leave too."

She knew she should hang up, but she needed to find out what else he knew.

"Your friend from the DA's Office told me you're a true crime junkie. Says you're obsessed with that case where the lawyer was killed while visiting three of his friends. Pretty obvious at least one of them did it. The cops sweated them for hours. Even charged them all with obstruction, sure one of them would break. The odds of two people going down together? Very low. But three? It's so easy to pit three people against each other. Isn't someone always the third wheel? That's the person to peel away."

"You have no idea what you're talking about."

"So what caused the breakup? One possibility is that they figured out you were having an affair with David Smith and lied to them about it."

She said nothing. Josh was gesturing at her from the sofa, telling her to get off the phone and tell him what was going on. She held up a finger to buy more time.

"I called that investigator from the DA's Office again to see if he knew you well enough to have a read on that. Turns out he knew you were engaged—to Josh, he said, last name unknown. For what it's worth, he says there's no way you'd cheat while you're engaged. Or get wrapped up in a homicide for that matter. So that leaves me with another theory. Maybe the woman who would never cheat and would never find herself in the middle of a murder case—the law professor and former prosecutor—realized someone else in that house is a killer and got out of Dodge."

She watched as Josh marched to the kitchen, shaking his head in frustration as he jotted a note on a Post-it before pushing the pad in her direction across the island. *WTF?!*

May pressed her eyes shut to focus. "I've got nothing to say to you, Detective."

"You went back to that strip of Sag Harbor where you first saw David Smith. No reason to do that if you were the one who killed him.

You went because you cared, May. You knew your friend Kelsey had left that note and you thought there could be a connection. I couldn't figure out why you'd be willing to lie about that. But I see it now. You all have something to lose. You don't want to be DA Karen again. Your friend Lauren has a fancy job with people who wouldn't approve of drunken practical jokes in the Hamptons. And don't get me started on Kelsey. But David Smith was only missing then, May. There are things more important than your privacy or reputation."

"You are completely off base," she said.

She made out the words "un-fucking-believable" as Josh muttered under his breath on his way to the bedroom.

"One thing I'm not wrong about? That video from the subway. You had no idea who said what. You were scared. Justifiably. I don't know you, but I don't think you're a bad person. That guy Brennan told me as much. And when you watch that video with the assumption you're not a bad person, it's pretty obvious. So I'm sorry other people judged you for something you didn't actually do, but I just had to ask David Smith's mother to identify him from a tattoo on his ankle because the gunshots to his face made him unrecognizable. We only knew it was him because the killer left his driver's license on his lap before taking his wallet, watch, and shoes."

"That sounds like a robbery," she said.

"Or a jealous girlfriend making it look that way."

"I can't help you. And stop following me," she added, before hanging up.

She found Josh sitting against the headboard of their bed, his phone in one hand as he popped in a second AirPod.

"I'm sorry about that. I had to talk to him."

He didn't respond, and she could hear the faint sound of whatever song he was blasting. She leaned forward and waved, and he freed up one ear.

"I said I'm sorry about that. I really had to talk to him."

"So I gathered. A detective? He's watching you? What the hell is going on, May?"

"Just give me a second, okay?"

When she turned to walk away, he rose to follow her. “It’s not okay to shut me out like this.”

She pulled an open bottle of chardonnay from the refrigerator and tipped herself a big pour before going to the sofa. She hugged Gomez on her lap as she told Josh everything.

32

May sat at the desk in the dimly lit remodeled closet that served as their shared home office space. Gomez was plopped on the floor, his chin resting on her foot. He always knew when she was upset and in need of comfort. She hoped that a few minutes alone would help clarify the emotional chaos that had her head throbbing.

At least Josh hadn't argued when she said she needed a minute to calm down and think. He was definitely angry, but his ire wasn't aimed at her—at least not exclusively. He was furious at Lauren and Kelsey, calling Lauren a narcissist who got off on the admiration of others and Kelsey a spoiled, emotionally stunted cool girl forever stuck in adolescence. He wasn't a hundred percent *not* right.

She wondered what that made her in his eyes, but decided it was better not to press the issue. It wasn't the first time he'd raised concerns about the intensity of her renewed friendship with Kelsey and Lauren—concerns she had always batted away dismissively. How had Lauren put it? *You have never known what you don't know—but you're always so damn certain.*

She had lied to him over and over again for days, and she had done it because she had placed her friends before him. He had a right to be mad.

Perhaps she had been blind to the warning signs, too wrapped up in the allure of a friendship that had felt so complete and unconditional. According to Josh, it was like the three of them had become obsessed with pleasing each other. He thought it was weird that neither Kelsey nor Lauren had a real relationship and always seemed to have time to text and do puzzles with her all day.

He said it was clear she needed to make a clean break. May couldn't imagine how silent her days would feel without them, but that choice had likely already been made for her.

Josh's other request was trickier. He wanted her to call back the detective on Long Island and tell him everything she knew about Kelsey and her connection to David Smith. It would mean admitting that she had initially misled both him and Danny, which could get her disbarred and fired. But Josh said it would be better for her to raise the issue first before the detective could eventually prove she was dishonest on his own. More importantly, there was a homicide investigation at stake.

She sought solace, as she so often had in the past few years, on the internet. She opened the Spelling Bee on her computer, searching for the final two words that had eluded the three of them that morning. By the time she found the word *ganglia,* she had already lost interest.

She typed *Lucas Freedman murder Boston* into her browser's search window. The first two hits were an article from *The Boston Globe* and a Wikipedia entry, followed by YouTube videos uploaded by different true crime vloggers. She scrolled down until she found what she was looking for—a page dedicated to Luke's murder on KillerInsights, one of the more respectable true crime message boards. The pinned post at the top outlined the basics of the case, including the wedding photo from the *Globe* when Kelsey and Lucas still seemed like giddy newlyweds.

Kelsey's blue eyes gazed right through the camera, while Luke wore the knowing smile of a man with a secret. The top comment read, *Why does she look so sinister in her own wedding picture? Like she's about to unhinge her jaw and swallow the photographer whole.*

But the couple's facial expressions made perfect sense to May. She had noticed the critical detail the first time she saw the picture after searching for news of the wedding she declined to attend—the groom's fingertips placed confidently on his bride's side, right at the top of her rib cage. A light tickle. It was Kelsey's "spot," the move that had earned Matt Lenox a dry hump in the eighth grade. Kelsey was smiling because she was thrilled in all the best ways.

May couldn't believe she was entertaining the idea that Kelsey may have been involved in the murders of two men. *My former BFF the serial killer?* But either Kelsey was the unluckiest woman in the world or it wasn't a coincidence that first her husband and now a boyfriend had been shot to death in their cars.

What could bring Kelsey to the point of wanting to end the lives of two men she supposedly loved? Luke had wanted out of their marriage. David Smith had ended things against Kelsey's wishes. Could it be as basic an explanation as rejection?

May remembered Kelsey boasting in college that she had never been dumped. *I'm the dumper, not the dumpee.* May could definitely not say the same. Rejection sucked. It wasn't only the loss of the relationship. It was the sting of putting yourself out there, allowing yourself to be vulnerable, and the inability to force a person to want you back. But was that really enough to bring Kelsey to wish a man dead?

May couldn't claim to be an expert on what Kelsey was like five years ago when Luke was killed, but she knew both younger Kelsey and present-day Kelsey pretty darn well. She knew the things that really mattered to her—earning the right and the skills to run her father's business at some point, being a good friend and sister, and eventually having children of her own. It all boiled down to family.

And for her to have biological children, she would need to use the fertilized eggs she and Luke had created before her surgery. That's why she had supposedly been crying to Nate on the phone that Friday night: David Smith wanted to father his own kids, which meant Kelsey wouldn't be their biological mother.

It was as if a switch suddenly flipped in her brain. The chaos in her mind was replaced by clarity.

All Luke had wanted was to make a clean break from Kelsey's overbearing family. Having children with Kelsey didn't fit into that plan.

She opened Westlaw, clicked on a database of Massachusetts law, and entered "disposition of frozen embryos after a divorce." It was a legal issue she had offered to research for Kelsey, but Kelsey assured her she had lawyers all over it. Within ten minutes, May had the answer: Kelsey would not have had unilateral control over the embryos if the divorce had been finalized. Courts were reluctant to permit one party to force the other to become a biological parent against their will. Instead, both parties would have to consent to any future use of the embryos.

She searched next for the disposition of frozen embryos in the event of one parent's death. *Unlike the situation of a dissolution of marriage, if one member of the couple passes away, control usually goes to the surviving spouse.*

She jumped at the sound of the office door sliding open. Josh popped his head in. "You okay in here?"

"Yeah, just figuring some things out."

"Got to say, I'm getting a little worried. I'm used to you being on the same side as cops. This is so out of character for you."

"I get it. Things are feeling a lot clearer already."

He peeked at her screen, the Westlaw heading clearly visible. "Are you working on your article?"

"No, I'm actually reading about Kelsey's husband's murder."

"Detective Hanover down the rabbit hole again?"

"Very."

"In a good way, or in a we-might-need-to-step-away-from-the-internet way?"

"In a good way."

"Let me know if you need anything?"

She handed him her empty wineglass. "Refill? A big one?"

Gomez followed him out, apparently satisfied that she no longer needed his emotional support services.

Halfway through her bucket of wine, she had completed a read of every last message-board post about the shooting of Lucas Freedman.

She scrolled back up to a batch of redacted photographs from the crime scene that the *Globe* had obtained pursuant to a public records request. The driver's-side door was wide open, but most of the window's shattered glass was inside the car. The consensus was that the shooter had fired through the window while the door was still closed and then grabbed the money Luke had been taking to the bank.

The glove box was open. Most of the amateur sleuths on the board agreed that the killer had been in a rush to make off with the deposit envelope that must have been stashed inside. But May found herself agreeing with the commenters who thought the cash had been stored somewhere else. When she was the only person in the car, she always threw her stuff on the passenger seat. The glove box also looked like it was already crammed full of papers.

At least when May had worked service jobs in high school and college, the bank envelopes that managers left with after closing had been floppy vinyl bags. She wasn't convinced one would fit in Luke's glove box. Even if Luke had wanted to conceal the money for some reason, it would be easier to simply stick it under the car seat. Glove boxes were for longer-term storage, things like service receipts, owner's manuals, and proof of registration and insurance.

She pictured Luke, alone in the car, pulled over to the side of the road. A bullet through the window into his left temple. Had he even seen the killer? Why had he stopped there? Was he still alive as his shooter rifled through the car for the cash?

She replayed the scene in her head again, this time rewinding even further to imagine Luke slowing his car and pulling over. Looking in the rearview mirror. Seeing someone approach. Someone who would have first stepped from their own vehicle. She imagined Luke reaching for the glove box. In the scene playing out in her mind, he was the one who opened it, not the killer. He needed something.

His insurance and registration. Then the gunshot.

She recalled the sound of Detective Decker's voice imploring her to stop thinking only about herself and her friends. *I just had to ask David Smith's mother to identify him from a tattoo on his ankle because the gunshots to his face made him unrecognizable. We only knew it was him because the killer left his driver's license on his lap.*

It was so clear now. She knew exactly what had happened, first to Luke, then to David Smith.

When she stepped from the office, Josh was on the sofa with his laptop, Gomez at his side.

"Another refill?" he asked, starting to get up.

She shook her head and picked up her cell phone from the coffee table.

"I'm calling that cop."

"I'm so relieved. It's the right decision."

"Kelsey did it, and I think I know why."

33

Today was the fourth time Carter Decker had to tell someone they'd never see a person they loved again. For all the complaints he'd heard from other cops about the job's burdens, he'd carry them all at maximum weight if he never had to be the one to shatter a person's world like that again. It would have been easier to keep Tinsley Smith in the dark when he first heard about the body found inside the car on Old Stone Highway. But after meeting her in person, he could no longer think of her as the rich lady used to getting her way with peons like him. She was a mother who loved her son. He didn't want to leave her clinging on to a nonexistent glimmer of hope any longer than necessary.

We do have new information about your son. We located him, and I'm very sorry—

No, please—

It's not the news I had hoped to be giving you.

Her sobs had filled the living room of the friend's home where she was staying. Carter stood and placed one hand on her back, patting gently in a steady rhythm to help slow her breath. His father had done the same thing for him after their beagle Joey had gotten out of the yard and was struck by a speeding car right in front of Carter, and twenty years later, Carter had found himself offering the same attempt at comfort the first time he had to notify a homicide victim's family.

He was my only son. The last remaining piece of my husband.

Carter had promised to do everything he could to find her son's killer.

The medical examiner was at work on David Smith's autopsy. The cause of death was obvious, two bullets fired through the open driver's-side window, directly at his face. Carter was eager for the toxicology results, but thanks to the fentanyl crisis he could be waiting for up to two months. He still had not written off the possibility that it was a drug deal gone bad.

David's friend Simon said that a younger David had gone on a binge during a rough period after college. Carter now knew that the rough time was over Marnie Mann's death. It was possible that Christine's calling things off, plus the end of the relationship Carter suspected David was having with Kelsey Ellis, had been enough to send him searching for drugs to dull the pain.

If nothing else, Carter could look himself in the mirror, knowing that he had made the right calls from the case's outset. And one of his calls now was to circle back to Gurney's. He had already overseen a thorough search of Smith's hotel room after he was assigned to the case, but he now knew that the staff had failed to notice the absence of the black clay bird that Christine had admitted to throwing once she confirmed he had been seeing other women. He wanted to make sure he didn't miss anything else before having a crime scene team do a thorough search for forensic evidence.

As he was pulling back the yellow crime scene tape from the hotel door, a woman stepped into the hallway from the next room. She did a double take.

"Are you with the police?" she asked. Her long gray hair was piled on top of her head in a bun. Her beach dress reminded him of Mrs. Roper from the *Three's Company* repeats his mother used to watch while she cooked dinner.

He produced his badge from his back pocket.

"That yellow tape is all anyone's been talking about—even more than the supposed influencer taking pictures of her butt all day by the pool. The management assured us there's no risk to any of us, but it's still so disconcerting."

"I can second the assurances. Nothing to worry about, ma'am."

"Was someone hurt?"

"It really has nothing to do with the hotel," he reassured her in a casual tone.

"I was wondering if it was about the people who were arguing in that room on Saturday."

"You heard an argument?"

"I certainly did. I had come back to the room to—well, I guess I can tell you the truth now that it's legal. I came back for"—she lowered her voice to a whisper—"a little toke on a vape." She mimed taking a drag. "How utterly delightful to say that to a cop! Never could have predicted that in 1970."

"Don't tell anyone, but I've been known to partake a little now and then."

"Oh, that is wonderful!"

He rocked on his heels. "So . . . the argument?"

"Yes, I could hear their voices even as I was coming down the hall. The woman was definitely not happy. She was calling him every name in the book. My husband would have walked right out the door if I went off on him like that. I could hear the man's voice but it was lower. I wasn't able to make out what he was saying. I enjoyed my little toot, and back out to the beach I went. They were still at it when I left."

"Could you tell what they were fighting about?" He was inclined to believe Christine's account of the argument, but a third party's corroboration would lock that piece of the picture in place.

She shook her head. "Of course, that didn't keep me from speculating. My theory was that it had something to do with him being on the phone Friday night—or I guess it was technically Saturday morning."

This woman in the muumuu was just full of information. "You could hear that, too?"

"Not the actual words, no. But I could tell it was a man's voice. He was out on his terrace. I peeked through the curtains and could see he was on his cell. I wanted Hal—that's my husband—to tell him to keep it down, but Hal said that's how people get shot these days. Isn't that insane?"

That was one word for it. "Did the phone call sound acrimonious? Was he yelling or any other indication of an argument?"

She squinted as if she was trying to remember. "I honestly don't know."

"What time was this?"

"Late. The clock said one-forty when he woke me up."

It was the call he had seen in Smith's phone log, the Rhode Island number that he had not been able to trace. "Anything else you remember about the couple or what you may have heard?"

"Well, when I came back to the room later on Saturday, the male half passed me in the hallway in the other direction. He was carrying a black plastic bag tied up at the top. I think it was garbage."

"Got it." It would line up with Christine's account of the broken bird figurine that had disappeared from Smith's room. "Anything else?"

"Nope. That's it. But you're sure we're safe? Like, wink your right eye if you think Hal and I should get the hell out of here?"

"You and Hal are all good," he said with a chuckle. "Don't toke and drive though, okay?"

She smiled slyly. "It's a deal."

Carter was finishing a second search of David Smith's suitcase when his phone rang. The city number was familiar.

"Decker," he said.

"It's May Hanover. I need you to listen to me." The trepidation that had been in her voice when he called her two hours earlier was gone now. Her tone was confident and urgent.

"I'm definitely listening," he said.

"You know that Kelsey's husband was shot, right? In Boston? They were on the verge of divorce."

"Luke," he said.

"He was also shot in his car—like David Smith. He owned a restaurant and was on his way to make a bank deposit—"

"I already know the basics."

"The glove box in his car was found open. The assumption was that either the cash for the bank drop was in there or the killer left it open after searching for valuables."

He remembered coming to that conclusion himself but could already tell that Hanover knew far more about the details of the murder of Kelsey Ellis's husband than he did. He had been hoping May would take the bait he had planted earlier to convince her to cooperate, but he had been expecting her to spill what she knew about whatever relationship Kelsey had with David Smith. Instead they were talking about Lucas Freedman. The car. The glove box.

Why hadn't he seen it earlier? Before he realized it, he was speaking his thoughts aloud. "It was a traffic stop."

"Or at least he thought it was a traffic stop," May said. "David Smith's killer didn't intentionally leave the driver's license on David's lap."

"David had it out for the police officer he thought had pulled him over," Carter said. He had already run Smith's license and rental car tag. He'd had no law enforcement contacts at all except for reporting a car accident six years earlier and the San Francisco robbery his mother had mentioned. "From the shell casings, Smith's killer used a nine-millimeter. Luke Freedman was shot with a thirty-eight. But the MO's still the same."

"There's something else," May said.

This woman was whip-smart. By the time she was finished, he felt like he could give a tutorial about the legal and ethical complications of in vitro fertilization and the handling of genetic materials.

Carter himself really didn't understand the appeal of parenthood, but he did know from multiple failed relationships that for some people, it felt as vital to their existence as air or water. *You only get one life,* as one woman had told him after breaking things off because of his disinterest in having a child. *I want to spend mine as a mother.*

"So just to make sure I understand," Carter said, "under the law,

Luke could have forced Kelsey to destroy the embryos once they were divorced. But with him deceased, she gets to make the call on whether to implant them or not? His parents can't stop her?"

"That's exactly what I'm saying. You should be able to subpoena the records from the fertility clinic they used. Whatever documents they signed will provide the exact terms of any legal agreement they had about the disposition of their embryos in the event of either divorce or death, but apparently the scenario I've laid out is pretty much the standard."

He had no other follow-up questions, so he ended the call as he usually did. "Is there anything else you can think of that might be helpful for me to know?"

"Marnie Mann," she said. "The girl from the Wildwood Camp who dated David Smith in college."

"What about her?"

"Kelsey really couldn't stand her. Frankly, I couldn't either. But I had been making an effort to get to know her better and stop bickering with her the way we did when we were all kids."

He didn't understand why they were now talking about the girl who drowned at camp fifteen years ago, but kept his confusion to himself.

"The night she drowned," May continued, "Kelsey said she saw Marnie and me off whispering to each other. She said it looked almost like we were conspiring. And that seeing the two of us together like that, she felt jealous. Left out."

"And you think she drowned her because of it?"

"We keep calling it a drowning, but it was due to a head injury. The coroner's theory was that she dove into the lake from an elevated spot and hit her head and that's why she drowned. But there are other ways of getting head injuries."

"Like from another camp counselor who doesn't want to share her best friend."

"Trust me, Detective. I'm having a hard time believing that I'm even entertaining the possibility, but female friendships are no joke. Losing a friend can break you far worse than losing a man. And three dead bodies in one person's path—it's just weird. She's either the unluckiest woman in the world, or—"

"They're somehow linked, and your friend's the common connection."

"My former friend." He couldn't tell if the edge in her voice was anger or sadness. "That ship has sailed."

34

May opened her eyes, aware of something cold and damp against her ear. It was Gomez sniffing at her. She gave him some neck scratches and then fumbled for her phone in the bed, searching for it in the blankets twisted around her legs.

It was almost ten in the morning. She didn't realize she had fallen back asleep after waking up while it was still dark outside. She must have nodded off while she'd been toiling away on the Spelling Bee.

She had three new message alerts and felt a glimmer of hope when she saw Lauren's name. The day and a half that had passed since Lauren told her to go back to the city had felt so quiet. Last night, she found herself rereading messages in the endless Canceled Crew group text thread. She had grown accustomed to days where they would exchange hundreds of messages. Now the most recent text was nearly two days old.

She had started to delete the entire thread, but stopped herself when her phone asked for final confirmation. Instead, she had sent a new text to Lauren. *I understand if you never forgive me, but I do want you to know how deeply sorry I am. I never meant to hurt you. I thought you were being taken advantage of and was trying to help. I should have gone to you instead to see if you were okay.*

She held her phone in front of her face to unlock the screen, skipping over new messages from Josh to read Lauren's response. *It's a lot to get my head around and right now I'm focused on Kelsey. I hope you are well.*

I hope you are well?

Best wishes. Warmest regards. She regretted it immediately after hitting send. *I'm sorry. That was obnoxious. I truly am sorry. For everything.*

She held her phone, waiting to see the dots indicating that Lauren was composing a reply. Nothing.

She jumped back to Josh's messages. *Good morning, sleepyhead. Glad you were finally able to fall back asleep. Hope today is better.*

And oh, you told me at 3 am to remind you today to call the caterer about the oyster bar, whatever that means.

May never used to have insomnia. She used to go to sleep a little after eleven and wake up by six-thirty, usually beating her alarm. But in early 2017, she began doomscrolling in the middle of the night. When the alarm went off, she had to drag herself to the shower to go to work.

Then, during the shutdown, schedules no longer mattered. She began staying up and sleeping in a little later. Most nights came with the dreaded eyes-suddenly-open at four a.m. on the dot, like her brain knew it was time to freak out. The only structure she managed to force upon herself was to get out of bed by eleven-thirty in time for the governor's daily briefings, the 2020 version of must-see television.

Poor Josh. She didn't even remember talking to him at three o'clock, but she was glad she had or she probably would have forgotten her middle-of-the-night decision. They had been struggling to come up with a wedding plan that would fit their budget without sacrificing the things that were most important to them. They had already resigned themselves to having beer and wine only, even though May knew their fancier friends thought cash-bar weddings were tacky.

But May was the one who really wanted the oysters. She could eat four dozen Wellfleets if someone else would pay for them. But even at wholesale prices, the cost of a raw bar with a designated shucker was exploding their budget. May would simply have to pick another day to have all the oysters she wanted. Problem solved.

Gomez was sniffing her again, this time on her neck. "You making sure I'm still Momma? No one switched me out while we were sleeping, baby. I love you too."

He jumped down from the bed, landing with a thud like a dropped bowling ball. Gomez's voluntary departure from a human bed was a sure sign he needed a walk.

She left her phone at home on their walk, a self-imposed rule she had adopted after she saw the video and realized her terrible mistake about who had spoken those disgusting words to her on the platform. She must have watched it a hundred times. The two men's voices sounded nothing alike. Why did she just assume that it was Darren Foster? She knew why. Unconscious bias might be unconscious, but it was still bias. If she had seen the man who actually said that to her—the white man whose name she would never know—would she have feared for herself physically or just rolled her eyes in disgust? Would she have even contemplated calling the police? May had never felt as ashamed of herself—not even over that note about Lauren and Thomas—than when she watched that video. Having to walk around her very safe block without her phone from now on was small punishment and ensured she'd never call the police on an innocent person again.

When they got back to the apartment, she gave Gomez his breakfast and then reopened the Spelling Bee on her laptop. She was missing three words and hoped that seeing the letters on a larger screen might help, but she was still completely stuck. Yesterday, she had missed Queen Bee by two words, *colleen* and *leonine.* When she looked at the solution this morning, she had searched the Canceled Crew thread and found a conversation from the previous year where Kelsey had given her one hint ("think Irish lass") and Lauren had given her the other ("with thick, shaggy hair"). If nothing else, she'd keep the thread for the word hints.

She turned off the wifi on her laptop, setting a timer for two hours to force herself to work on the law review article she had been ignoring since she first left for East Hampton. By the time the alarm went off, Gomez was snoring at her feet, and she had managed to finish the entire introduction. She realized how much longer a day felt when she wasn't constantly texting.

She turned her wifi back on and saw that a new message had arrived from Lauren, responding specifically to her snarky *Best wishes* remark. *FWIW that actually made me LOL. Look at me using the dumb acronyms.*

The reply was better than silence, but it didn't feel like a return to normalcy. Had May really expected Lauren to absolve her already, just from a text message? When she wrote that note, she had no way of knowing that Marnie would die or that Lauren would be forced to leave a job and a place that she loved. By the time Lauren announced her resignation, the three of them had developed a bond that May didn't want to break. She rationalized her silence, convincing herself that Lauren would have gotten pushed out of Wildwood anyway over Marnie's death, whether May had sent the letter or not. She even let herself believe that Lauren's departure might have been for the best if it got Lauren away from an abusive employer.

Part of May wanted to beg for forgiveness, but she also wanted a chance to defend herself. May's mistake was a long time ago. And, yes, she had been hiding the truth for all these years, but Kelsey had been lying to them left and right for months. And Lauren wasn't completely innocent either, telling her so many times she wasn't seeing anyone when it was obvious Thomas had been in the picture the entire time. But pointing all of that out to Lauren would only get her angrier. For now, May would have to settle for an LOL.

She opened her browser window and searched for *David Smith murder*. The East Hampton police department had announced the homicide the previous day, releasing the victim's name but not identifying any suspects or including any details other than to say that the victim had been shot, that there was no reason to believe the general public was in danger, and that the investigation was ongoing.

She clicked on her bookmarks and pulled up the KillerInsights message board. A search for David Smith's name had yielded no results every time she checked yesterday.

Now, however, there were new hits, the first of which was posted shortly after ten p.m. the previous night. The name of the thread to which the new messages had been added hit her with a wave of confusion. *Boston Restaurant Owner Lucas Freedman Murder.*

She clicked on the link. It was a message from a user named BostonGirl. *I live in Boston and have followed this case for years. I can't say how I'm related because I don't want to be identified as a leak, but I promise I have a relative who's Boston Police. There's a new break in the case. A man named David Smith was shot last weekend in East Hampton, NY—also shot in his car like Luke. The police think there's a connection. And guess what the connection is? Kelsey Ellis!! You guys, I'm telling you. This is it!!! Stay tuned.*

A user named AmateurSloth replied two hours later. *Wow, that is HUGE! Can you tell us more about the connection between Kelsey and the new victim?*

BostonGirl answered almost immediately. *Kelsey was dating him but he dumped her.*

AmateurSloth: *Wow. Sounds like someone doesn't handle rejection well? LOL.*

BostonGirl: *Right? I mean, you've got to know you're taking a risk getting involved with her. Sleep with one eye open. Oh, and guess what else I found out? Kelsey was ALSO IN THE HAMPTONS when he was shot. And she was with two friends as notoriously toxic as her. Well, not suspected-murder notorious (LOL) but google them. May Hanover (aka AsianDAKaren) and Lauren Berry (uppity slut who gets jobs by being a mistress). What a combo.*

There were May's first and last names, right there in black and white on her computer screen, once again, for anyone to see. How many people were already online, scrounging for more dirt on her? Would her fellow faculty members see this? Her students? It was happening again.

She was on Reddit, trying to see if anyone had reposted BostonGirl's insider information for wider distribution, when a new email alert flashed at the top of her screen. It was from someone named Tlinton at Newsday.com. She assumed it was junk mail until she saw the subject line: *Kelsey Ellis.*

She clicked to open. *Hi, Professor Hanover. My name is Tamara Linton and I'm a reporter working on a story about the shooting of David Smith in East Hampton. I've been told that you were there with Kelsey Ellis, whose name has come up in my reporting. I'm hoping you can help provide some background information and context. Please call me.*

She could not hit the delete key hard enough.

It was only the sight of a startled Gomez running away to the living room that made her realize she was screaming at the top of her lungs.

35

Lauren took the liberty of switching the pool speaker to her favorite "yard party" playlist as a break from the reggae Nate had been streaming nonstop for the past two days. Nate had volunteered to make a grocery run for their dinner provisions, and Kelsey was reading a Megan Abbott novel on the chaise longue next to hers. As "Lovely Day" by Bill Withers came over the speaker, Lauren tried to gauge if Kelsey's eyes were actually scanning the pages. She could tell that Kelsey was struggling to cope with David's death and all the questions it raised.

Lauren moved from the playlist on her screen back to the daily bee, knowing that Kelsey would appreciate the distraction. Nate had chipped in with a few hard-to-find compounds, and now she and Kelsey were missing only two words. They had cheated by looking at the hints and knew that both missing words started with *b*. One was a musical instrument and the other was related to bacteria, but they were hopelessly stuck.

"Have you found them for us yet?" Kelsey asked, resting her book open against her flat belly.

"No, and it's driving me batty. I'm certain we've had these words before—multiple times—but we never remember them."

"You know who probably has them, don't you? She always gets the science words, and I distinctly remember her knowing about a certain kind of musical instrument that not even *you* had heard of."

May had texted Lauren this morning to offer another apology, but Lauren wasn't ready to accept it. *I never meant to hurt you. I thought you were being taken advantage of and was trying to help.* Lauren knew her relationship with Thomas was complicated and unconventional, but she had never questioned her own voluntary participation in it until the Me Too movement made it clear to her that modern notions of consent were different than the ones she had always accepted.

May was only nine years younger than her, but even that age gap was enough to explain why May would simply assume that the dynamics of wealth and power would make Lauren a victim in any sexual relationship with Thomas. But when those conversations became omnipresent after the Weinstein stories opened the floodgates, Lauren had replayed her entire relationship with Thomas and still saw it for what it was—two people who loved each other without needing the confines of traditional monogamy. And it wasn't May's place in 2008 as a twenty-two-year-old busybody to question the decisions of a grown woman with agency.

She did have to admit that May's text reply of *best wishes, warmest regards* after Lauren wished her well had made her laugh. May was always trying to be the nice girl, but someday she'd realize that the people closest to her loved her for the other parts, including her inner snark.

"Okay, I'm giving up," she announced. She pulled up the Canceled Crew group thread and searched for *bacteria* and then *musical instrument.* "Got them both. Sure enough, May was the one who found these same words five months ago."

"Just tell me. I'll never get them."

"Bacilli and balalaika. Seriously, how does that girl know these things?"

When she looked up from her phone, Kelsey was studying her with a puzzled expression. "You're really not going to talk to her again?"

"I honestly don't know."

"She's not the only one who was keeping that information from you," Kelsey said. "I also could have told you."

"But only if you betrayed your best friend. It's not the same."

"We were just kids, and it was before Marnie died and the three of us got closer to each other. You never would have known except she pissed me off and I acted like an asshole."

"She was out of college, on her way to law school. That's a grown-ass woman. And honestly? Has she even changed? We call her the 'little sheriff' for a reason. There's a self-righteousness that borders on the edge of sanctimony. I think deep down, May is a really angry person."

"May?" Kelsey said, shaking her head with a chuckle. "Who apologizes twenty times a day? I think I've seen her mad, like, three times in our whole lives."

"Well, she was running red-hot at you the other night."

"I can't really blame her. I dragged you all into this mess with Dave."

"No, I'm telling you. She's been pressured her whole life—by her mom, by society—to be a smart, perfect, docile little girl. She hates it. That incident on the subway platform might have been the tip of the iceberg. One of these days, she might completely lose it. Like Celie in *The Color Purple* with a knife to Danny Glover on Thanksgiving." Lauren made an explosion sound with the accompanying *boom* hand gesture. "Speak of the devil."

A new text message from May. *Hey, I know I'm not your favorite person right now, but I just got an email from a Long Island reporter named Tamara Linton asking about Kelsey, and I think it has something to do with this. Thought you should know because if I'm right, she'll probably contact you too. And not that you want my advice, but I would at least keep an open mind about what else Kelsey might be hiding.*

The text was followed by two screenshots from some message board called KillerInsights. The conversation thread made clear that someone knew that the police were looking at Kelsey as the common link between David Smith and Kelsey's husband. May and Lauren had both been named as the friends who were in the Hamptons with her.

She checked her email and found a recent message from the same reporter.

"I think you need to see this," she said, switching her screen back to the message from May. She scrolled past the part about doubting Kelsey's innocence to show the two screenshots from the Killer-Insights message board.

As she read, Kelsey chewed at her lower lip so hard that Lauren was afraid she might draw blood. "And a reporter from *Newsday* emailed both May and me asking about you."

She was shaking her head as she returned Lauren's phone. "I can't believe this is happening again. Why in the world would I hurt Dave? We were on the verge of getting back together. He was going to be my future. Now that's all gone and they think I would do that not only to him but to myself?" Kelsey was practically yelling by the time she was finished.

"It's going to be okay, sweetie." Lauren reached over and gave Kelsey's hand a reassuring squeeze. "They can't prove something that didn't happen."

"Tell that to all the people who rotted in jail after wrongful convictions."

"Oh, but they weren't pretty rich white girls like you," Lauren said with a straight face.

"Okay, that was funny."

"I aim to please."

"God, Lauren, I'm so sorry you're getting dragged into this. What that person said about you online is disgusting. That actually does make me want to kill someone."

"Don't worry about me," she said. "My skin might be gorgeous, but it's calloused where it matters."

Despite her words, Lauren *was* worried about the potential blowback. She was certain a couple of those biddies on the symphony board had Google alerts at the ready, searching for a reason to get rid of her without making it about their buddy, Jessica. In her letter, Jessica had portrayed herself as a victimized woman shocked by her husband's tawdry infidelity, but her arrangement with Thomas predated Lauren. Jessica only got resentful about it when the woman Thomas had chosen for his long-term unconventional relationship was Lauren instead of some Twinkie. Lauren knew for a fact that Jessica had been seeing her current gentleman friend for the last seven years and was on Xanax and Ketel One martinis when she'd written that email to her friend trying to get Lauren fired.

She turned her head at the sound of a car pulling into the driveway. She hoped Nate had followed her shopping instructions. She was cooking her famous enchiladas with chili con carne and green rice tonight, and she wasn't sure she trusted a bachelor to know a corn tortilla from flour, cilantro from parsley, or a poblano from a jalapeño.

She was rising to her feet when she heard another car engine and then the distinct sounds of car doors opening and closing. She turned down the music on the speaker and exchanged a glance with Kelsey. Something wasn't right. The knocking on the front door quickly escalated into pounding.

It wasn't until she was opening the door that she made out the words. "Police, open up!"

Detective Carter Decker was flanked on each side by two uniformed officers. The folksy just-have-a-few-questions demeanor from two nights ago was gone.

"Who else is on the premises?" he asked.

"No one," Lauren said.

"My brother will be back soon though," Kelsey added.

The detective nodded toward the uniformed officers, who swept past them and began moving quickly through the house. Lauren wondered why the detective hadn't asked about May. Was it possible he knew she had returned to the city?

"Kelsey Ellis, we have a search warrant for this house, your vehicle, your telephone, and any other electronic devices that might contain evidence of your communication with David Smith. Turn around and place your hands behind your back."

Kelsey looked to Lauren in panic.

"You can't possibly—"

"Ma'am," Decker said to Lauren sharply, "you need to step outside to the front yard until this matter is handled. Now!"

As she walked away she heard the detective tell Kelsey she was under arrest for falsely reporting an incident in the third degree and obstructing governmental administration in the second degree. She repeated the words over and over again in her head so she wouldn't forget them. As soon as she could get her phone from the back deck, she'd text them to herself. A lawyer would want to know the charges.

Decker was escorting Kelsey toward a patrol car in the driveway. The sight of her in handcuffs felt surreal. Kelsey's eyes pleaded with Lauren silently as she passed. "I'm going to call your father, okay? We'll get you a lawyer. Stay strong."

She tried to tell herself that it could be worse. At least they weren't charging her with murder.

Lauren spotted Kelsey's little Audi accelerating toward the house. It screeched to a stop in front of the driveway, and Nate sprang from the driver's seat toward the commotion. "What's going on? What are you doing to her?"

Decker held up a hand to halt Nate's movement and guided Kelsey into the patrol car's backseat. "Slow your roll and back up, sir, or we're going to have a problem."

Kelsey had vowed to always take care of Nate since her father had turned his back on him. His mother was still alive, but in light of the rapid progression of her Alzheimer's disease, Kelsey was in some ways the only family he had left. Lauren could see now that the loyalty was mutual. Nate looked ready to charge at the police car if necessary.

"She's my sister," he yelled.

"And that doesn't give you the right to interfere with a lawful arrest."

"Arrest? For what?"

"I'm going to ask you one more time before you end up next to her in cuffs. Back. Up."

Nate's shoulders sagged as he stepped away as instructed.

"I left copies of our warrants on the front porch so you'll see the two charges listed there. We'll be transporting her to the East Hampton Town police station, and she'll be arraigned tomorrow at two p.m. at the Justice Court behind town hall. Now I'm going to need you to move that car."

Lauren could see that Nate was assessing his choices, but there were none. As soon as he'd inched the Audi forward the necessary distance,

Decker rapped his knuckles two times on the patrol car's passenger window and stepped away.

Lauren tried to give Kelsey one more reassuring look as the car backed up, but her head was slumped forward, her shoulders trembling. She watched as the patrol car got smaller and smaller until it reached the curve at the end of the road near the bay. And then Kelsey was gone.

PART FOUR

THE PEOPLE V. KELSEY ELLIS

36

The detective gestured for Lauren and Nate to follow him to the front porch. He handed Nate a set of documents he had tucked beneath the cushion of one of the Adirondack chairs.

"I guess I'll give this to you since you're family—copies of the search warrant and arrest warrant." Nate began skimming the papers while the detective continued. "What's going to happen now is a thorough search of the house. To be honest, that's not going to be done until early tomorrow morning. You have somewhere to go until then?"

Nate's attention remained on the documents. He was not about to accept some token effort at kindness. "We'll figure it out."

"You won't find a hotel room out here. Not this time of year. You might have a better chance in maybe Riverhead or Islip."

Lauren folded her arms. This asshole was pretending to be helpful now? "Like Nate said, we'll figure it out."

He explained that they could go inside the beach rental with police supervision to retrieve their personal belongings, and could return to the house once the search was completed tomorrow. "And if you could hand over the keys to Kelsey's Audi, that'll make the search a little faster."

Nate's jaw was clenched as he handed Decker the car key.

"My phone's in the backyard," Lauren said. "Can we make some calls from there while you're wasting your time searching the house?"

"That's no problem."

The first call Lauren made was to Suzanne Kim. Kelsey had given Nate and Lauren the lawyer's number after Decker's initial visit to the house just in case they needed it. Suzanne had represented Kelsey's family after Luke's murder. A call to her firm reached a voicemail saying that the office was closed but providing an after-hours number in the event of an emergency.

That number picked up after two rings. "Call center."

Lauren put her phone on speaker as she explained who she was and why she was trying to reach Suzanne Kim. The three minutes that passed before she got a return call felt like days, but she spent the time organizing her thoughts so she was able to lay out the facts for the lawyer succinctly.

"Are there statutory provisions listed there with the names of the charges?" Suzanne asked. Lauren recited them from the section of the arrest warrant Nate was pointing to. "Okay, I'm going to have to look those up since it's New York law, but it's probably for lying to the police about the fact that she knew David Smith before that incident with the parking spot. I'd be surprised if it's more serious than a misdemeanor, but they're obviously looking at her for more serious offenses, both there and in Boston."

Lauren still could not believe that what she had thought was a practical joke had turned into murder investigations of two men in different states. "They said she's being arraigned tomorrow. Can you get here for that?"

"No, that's not how this works. I'm not licensed in New York and don't know anything about those offenses. I can reach out to some referrals, but it will be hard to find someone on short notice for a new client on what's likely a misdemeanor. Worst-case scenario, she could ask for more time to locate counsel since she obviously won't qualify for a public defender."

Next to her, Nate was holding up his hand like a child asking permission from the teacher. Lauren nodded for him to go ahead.

"Hey, this is Kelsey's brother, Nate," he said. "I looked up the statutes. They're both Class A misdemeanors."

"Okay, could be worse. Let me make some calls and get back to you."

So Kelsey was too rich to get a public lawyer, but apparently not rich enough to make a top-notch lawyer scramble out to Long Island.

"We should probably call her father," Lauren suggested. "Well, your father too. Sorry."

"An understandable mistake," Nate said as he pulled up the number on his phone. She could hear one ring after another, followed by a recorded message and a beep. "Hey. It's Nate. Can you please call me as soon as you get this. It's about Kelsey. She's in trouble."

"Do you have another number for him? His office maybe?"

He shook his head. "He's glued to his cell phone. I guarantee you he saw my name and just didn't pick up. That message will light a fire—"

The phone rang in his hand. "Told you," he said, extending the screen to show a single name—DAD—before answering. "Hi. I'm not sure exactly how to say this, but we're in the Hamptons, and Kelsey's been arrested." She listened as Nate explained the series of events that had led to her charges. "She was out here with her girlfriends . . . Yes, May and Lauren . . . I only came out because May went back to the city early and there was an extra room . . . Okay, none of that is relevant right now, Dad . . . Fine, Bill. I can't believe that's what you're focusing on, but all right . . . Yes, we're trying to find her a lawyer now. Suzanne's calling people in New York . . . I know about Suzanne because I know Kelsey and she tells me things . . . Fine. I'm really just trying to help."

His eyes looked flat as he extended the phone to Lauren. "He apparently prefers to talk to you."

She had no idea the situation between Nate and his former stepfather was that estranged. "Hi, Bill. I'm so sorry to be speaking under such awful circumstances."

She had not seen Kelsey's father since the wedding. Even though Kelsey had mentioned that the prostate surgery and subsequent radiation had taken their toll, she was taken aback by how frail he sounded. "Well, at least you're there with her," he said. "I had no idea Nate was involved in this trip. She told me it was with you and May."

"It was. Nate came out last minute when May left early. I was the one to suggest it, in fact, because I haven't seen him in years." It was a lie, but she found herself wanting to protect Nate from his former stepfather's iciness.

"They really put her under arrest? Like actual handcuffs in a police car arrest?"

"Yes. She's her father's daughter, so she handled it like a boss, but I could tell she was afraid."

"Couldn't you have stopped it? I mean, we could have posted any amount of bail they needed for her to come back tomorrow for court."

Lauren pressed her lips together and counted to five in her head to gather her patience. "That wasn't an option, Bill."

"Don't be naive, Lauren. Everything's an option if you find the right people."

She shifted away from what sounded to her like a suggestion that she should have bribed the police, telling him what she knew about the timing for the arraignment the next morning.

"I'll start making calls," he said. "I'll get her the best lawyer in the city. She's such a good girl, Lauren. She's had terrible misfortune in her life. I know not to speak ill of the dead—but for Luke to leave her after everything she went through with the surgery . . . I saw her inner light dim even from the separation. Then for her to be blamed for the shooting? It was ridiculous. I don't know how any one person can be expected to bear the pain she's gone through."

She knew that in William Ellis's eyes, Kelsey would forever be a child who lost her mother at the age of seven and needed his constant protection. Kelsey had complained that her father could be overly involved in her life, but Lauren hadn't realized until now the extent to which he infantilized his daughter. Kelsey had never been helpless, not even as a child. As he continued to rant about how unfairly she had been treated—by fate, by the media, by internet "looky-loos"—and how he was going to use his money and influence to protect her, she recalled the screenshot May had sent her from the true crime message board.

The police think there is a connection. And guess what the connection is? Kelsey Ellis!!

But Kelsey wasn't the only connection. Luke Freedman broke the heart of William Ellis's beloved daughter. And David Smith was a player who had misled William Ellis's poor, heartbroken, vulnerable daughter into believing they might have a future together.

And William Ellis had money. A lot of money. Enough money to make extraordinary things happen—as long as you, in his words, could "find the right people."

She lied and told Kelsey's father that a call was coming in that might be one of the New York lawyers. When she hung up, she asked Nate why Bill had been so cold toward him.

"Aah, the question I've explored for countless hours with many, many therapists. One theory is that, despite all the words to the contrary, he never really saw me as a son. I was an extension of my mother, not an actual person. And when he left her, he left me."

Lauren pictured younger Nate, who always seemed so sweet and a little awestruck around her. She couldn't imagine how Bill Ellis could treat him so cruelly. It was amazing he had turned out as well as he had under the circumstances. "I'm sorry. That's . . . awful."

"To be honest, I've got another theory. Mr. Ellis's wives may have come and gone, but his one and only is his most beloved, Kelsey."

The idea of it made Lauren feel queasy. She knew it happened, of course. Back in Louisiana in her childhood, they thought it was only in certain types of families, but that kind of abuse wasn't confined by class. "You don't mean like he ever—"

"No," he said, shaking his head quickly. "She would have told me. But he'll never accept her as an adult who can make her own decisions. He wants Kelsey to be his little girl, running off to Daddy for help, for as long as he's on this earth. It's like he gets off on coming to her rescue."

She saw it so clearly now. "So much so that he might hurt other men for hurting her?"

The words felt like a weight that she had removed from herself and dropped onto him. He took a deep breath.

"I actually asked Kelsey if that was possible after Luke was killed. She got so mad, she didn't talk to me for a month. She managed to convince me it was a ludicrous theory cooked up by those true crime vultures online. I can't believe I didn't think of him again after all this stuff with Dave came up."

"And now?" she asked.

Nate stood up silently and put his hands in his pockets, staring out toward the bay.

"I'm sorry. I'm sure this is digging up a lot of feelings about your father, but this is for Kelsey. Is it possible—"

He turned to face her abruptly. "Look, there's something I've never told anyone, not even Kelsey." He sat back down on the sofa, his voice low. "When everything first went down with Luke and people were questioning if Kelsey and her dad were involved, my mother told me she had a feeling he had something to do with it."

"What?"

He nodded, and when he spoke again, he sounded more confident. "This was after she started struggling to find words here and there, but her memory was still spot-on. She said Kelsey's grandfather had been wrapped up with the Boston mafia, just like the rumors said, and that Bill had taken the business legit for the most part, but still had contacts with people she described as dangerous. He had . . . How did she put it? *The moral code of a lizard.* That's why she didn't even try to challenge the prenup. She told me she was afraid he'd find a way to *deal with her,* as she put it. When I clarified to make sure she was talking about murder, she said he'd do it in a heartbeat if he thought someone deserved it."

Lauren could almost hear Jeanie's voice uttering the words. "She didn't think to tell the police any of this?"

"Tell them what? That she thought her ex-husband was a bad guy? She didn't know anything concrete. And at the time, even I sort of chalked it up to her being resentful toward him about the divorce and for being such a dick to me. But now that this other guy is dead too? I should have said something earlier. Maybe the police would have—"

Lauren's cell phone rang. It was a Boston area code. "That's probably Suzanne Kim about the lawyer referrals."

"Lawyers that will be paid a fortune by my father," he said. "They won't pursue what we're talking about now."

They let the call go to voicemail.

Nate rubbed his temples with his fingertips. "Guess what really smart former prosecutor already researched all that complicated stuff about the laws covering lying to police in New York?"

They needed May.

37

"Babe, you really need to stop looking at all that stuff."

May sat cross-legged in her living room, parked in front of her laptop at the coffee table while Josh washed dishes on the other side of the kitchen island.

All that stuff meant the entire internet, which she had been searching compulsively all day for any other mentions of Kelsey and her connections to Dave Smith, Lauren, or May.

In addition to the initial post on KillerInsights from someone claiming to be a Boston cop's family member, she had found a Hamptons-focused TikTok account where the user had named all three of them, suggesting that Andy Cohen should build a Bravo reality television show around them—if Kelsey didn't end up in jail first. That video was reposted almost immediately by an Instagram page called HamptonsTea. It had been shared two hundred and twenty-two times since.

She had stopped looking long enough to eat the sushi takeout Josh had ordered, but then immediately plopped down in front of her laptop once he began clearing dishes. She hit the refresh page on her search again.

"You didn't do anything wrong." Josh sounded more irritated than concerned. "You told that Long Island cop everything you know. You can wash your hands of the whole situation now."

"I mean, I know you're right, but I need to know what people are saying."

"How does it help to know if total strangers are shit-talking you online?" The clink of their plates into the dishwasher seemed louder than necessary. "You can't do anything about it. And you've been working so hard at managing your anxiety. This really doesn't seem good."

"Okay, Dr. Freud."

"Really, you want to go there? Fine, why don't you call Marissa?" Whenever he referred to May's therapist, it sounded like he resented the fact that May was still seeing her after all this time. By now, it was obvious the focus had moved beyond the subway incident and onto other issues. She talked about everything, including Josh. "Does she have emergency hours or something? Because I think this qualifies. You didn't even take a shower today. It's like you regressed to three years ago."

She lifted her tank top away from her chest and took a quick sniff. She was fine. A new call came into her cell—a Long Island area code. "Hello?"

"Hi, this is Arianna Hensley. I own the house you're renting. Are you the woman who called me Wednesday night? I think you said your name was Kelsey?"

So much had happened since that phone call. May had to remind herself that she'd claimed to be Kelsey when she called the homeowner to confirm the timing of the rental. "Yes, is everything all right?"

"You tell me. My neighbor said there are cops all over the house and someone was carried off in handcuffs. I tried your friend Callie—it was disconnected, so I found your number in my call log. What exactly is going on there?"

"I'm not at the house right now, so let me find out—"

"Not necessary. The neighbor sent video. I'm terminating the agreement and will call the police directly to make sure they know I have nothing to do with whatever you guys are doing."

"Let me call my friends and—"

"Yes, do call them. Make sure they know I'm notifying the police right now that under no circumstances can they reoccupy that house."

The other end of the line went dead.

"Can we please talk about this before you call them?" Josh asked when he saw May opening FaceTime on her laptop and carrying it toward her office.

"I need to tell them—"

Lauren answered almost immediately. "Hey," Lauren said. "I was literally about to call."

May could barely make out Lauren's face on the screen. She was sitting outside in the dark.

Lauren's screen shifted for a brief shot of Nate, who looked exhausted. "Hey, I know things got weird the other night, but Kelsey really needs your help."

As far as May was concerned, Kelsey was on her own, but she didn't want Lauren to be stranded without a place in East Hampton. "The owner of the rental just called me," May said, making her way to the office. "Are the police at the house? Did they arrest Kelsey?"

Once Lauren spelled out the charges listed in the arrest and search warrants, May could see the logic of the prosecution. "My guess is they're looking at her for murder but don't have their case together yet," she said. "Going after her for lying to the police gave them leverage for the warrants. Technically, they're searching for evidence she lied about her ties to David, but if they find anything related to his death, they can use it against her. And even a misdemeanor charge could be enough to hold her if they're worried about her fleeing the country before they get the evidence they need."

"They're allowed to do that?" Nate asked. "That doesn't seem fair."

It's exactly what May would have done as a prosecutor. "I was calling because the homeowner terminated the rental agreement. She's notifying the police that you can't stay there anymore, effective immediately."

"We were already eighty-sixed for the night because of the search warrant," Lauren said. "We'll figure something out, but we were about to call to ask you—beg you if necessary—to represent Kelsey tomorrow at her court hearing."

The office door slid open. Josh looked incredulous. She didn't need to be a good lip-reader to make out his mouthed words: *What the fuck?*

She shook her head and made a slashing gesture across her throat.

As the door slid closed again, she told them that she couldn't possibly do that. She had hung up her practitioner hat when she joined the academy.

"But you still have a bar license," Lauren said. "You even told me that Fordham gave you permission to work on pro bono cases if you wanted."

"Kelsey's not exactly pro bono."

"My point is you could represent her if you wanted."

She couldn't bring herself to lie to Lauren—not after being caught in the big lie she'd been holding on to for fifteen years. "Yes, I could. But I won't."

Nate leaned into the screen. She felt like she was looking directly into his eyes, even though she knew it wouldn't look that way to him on camera. "Please, May. You're the perfect person for this. You made it clear you know these laws cold the other night, and, most importantly, you wouldn't be beholden to Kelsey's dad."

"Why would that matter?"

"Hey, let me call you right back on a regular line," Lauren said, ending the FaceTime stream abruptly.

As May walked through the living room to get her phone, Josh blocked her path. "Do not answer that call, May. They're trying to pull you into something really stupid, just like they did before. Do I have to remind you that you lied to a police officer because of them?"

"They were saying something about Kelsey's father," she said. "Let me just hear them out." Her cell phone was already ringing on the kitchen counter.

"I'm telling you—"

She picked up anyway. "Hey." As she made her way back to the office, Josh began walking toward the bedroom.

"Sorry about that," Lauren said. She could tell that Lauren's phone was no longer on speaker. "The police told us the landlord called them. Nate's going to go pack up our stuff, but here's the deal. If there really is a connection between Luke's murder and David's, it could be Kelsey's father—not Kelsey. Think about it. He's super protective of her and is used to getting his way. You should have heard the way he talked to Nate tonight when he was only trying to help. Nate thinks Bill has this weird hang-up where he wants Kelsey to depend solely on him. There's always been rumors that he was mobbed up."

"Kelsey's pretty damn used to getting her own way, too," May said. She explained what she had figured out about Kelsey's motive to retain control over the embryos, plus the possibility that David and Luke were both killed after someone initiated a fake traffic stop.

"There's no way Kelsey could be involved," Lauren said. "The police think David was killed Saturday night. We were all together that whole time."

"And Kelsey and her father were both at that Golden Plate Award banquet when Luke was killed. Whoever pulled the trigger was hired."

"But by her father, not Kelsey," Lauren said. "Nate told me that when Luke was first killed, his mother even said she thought Bill did it. She said he's mobbed up and knows the kind of people who can have someone killed."

"Which means Kelsey probably knows them too. She's the heir apparent."

"No way. You saw the way she responded when you told her David had died. She completely broke down."

"Because she realized the police had connected the two of them. She knew she was busted." May couldn't believe how callous she sounded. They were talking about Kelsey.

"No, you're wrong about that, May. I'd bet my actual life on it. You weren't close to Kelsey when Luke died. I was. She was a complete mess. She had truly been hoping that Luke would change his mind about the divorce. And she definitely assumed at the time she wouldn't be able to use the embryos after he died, so that added to her depression. She only found out later from the clinic she'd be able to use them as she wanted."

"How do you know that?" May asked.

"Because when the divorce was happening, she knew she'd need his permission to implant the embryos in the future. After he died, she wouldn't be able to get his permission, so to her it was the door slamming shut. I told her she shouldn't just assume that, so she called the clinic, and they told her the law gave her control over the disposition. It at least gave her some consolation, but she was still devastated."

If it were true Kelsey didn't realize how Luke's death would affect the situation with the fertility clinic, it was a devastating blow to the case May had built in her mind against Kelsey—the case she had shared with Detective Carter Decker. She felt her face begin to grow hot.

"She really did seem upset about David's death," May said, replaying the image of Kelsey opening her mouth wide and letting loose that full-throated, primal scream. Like May on the subway platform. Like May, alone in her apartment this morning, sending poor Gomez scattering for cover. When May had those outbursts, she knew they were uncontrollable. She couldn't stop them.

She also wouldn't be able to fake them.

"I'm telling you, May. She was even worse about Luke. I'm convinced she was in love with both of them. She had nothing to do with this. But Bill? He could have done it. And there's no way he would tell Kelsey about it. That would be the way he protected her—to keep her completely in the dark. And here's the thing: The night Luke was killed, Bill was the one who insisted that Kelsey go with him to that award ceremony. She canceled a date to appease him. She even tried to turn it into a joke. *I never got a third date, but I did get filet mignon and an alibi.*"

These were things that May would have known if she had never lost touch with Kelsey. If she had called her all those times she was in Boston for depositions when she was still at the law firm. If she had gone to the wedding. If she had gotten to see her in love with Luke, the man who knew the special spot to tickle as they stood for wedding portraits. If she had helped her after her husband was murdered.

She would have known Kelsey better. She wouldn't have fallen prey to the uninformed speculation of strangers who posted at whim on anonymous message boards. She wouldn't have teed her friend up to Carter Decker, a cop hungry for a suspect.

She had messed everything up. "Send me pictures of everything you got from the police."

"So you'll represent her tomorrow?" Lauren asked. "If not, I need to find someone else."

Maybe it wouldn't even come to that. "Let me make a call and get back to you."

As May pulled up Decker's number, Josh opened the office door again. "That didn't sound like a 'no' to me. You really need to explain right now." She noticed him clenching and unclenching his fists.

"Just give me a second. I messed up. This is an emergency."

As he walked away, she reached over to slide the doors shut behind him. Two rings followed by an answer. "Decker."

She was in lawyer mode, so she didn't give him everything—just enough to negate the motive she had previously offered. "I know everything I said earlier, but I have new information. Kelsey didn't even know she'd be able to use the embryos until after Luke died, so I was wrong. She didn't have any motive to kill him."

"People kill soon-to-be-exes without having baby problems all the time," he said dryly.

"She didn't do it—"

"Well, that's not what you thought forty-eight hours ago. More importantly: I don't care what you think, and she's not charged with murder. Not yet. She lied to me, point-blank. And she's not the only one—but, unlike her, someone else corrected the record before I took the case to the DA. You wouldn't have stormed in to tell Kelsey to lawyer up if you didn't know more than you let on."

His point was not lost on her. He could have charged May, too. The call Josh encouraged her to make had saved her. "Does your DA know?" Even if he didn't charge her, he could report her to the bar association.

There was a long pause at the other end of the line. His voice was gentle when he finally spoke. "No. And I didn't call your investigator friend in the city either."

She was worried he could literally hear her breathing. She was the one to break the silence. "Why didn't you?"

"I don't know."

"Well, thank you for that."

"Don't make me regret it."

Her mind raced. She wanted to say so much, but it was clear she wasn't going to be able to stop Kelsey from being charged. She wasn't sure how much information to share with him at this early stage of the case. "Kelsey needs a lawyer for her arraignment attorney—one that isn't paid for by her father."

"Is that lawyer going to be you?"

"Probably. Will that change your mind about the other thing?"

He answered immediately. "No."

"Can I ask why not?"

"Well, you just did, but does it really matter? Because I think you might be a good person who tries to do the right thing."

She realized they were both whispering now. "I am."

"And is that why you let it slip just now that Kelsey doesn't want a lawyer who's paid by her father?"

She said nothing.

"Did you find out something else new since you called me the other night?" he asked.

"You're a good cop, Decker."

"I certainly think so. See you tomorrow at the courthouse?"

"You're going to the arraignment?" A detective's police report was more than sufficient for an initial probable cause hearing.

"The DA wants me there."

It was further confirmation that this wasn't any old misdemeanor case. Tomorrow's hearing was one small step in a homicide investigation.

"Thanks for letting Lauren and Nate get their belongings out. They're free to leave now, right?"

"Yep, standard protocol for non-suspects. And trust me, from what I heard about her phone call to the station, that landlady does not want any of you stepping foot near this house again."

She felt herself smile involuntarily.

When she stepped out of her office, Josh was staring at her from the sofa, a glass of what appeared to be whiskey in his hand. "Is this the way you plan on treating me now? I thought we got past your little secrets with your friends when you came back from the Hamptons. Now you're holed up in your office whispering? That's not okay."

"Josh, there's a whole situation out there that I'm trying to handle. They arrested Kelsey for providing false information. Lauren and Nate think her father might be behind all of this, so she needs a lawyer who's truly independent from him."

"Meaning you? No, May. That is a terrible idea."

"It's just a first appearance. It's no big deal. She enters a not guilty plea and I get her released from custody. We can deal with the rest of it afterward."

"And I don't get a say-so in this?" He took a sip of his drink, holding her gaze.

"In what I do for a friend in my capacity as a lawyer? No, you actually don't. This doesn't affect you."

"No, but your whole relationship with your crew or whatever does affect *you,*" he said, his voice rising. "It's too much. And you and I are supposed to be getting married, so of course it affects me."

"*Supposed* to be?"

"You know what I mean."

"I'm sorry, Josh." Was she really sorry, though? "I don't have time for this. I just need to get through the hearing tomorrow, okay? You and I will be fine."

"And a couple of days ago, you just needed to call that police officer, and now here we are again. You're never going to extract yourself from this, are you?"

"Just when I thought I was out," she said, slipping into her best Michael Corleone imitation.

"It's not funny, May."

"Little bit, little bit." Now she was De Niro. "I swear it's just an arraignment. A well-trained monkey could probably handle it. Then Kelsey can find another lawyer for the hard stuff. I promise."

"Fine," he said grudgingly. "Okay. Tomorrow."

"I love you." She leaned in for a quick kiss and he kissed her back.

"Love you too, even if you are being infuriating right now."

He walked away toward the bedroom as she redialed Lauren. "So I tried to see if Decker could do anything to drop the charges, but no luck. I'll handle the first appearance tomorrow and then help her find a lawyer for the long run."

"Or that can be you," Lauren said. "You're Sasha Fierce in a courtroom."

"I'm a dusty old law prof now. If this turns into a murder trial, she's going to need a whole team. Just take the bird in hand, okay? You guys must be exhausted. Carter said you're free to go now, so call an Uber and come to the city."

"Carter? Is that the detective? He's Carter now?"

May hadn't even realized she'd used his first name. "Nate has his place, and you can stay with us."

"Oof. Forty-six years old on a pool raft, and then we'll have to turn around and come back tomorrow. No bueno."

"It's one of the good ones with the platform on the bottom. And trust me, you're going to have to drive mid-island to a fleabag motel and you'll spend an hour making calls to lock even that down. Just head here and we can use the car time tomorrow to strategize."

Having convinced Lauren of her plan, she hopped onto Westlaw and searched for reported cases interpreting the two statutes under which Kelsey was charged. The search warrant covered Kelsey's phone, and her calls with Smith would prove that she had lied to Carter—*Decker,* she thought, correcting her internal monologue. But it wasn't obvious that the lie fell within the scope of the statutes charged.

Gomez rose from his spot on her feet and walked to the office door, nudging at it with his flat face. "Josh, I think Gomez needs to go out," she called, sliding open the door. "Josh?"

When she didn't see him in the living room either, she checked the bedroom, bathroom, and terrace.

That's when she saw the note on the kitchen island. "I didn't realize we'd have a houseguest too. I'm going to my brother's to get out of your way. Good luck with your hearing tomorrow." His car key was next to the note.

Four rings to his phone. No answer.

"Josh, I'm sorry. I should have asked you about Lauren. It's just one night. I want to make sure I know everything that happened at the house before court. Just come home, okay?"

Two minutes later, he sent her a text. *Busy day at work tomorrow, and you guys will be up late talking. It's fine. Good night. I love you.*

OK, thanks. Love you too.

It all made perfect, logical sense. He gets his sleep. She and Lauren get the apartment to themselves. But she knew there was so much more he wasn't saying. She was losing him.

38

May hadn't worn heels—like, actual, real, non-wedge, non-platform, expected-to-stand-on-the-balls-of-your-toes high heels since March 13, 2020. Her toes were scrunched at the front of her shoes as she clomped, Lauren at her side, toward the criminal arraignments courtroom of the East Hampton Town justice center. She was counting down the steps before she'd get to sit down when she spotted a man, familiar but so much older than she remembered, as they turned the hallway corner.

"Finally." William Ellis had lost his physically imposing frame, but still carried himself like a man in power, wearing a perfectly tailored suit and Ferragamo tie, hands on hips, waiting for someone to yell at. "What is happening? Nate hasn't been returning my calls. I chased down your number from a friend," he said, looking directly at Lauren, "and have left a million messages. And I left messages for *you* at the law school. Suzanne Kim told me that she couldn't reach you either. I got up at four in the morning to make it down here. Does my daughter have a fucking lawyer or not?"

May took a deep breath. She knew Kelsey's father wouldn't be happy about her handling this court hearing, which is why they'd decided not to tell him, but she didn't predict that he'd drive down in person. Now that he was here, his presence seemed inevitable. His perfect baby girl's freedom was at stake, and—if their theory was right—perhaps his, too. What else could be more important?

"Mr. Ellis—Bill—I understand your concern." May placed a reassuring hand on one of his adamant elbows, and he at least dropped his hands to his sides. It was possibly the second time in her life that she had touched a murderer, the first being a defendant who made it a condition of his guilty plea that she look him in the eye and shake his hand. "I couldn't call you because I was preparing for the hearing and also driving here, but I assure you, I've got this. Nate is here, too. He's parking the car. But you causing a scene would be the worst possible situation for your daughter, and the judge will be calling the case at any minute. I need you to calm down before we go into the courtroom, okay?"

Ellis's eyes narrowed, but he followed her lead, taking a seat next to them in the third row, his displeasure still etched across his face. A young female lawyer probably a year out of law school was at the prosecution table, a stack of files in front of her. May recognized the more senior attorney next to her as Mike Nunzio, the Suffolk County DA's Office go-to ADA for major trials.

A couple of years before she left the DA's Office, May had coordinated trial strategy with Nunzio for a defendant who'd kidnapped his ex-wife in Manhattan and then taken her to his house in Babylon. Nunzio's attendance at a misdemeanor arraignment in a town court only confirmed that this hearing was the beginning of what they expected to lead to a murder charge.

While William Ellis had been bombing May's phone all morning, the man whose voice she wanted to hear still had her on mute. She'd called Josh twice, but he had responded with terse texts, saying he was tied up in meetings and wishing her luck with the hearing. She could accept that he was mad at her in the moment, but this felt bigger. Not anger, but disappointment. Worse yet—disillusionment.

His feelings mattered to her. Of course they did. She cared. She loved him. But she was also angry. What was a marriage if she wasn't allowed to make choices he might not agree with?

She turned her head at the sound of Nate's approaching footsteps echoing in the nearly empty room. She and Lauren scooted down to make room for him, but Kelsey's father remained planted in place. May noticed William Ellis's lips purse when Nate took a seat in the row behind them.

After arraigning two other defendants on charges of domestic assault and reckless driving, the court clerk called the next case, his voice reverberating in the cavernous space. "People versus Kelsey Ellis."

Only as May stepped toward the defense counsel table did she realize that the lone person sitting in the front row was Detective Carter Decker. They exchanged a glance before she took her seat. There was a time when May could have handled something as simple as an arraignment and detention hearing after downing two martinis. But it had been well over three years since she'd physically appeared in a courtroom, and almost a year and a half since her last virtual hearing. She kept mentally replaying the words she'd been rehearsing since last night. She couldn't mess this up.

She felt the weight of the situation all over again as she saw Kelsey being walked in by the correctional officers. Kelsey—hilarious, irreverent, shining, beautiful Kelsey—was haggard and disheveled in yesterday's clothes, a stark reminder of the night spent in custody. Her eyes searched the courtroom and a glint of her usual spark appeared as they landed on Lauren, her brother, and her father. When she saw May at counsel's table, her lips parted with a gasp of gratitude. May fought back the urge to break into tears.

As soon as Kelsey's handcuffs were removed, she turned to give May a hug, but May shook her head subtly. This wasn't the time.

"Your Honor, May Hanover, appearing for Kelsey Ellis."

"I'm not familiar with you, Ms. Hanover." May had looked up the two East Hampton town justices and recognized this one as Dennis Knoll, described in his online bio as "a lifetime East Ender." He'd had a brief stint as a prosecutor for Suffolk County, followed by fifteen years as a solo practitioner before being elected to the bench.

"It's my first appearance in this courtroom, Your Honor."

"From the city?" he asked.

"Yes, sir, but that's not my client's fault."

She was relieved when he snickered. "Touché. Now, Mr. Nunzio, I've seen you lurking over there and now you have a file open in front of you. Have I finally solved the mystery of what brings you to my courtroom today?"

"Yes, Your Honor."

"Well, let's do the easy part first. Will the defendant please rise?"

The judge read the two charges aloud and asked if Kelsey was prepared to enter a plea. Without coaching, she said clearly and confidently, "Not guilty."

"Typically on a misdemeanor, no convictions that I see here, I'd order the defendant released on her own recognizance, but let me take another guess, that's why you're here, Mr. Nunzio?"

"That's correct, Your Honor. The allegations here arise from the defendant's false statements to East Hampton detective Carter Decker during an ongoing homicide investigation." Nunzio didn't name the murder victim, but murders in East Hampton were almost nonexistent. It was obvious which case they were dealing with. "And the defendant was well aware of the severity of the investigation, because her lawyer—Ms. Hanover, in fact—interrupted Detective Decker's conversation with the defendant to notify her that it was likely a homicide investigation. Our investigation has revealed connections between the defendant and the victim that the defendant went to great lengths to conceal, hence her deception in her conversations with Detective Decker."

Judge Knoll leaned back in his chair, peering down at Kelsey, as if he was trying to imagine her being responsible for a man getting killed.

May half stood from her chair. "If I may, Your Honor?"

"Yes, May, you may. I'm sorry, I couldn't resist. Please proceed, Counselor."

"Just to correct the record, whatever encounter Detective Decker was having with my client terminated at the same moment I intervened for the purpose of facilitating her right to counsel. Therefore, anything I said could not possibly be relevant to Ms. Ellis's state of mind during any interactions she had with law enforcement."

"Point taken," he said. "So what exactly are you requesting, Mr. Nunzio?"

The prosecutor wasted no time laying out the facts in the state's favor. Kelsey's lack of ties to the region. Her access to a prominent father's resources. Her potential involvement in a very serious offense triggering a possible life sentence.

The judge finally cut him off. "I don't like where this is going. Let me hear from our newcomer, okay? Ms. Hanover?"

May rose to her feet, ignoring the pain of the blister forming at her right heel. "Mr. Nunzio sounds like he's at a murder arraignment asking for preventative detention. This is a misdemeanor case in a state that reserves even a cash bail requirement for the most serious of charges, and these aren't that. If the prosecution believes it has probable cause to hold my client over on the kinds of allegations he's bandying about without evidence—and he surely does not have it, because it does not exist—then let him file a superseding charging instrument and put that to the test. Short of that, it sounds like he is using these threadbare charges and your courtroom as a pretext to obtain presumptive detention without demonstrating probable cause, which is patently unconstitutional."

Knoll was nodding along as she spoke. "Wow, okay. Not the usual discourse of a misdemeanor arraignment. I'm having flashbacks to my 1L year. You'd be a good professor."

"I actually am. Well, a professor, Your Honor. I'd leave it to my students to say if I'm any good."

Another chuckle. "You'd make my job here a lot easier, Ms. Hanover, if you could stipulate to some assurance that your client's not going to leave the state while this investigation is pending."

"That's not a requirement of pre-trial release on a misdemeanor, Your Honor. She lives in Massachusetts but will most certainly return for all court appearances."

"Take off your law professor hat, Ms. Hanover, and listen carefully again to what I said. You'd make my job here easier if your client weren't running straight back to Massachusetts."

"Yes, Your Honor, I understand." May had almost forgotten that formal law was not how law actually worked in the real world. This judge would have to stretch the law to creative places to detain Kelsey, but May had researched it long enough to know it was technically possible. Whether this town justice was quick enough to figure it out remained to be seen. But what mattered is that he did not want to be the judge who ROR'd a murderer only to see her jet off to a private island. "She has a brother who lives in New York City," May said. "She could remain there for now with the possibility of revisiting this issue more completely at her next appearance."

Kelsey tugged at the edge of her blazer. May leaned down to hear her.

"Not at Nate's," Kelsey said. "Plus, his place is in Jersey City. I can get a hotel."

"I stand corrected, Your Honor," May said. "He's located in Jersey City." She knew that the solution the judge was looking for had to be more reassuring than a well-resourced defendant on her own in a hotel room.

May was about to present her own suggestion when a voice suddenly boomed behind her. "Judge, I'm Kelsey's father. I'm more than happy to put up whatever bail would put your concerns at ease."

As the judge squinted toward the source of the courtroom outburst, Nunzio rose to his feet again. "Your Honor, I think this encapsulates the validity of the state's concerns."

"Indeed," Knoll agreed. "That was quite the grand gesture, sir, but I suggest you take a seat, and I suspect your daughter's lawyer would request the same. The issue at hand is whether I trust this woman to come back to this courthouse for her trial. Bail is not a panacea. It is about securing the defendant's presence, not about buying one's freedom to do as they wish—perhaps even fleeing the country to avoid future law enforcement encounters."

May took a deep breath, ready to go all in. "Your Honor, as a member of the bar, I assure this court that I will personally ensure Ms. Ellis's presence at trial. I understand the gravity of this situation and have full faith in my client's commitment to the legal process."

"And how precisely would you assure her presence?" he asked.

"She will stay with me, in New York City."

The judge squinted at May with curiosity. If nothing else, she had surprised him.

"Mr. Nunzio?"

"I have to be honest, Your Honor. I have no idea what Ms. Hanover is even suggesting."

"Seems fairly clear to me," Knoll said. "Do you know her, by the way? Do you know Ms. Hanover as a lawyer?"

"Yes, Your Honor. We worked together on a matter when she was an assistant district attorney for the Manhattan District Attorney's Office."

"And did she handle that matter responsibly?"

"Yes, but that was more than three years ago, and I've heard things since then that—"

Knoll held up a hand. "I don't like the direction you were about to take, Counselor. I'm not interested in what *things* you may have *heard.*" His gaze shifted toward Detective Decker, his piercing eyes searching for insight. "Detective Decker, you were the one whose interview was interrupted by Ms. Hanover. Given that interaction, do you have any reason why I should question her good faith? Was there any indication she was attempting to hinder your investigation?"

If Carter noticed Nunzio's glare, he ignored it as he rose to his feet. "I have no reason to question Ms. Hanover's representations. While my initial encounter with her client was interrupted, I do not believe it compromises her dedication to upholding her responsibilities as an officer of the court."

It was a perfect answer.

"So ordered," the judge announced with a tap of his gavel. "My clerk will figure out a way to write it up. Ms. Ellis, I strongly advise you not to burn your attorney for sticking her neck out for you."

"Absolutely not, Your Honor." Kelsey couldn't help herself and flung her arms around May's shoulders with the best kind of Kelsey hug.

May glanced back at Kelsey's father, whose stony expression radiated dissatisfaction. She felt a sense of vindication that both the prosecutor and judge had scolded him for trying to take over the court proceedings. The schadenfreude was satisfying, but more importantly, she hoped his outburst proved to Carter Decker that William Ellis was the kind of man who was used to getting his way and would go to extraordinary lengths to protect his daughter.

As Ellis walked toward the courtroom exit, he did not say a word to either Lauren or Nate. Decker gave a slight nod in May's direction before following him out the door.

39

As they emerged from the Midtown Tunnel, billboards and skyscrapers towered over the snarl of cars escaping the bottleneck to claim their chosen traffic lanes. May gripped the SUV's steering wheel tightly, her gaze flickering between the lane she needed to force her way into and the screen of her phone, searching for a signal.

She had sent a text to Josh nearly two hours ago, asking him to call her as soon as possible. The tension in her chest expanded as she realized her fiancé might walk into the apartment to find a group of people he most certainly did not want to see in his home.

From the backseat, Kelsey leaned forward to rest her chin on May's headrest. "Are you absolutely sure Josh is going to be okay with me staying at your place? I mean, a jailbird on your sofa is a special kind of cockblock."

It was just like Kelsey to try to find the humor in her current situation. "Stop it," May said. "One, you're not on the sofa. I'll put the Aerobed out, because we're classy like that. And two, Josh is totally fine. You'll finally get to know each other. It'll be great."

May hoped her lie would help ease Kelsey's worries, but pretending that she had already spoken to Josh only deepened her own fears about his response.

"All I know is I am counting down the seconds to getting in the shower," Kelsey said. "I stink like the sewer."

Nate leaned toward his sister and pretended to sniff her. "Funk factor five."

"Stop it," Lauren said from the front passenger seat. "You don't stink."

"Well, try a jailhouse slumber party. It's like my nostrils are filled with this stench and I'm sure it'll never wash off. I never want to go back there again."

The car fell into silence at the reminder of what was at stake. They had spent most of the ride from Long Island trying to convince Kelsey of the possibility that her father might have had Luke and David killed, but she wasn't yet willing to look at the facts objectively. The furthest they had gotten with her was the chance that she might have to float the theory in her defense if she was eventually accused of murder. May could tell that Kelsey was mentally and physically exhausted, so that was as much progress as they were going to make for now.

Gomez was already wiggling with excitement when she unlocked the apartment door. At the sight of new visitors, he jumped up to give each one what she referred to as a "knee hug," wrapping his front paws around any willing participant's leg.

Kelsey plopped down on the floor cross-legged to give him a landing spot. "Hi, buddy. Do you recognize me from all our FaceTimes? Don't get used to how I smell right now though. I'm usually clean. On that note, point me to the shower? I wasn't kidding about wanting one ASAP."

"Down that hall," May said. "I'll warn you in advance our bathroom's super tiny. You can barely raise your arms to wash your hair. The only reason we don't move is it's the only thing we can afford with a terrace. Our landlord did finally break down and replace our leaky showerhead. We have one of those rainfall ones now."

"Ooh-la-la," Kelsey said. "You weren't kidding about *fawn-say*. Off I go."

"Oh, shoot." May realized that she hadn't fully thought through the logistics of Kelsey's housing arrangement. "Nate took your luggage to his place yesterday, assuming you'd stay with him. I've got clothes for you though."

In the bedroom, May swapped her suit out for jeans and a black tank top. Kelsey yelled "Thank you" from the shower when she left a pair of shorts and a T-shirt on the toilet. "Water has never felt so good. I may never leave."

When May returned to the living room, Lauren waved her over to the sofa. "So we were just talking about the level of denial going on with Miss Kelsey. She needs to snap out of it."

May took a seat next to Lauren. "I mean, it's not that surprising, is it? We're floating the idea of her father as a murderer after five years of people suspecting both of them. Of course she thinks he's innocent."

"Okay, but she did admit in the car that he knows the kind of people who would know where to find a hit man. Her assurances that those ties were all made by her grandfather doesn't change the fact that her dad would know how to put out a hit. I mean, that's not most people."

Nate rubbed the beard stubble that had accumulated since he first arrived in East Hampton. "I was sure she'd freak out when I told her Mom always suspected him, but . . . nothing."

May was having a hard time adjusting to the sight of her ex-boyfriend in her apartment. Not her apartment, but hers and Josh's. Even though Nate was here because of Kelsey, his presence in what was Josh's home—when she hadn't even had a chance to tell him—felt like a betrayal. "I think she's worn out from a night in jail, and it's a lot to take in. We can try getting her to focus when she comes out."

The room fell silent at the sound of the bathroom door opening. Wet-haired Kelsey managed to make May's workout shorts and David Bowie T-shirt look like an outfit.

"Very quiet in here. You guys were talking about the jailbird, weren't you?"

Nate spoke up first. "We're a little worried that you're not taking our thoughts about Dad seriously."

"Because you can't actually be serious. He didn't even know about Dave, so why would he kill him? And even if he wanted to, how would he have known where to find him?"

"I'm no expert," Lauren said, looking to May to back her up. "But I'm pretty sure hit men can follow people."

Kelsey sat cross-legged on the floor next to Gomez, tapping her fingers on the rug to coax him toward her. "Well, it doesn't change the fact that I never told Dad about Dave."

"So where'd you tell him you were all those weekends you went to Providence?" Kelsey's father made a habit of knowing where Kelsey was at all times.

"Girls' trips, spa days, stuff he wouldn't worry about."

Nate rubbed a palm across his eyes. "Kelsey, get real. Worrying about you is Dad's twenty-four/seven job. He must have known something was up if you weren't giving him specifics. Even with the Hamptons, he knew you were with May and Lauren and was mad he didn't know I was going."

"You've told us before that he has a private investigator to dig up dirt on his business rivals," May said, trying her best to sound as if she hadn't yet made up her mind about Bill's guilt. "Isn't it possible he wanted to know for certain who you were spending your time with?"

"May, I normally love your wild imagination, but this is getting silly. My dad didn't investigate me." Kelsey's tone was growing increasingly impatient.

"I know for a fact he spied on my mom," Nate said.

"That email thing?" Kelsey was practically shouting now. "That's not the same. You mean to tell me you wouldn't read your ex's emails if you could? Apparently during the divorce Jeanie kept finding emails that had already been read even though she hadn't opened them. She was convinced it was my dad logging into her account."

"It definitely was," Nate said. "He knew her passwords. Once she changed them, it stopped."

Kelsey shot her stepbrother a scathing look. "That's not murder."

"No," May said, attempting to defuse the tension with the law professor voice she was still learning to master, "but it is controlling and prying, which he has always been with you. Which means he definitely could have found out about Dave. If he was having him followed, and then saw he was going to East Hampton at the same time you were, or thought he was cheating on you, or knew that he had hurt you? You have to admit your dad's super protective."

"Not like murdery-protective, though."

"Two guys both connected to you," Lauren said. "Both shot in their cars. You've got to at least acknowledge the possibility."

Kelsey opened her mouth to speak, but when she did, her face crumpled. She saw it now. It was too big of a coincidence to deny. There had to be a connection, and she knew it wasn't her.

Her eyes scanned the room before she realized she was looking for something that wasn't there. "Jesus, I don't even have a phone. Can one of you pull up the number for the James Cummins Agency in Boston?"

The website May landed on made clear that Cummins was a private investigator.

Kelsey reached out her hand for May's phone. "Just give me a second," she said, heading toward the bathroom.

When she returned, her gaze appeared unfocused. Her voice was distant as she returned May's phone. "You got a call while I was talking. From your mom."

"Okay, but did you talk to the PI?" May asked.

"Yeah. It took some pushing, but you guys were right. My dad got worried that I was leaving town so much. Jimmy followed me all the way to Rhode Island."

"Oh my god," Lauren said. "Did he follow Dave to East Hampton?"

"No, he said this was two months ago. But there are PIs in Providence. And Jimmy's legit. He's not some mobbed-up hit man. But this changes everything. It proves my father knew about Dave."

40

Carter was watching the video of May Hanover on the subway platform for the umpteenth time. He could not believe the person unleashing that ear-splitting scream in her N95—Asian DA Karen—was the same woman he'd been dealing with the past few days. The woman he'd been talking to was confident, one step ahead of everyone around her. What he called a TCB-er, taking care of business. He thought of the quintessential Karen as a person looking to assert their power over other people. That's not what he saw in this video. He saw a person who wanted control over her own fears.

The sounds of the subway were interrupted by his ringtone. He had the name in his phone now. Incoming call from May Hanover. He snatched his phone off his desk.

"Decker." His earbuds switched over to his cell.

She didn't bother identifying herself. "I'm about to go through the Holland Tunnel so the call might cut off."

"That's a lot of miles today," he said. "You and your friends aren't on another road trip, are you? Bad things seem to happen around you guys."

"No trips. I'm dropping off Kelsey's brother and picking up her luggage. I saw you follow William Ellis out of the courtroom today. Did you talk to him?"

"Nope. More like he talked to me. Told me I was abusing my power, had it all wrong, along those lines. He even told me he'd have my badge when this was over. Do people really think that if you get a cop fired, you get to keep their badge?" He heard the blast of a car horn in the background.

"Look, I'm going out on a limb here. I don't want to wait and see if you charge her and then save all my evidence for trial, which is what I would do if I didn't trust you. But I told Kelsey I think you'll actually listen and try to do what's right."

"And I will."

He had asked a city ADA he knew about her. He said she'd been one of the best lawyers in the office—book smart but also an animal in court. Everyone thought she'd be a lifer until she suddenly announced she had accepted a job as a professor. Based on the engagement ring that had recently appeared on her finger, there was speculation she might be looking for a more mommy-friendly job.

She laid out the facts clearly and succinctly. By the time she was finished telling him about William Ellis's private detective and mafia connections, he knew he needed to call the Boston detective in charge of the Luke Freedman case to find out more about Kelsey's father.

"Do you believe me yet? Kelsey didn't do this."

"You know I'm not going to answer that, but thanks for the info. Drive safe."

41

Nate's apartment was on the third floor of a walk-up. It was small, but it was also clean and modern and thoughtfully decorated. When she'd been single, she noticed that most men had apartments that felt sterile, filled with cookie-cutter furniture they had circled in a chain store catalogue. Nate had managed to amass a nice collection of funky vintage pieces, filling the walls with framed prints that reflected his interests. A display of playbills from off-Broadway shows he'd appeared in. A sunglass-wearing, martini-wielding Vince Vaughan from the film *Swingers*. Milton Glaser's iconic Dylan poster. On a knee-high mid-century media cabinet, a crowded mix of framed photographs on either side of the flat-screen television made it clear that the apartment belonged to someone who wanted to live among his favorite memories.

"Wow," May said, taking it all in. "This place is . . . spectacular. I was proud of myself for finally committing to a couple of throw pillows to zhuzh up our place. I'm not the world's best decorator."

"I figure just because it has to be cheap, it doesn't have to be boring. An actor friend told me it's all about finding things that mean something to you."

"That's really nice. Do you remember when we rented *Swingers* when I stayed at your house before camp one summer? That was like after tenth grade?"

"Ninth for me, but yeah. And my mom was so annoyed. I kept running around saying everything was *so money*. The more she said, *stop saying 'money,'* the more I thought it was the coolest thing in the world."

"Hey, do you mind if I use your powder room? The car ride, you know."

"I am a man and do not have a powder room, but yes." He gestured toward a door past a small hallway lined by two closets.

As she stepped into Nate's bathroom, a familiar smell tugged at her memory and she felt like she was in college again. That smell. She used to live in it. When she was done, she picked up his shampoo bottle from the edge of the weathered tub, screwed off the top, and breathed it in. That had always been Nate.

She set it exactly back in its place, recalling the time she had bought some for Josh. *Not for me. That's a whole lot of scent.* He still hadn't called her, and she was terrified he would come home to find Kelsey and Lauren in their apartment. She had no choice but to break the news by text.

I was hoping you'd have a chance to call so we could talk, but the court hearing started to go south this morning. Kelsey may need to stay with us tonight. She's there now with Lauren while I'm picking up some things for her. Not completely honest. Kelsey would definitely be staying with them, and it wouldn't only be for the night. And no mention that she was picking up Kelsey's things from Nate's apartment. But it was enough to prevent him from being completely blindsided. She reread it twice before hitting send.

She found Nate standing in front of his kitchen sink, slamming back a glass tumbler filled with ice water. Her throat immediately felt parched. She accepted gratefully as he extended an identical glass in her direction. Between the round-trip drive and court, she realized the only hydration she'd had all day was her morning cup of coffee and the few nervous sips of water she'd taken during the arraignment.

"With everything that's been going on, I haven't had a chance to tell you how sorry I was to hear about your mother's condition."

He put his free hand in his pocket and looked away from her gaze. "Yeah, it's . . . not good. I've thought about moving back to Boston to see her more, but she usually doesn't know who I am." He suddenly rested his glass on the counter. "Hey, I just remembered. I need to run down to the laundry room to get Kelsey's clothes."

She remembered now how quickly he could pivot from a dark subject. "You did her laundry?" she asked.

"Yeah, this morning. Threw it into the dryer before you picked me up. Hope it's not too wrinkled. Figured after a night in the slammer, a suitcase of clean clothes might be appreciated."

May smiled. "Clean laundry's a treat even without the jail part. My mom made me start doing my own laundry when I hit middle school, and it's always been my least favorite chore. That, and unloading the dishwasher."

Nate's eyes met hers over the top of his glass. "I remember that," he said, a hint of nostalgia in his voice. "Okay, be right back."

As May continued to sip her water, appreciating how very, very cold it was, her eyes roamed over the collection of photographs by the TV. A few showed him onstage, either performing or posing with a full cast. Some were with friends she didn't recognize—at a baseball game, a bar, a Halloween party in a cop costume she recognized from one of Kelsey's old Facebook posts. Several were with Kelsey and their parents—back when they had been an intact family of four.

She found herself pausing longest on the photographs from the era when she had been with Nate. It was her first serious relationship, and she had allowed it to become such a source of stress. Looking at these pictures, she realized they were just kids. If they had stayed together, would she have stopped overthinking it? Would he have grown up enough for her to trust him to be reliable? Would that stupid night when she tried to videotape them have become a ridiculous memory they would have laughed about for decades?

As May stared at a photograph of the Ellises—Kelsey beaming in her high school graduation regalia, the brick and ivy of Choate behind them—she studied William Ellis's face. All those hours she had spent fixated on Luke's murder, and it never dawned on her that he could be guilty while Kelsey was innocent.

She was about to return her glass to the kitchen when she looked at the photograph again. She had been so focused on Kelsey's father that she didn't notice it before. Now that she had, the conversation she'd overheard between Kelsey and her brother on the patio came back to her. *You keep saying that, Kelsey, but it's not true. It's never been true. How do I convince you of that?*

But it's unnatural. It's not only a question of biology.

She had assumed they were talking about Kelsey's plans to implant the embryos that had been fertilized by Luke.

But in this graduation photograph, Nate's hand was wrapped around his sister's waist, the touch of his fingertips at the side of her rib cage gentle yet possessive. The excitement in Kelsey's expression took on a new meaning that made May's stomach lurch.

Was it possible?

She pulled her cell phone from her blazer pocket, scrolled to one of William Ellis's many unanswered calls from that morning, and hit enter.

"May," he said dryly. "So apparently now you have time to return my calls. Despite the delay, I do appreciate what you did for Kelsey today, even though I did *not* appreciate being reprimanded by that judge. We do need to get her a more experienced defense team, but you're of course welcome to stay on."

"I need to know why you and Jeanie got divorced."

"Well, I certainly can't imagine why you'd need that information."

"It's for Kelsey's case. It's important."

"It's ancient history. Water under the bridge. All the trite idioms. It can't possibly matter."

"And I promise you that it does. Did it have something to do with Nate?"

When he finally began talking, May could see it all so clearly. She even remembered—or at least thought it was possible that she remembered—what Marnie had been telling her that night before she drowned.

At the sound of keys in the door, she hung up abruptly, managing to slip her phone into her back pocket before Nate walked inside. His arms were filled with laundry that he rushed into his bedroom. Entangled with clothes she recognized from Kelsey's vacation wardrobe was a bundle of dark navy polyester.

"Let me just get this back into her suitcase, and you can be on your way."

"Can I help you fold?" she asked as her phone began to ring.

He stood at the threshold of the room. "Don't you need to get that?"

She pulled out her phone and rejected the call from Kelsey's father. "Spam. Seriously, let me help you. I'm a packing pro."

"No, I'm good. It's a sty in here. Just give me two minutes to get Kelsey's things together." He closed the door, but she kept picturing that bundle of laundry.

Kelsey wouldn't be caught dead wearing that thick blue polyester. It looked like some kind of a uniform.

She needed to get out of this apartment.

PART FIVE

THE TRUTH

42

It's only been three days and she's driving me bonkers." Kelsey was whispering into her new cell phone, as if she were worried about her temporary roommate overhearing. In truth, Lauren and May were on either side of her as she called Nate on speaker from May's living room sofa.

"You guys were bunkmates for weeks on end back in the day," Nate said. "You'll manage."

"I was eating my toast this morning at the kitchen counter and dropped maybe three crumbs. She appeared out of nowhere like a tiny little ninja to hand me a plate and a napkin." May silently objected beside her. That did actually happen. "It might be easier to live in jail."

"I still don't really understand what happened in that courtroom. Seemed like overkill."

"I think when Dad jumped up and offered to buy my way out of trouble, May was scared it was all going south and thought we needed to go big to make sure the judge let me walk out of court a free woman." No objection from May this time, since that was the precise explanation she had given Kelsey. "She contacted the court yesterday about modifying the order, but the judge said something like I should appreciate being here while it lasted."

"What the hell is that supposed to mean?"

"It sounds like the guy's a little shoot-from-the-hip. He let it slip that he overheard some cops talking at a local bar about connecting a bunch of dots with the Boston police. Honestly, Nate, I'm really scared. If Dad did this, he only did it for me, but how does any of this help me? It's ruined my life, so I keep thinking that's impossible, right?"

If Dad did this . . . It was almost as if she were talking out loud to herself about Nate, she thought. If *Nate* really did all this, then it had been all for her—or maybe in his mind for both of them. He knew that Luke would never agree to let her use those embryos once the divorce was final. Luke's entire reason for ending the marriage was to get a clean break from her and her family. He wasn't about to father the next generation of Ellis children.

At the time, Kelsey was still trying to convince Luke to salvage their relationship. How many times had she cried it out with Nate, confiding that she was not only losing her husband but also her chance to be a mother. It never occurred to her to research what would happen to the embryos if her soon-to-be ex-husband died. It turned out the answer was readily available on Google, if someone had a reason to look. Someone like Nate.

And that Friday night in East Hampton, she had turned to Nate again, this time about the possibility of making a life with Dave, a life that would mean having a husband and having children, but not ones with her genetic material. If Nate really was the one who killed Dave, had that actually been for her? Or was it for himself, because he needed her to be alone, depending on him to be her family?

She'd made it clear when their parents first started talking about getting divorced that nothing physical could ever happen again between them, but in every other way, hadn't they become almost a couple by now? No one wanted to date her, so she leaned on Nate for companionship. And Nate was alone by choice. The only woman he had ever tried to be serious with was May, and Kelsey wondered now if maybe the plan had been to marry her best friend so he'd always be close to Kelsey, too.

That Off-Campus Night, he had been so wrecked. She and Nate had gone almost four years without even speaking about the way they used to be. She had been the one to justify the little experiments initially. They were young. It was natural. They weren't biologically related. It was fun, comparing notes about what made a good kiss, what certain things felt like, the weird thrill she got just from a little tickle against her rib cage. It wasn't until their parents walked in on them and she saw what they were doing through their eyes that she realized how sick it was. It literally broke their family in two, and so they swore that would be the end of it.

But then that night, so much vodka, and then the Ecstasy that he and May had taken. He said he needed to talk to her and led the way into the woods. He said he saw it all so clearly. She told him he was high as fuck. He loved her, he said. He knew they could never be a normal couple, yet he would never be able to love anyone else. Couldn't they find a way to be together forever?

And then they heard a branch cracking behind the wood line and there was Marnie, collecting a new secret. And then there was Marnie again, huddled next to her new friend May at the lake. Kelsey felt guilty for the sense of relief that washed over her when no one could find Marnie in the morning and May was so blotto she couldn't even remember the previous night. But never once did she question the fact that Marnie died of an accidental drowning. Now? Lauren and May were convinced Nate had tracked her down, hit her on the head, and thrown her into the water.

Plus there was all the other evidence May and the police had found since May first began zeroing in on Nate. Kelsey understood how the pieces fit together on paper, but she refused to let herself believe it. There had to be an explanation for all of this, because Nate? It couldn't be him. It just couldn't.

Her brother had been quiet for so long, she wondered if she'd lost the connection. "Your life's not ruined," he finally said.

"Did I tell you May's dog has some serious GI issues and lets it fly whenever he sits next to me? My life is literally busted." She could have sworn Gomez flashed her a side-eyed glare. "Anyway, want to come by for drinks? I could use some other company for a while."

"Is that cool with Josh or whatever his name is? I got the impression from May he was sort of weird with the fact I'd been at the house."

"He's actually out of town on business." She noticed May's face fall. May had tried to give Kelsey the same explanation yesterday for his ongoing absence, but then finally conceded that Josh was staying with his brother, no end date specified. "Does five-thirty work?"

"Sounds good. Text me the address?"

"Will do." That was in four hours. In four hours, she'd prove to them that they were wrong about everything. First they thought it was her father. Now it was Nate. Tomorrow it would be her hairdresser. After the past five years, she was almost numbed to the false accusations. She'd survive the latest round. "He'll be here," she said, resting her phone on the coffee table.

May was more eager than she was for the next steps. "Great," she said. "I'll tell Carter. You going to be okay?"

She nodded, even though she was certain that nothing would ever be okay again if her friends were right about this.

43

It was five-sixteen p.m., fourteen minutes to go, and May was telling Kelsey that, no, she absolutely could not make herself a martini. Lauren had lost count of the number of times they had played out this argument in the past half hour.

"I'm freaking out right now, May." Kelsey was massaging her temples with her fingertips, pacing behind the living room sofa. "I don't know if I can do this. I mean . . . it's Nate. I feel like I'm setting him up."

She was most definitely setting him up, but as far as Lauren could tell, May had convinced Kelsey to think of the plan as a way to confirm that Nate *wasn't* involved while the police continued to investigate her father.

From the moment May had agreed to represent Kelsey at her arraignment, Lauren noticed the ways May kept putting herself on the line. Offering up her apartment in the courtroom to keep Kelsey out of custody. Working incessantly as both lawyer and investigator once she suspected Nate. Devising this entire plan. Calling in law enforcement favors to make it happen, despite the dangers involved. After watching May sacrifice time and again, it was impossible for Lauren to stay mad at her for a mistake she'd made fifteen years earlier.

"Okay, but drinking is not going to help." May interrupted Kelsey mid-pace and held her by the shoulders. "This is really important."

"Master of the understatement," Kelsey snapped. "Of course I know it's *important*. You guys think my brother murdered a bunch of people because of me, and what if we find out he did? And frankly, after the past few years, if Nate gets here and I'm not already drinking, he'll definitely be suspicious."

Lauren had initially tried to find a way not to be here for this. Being here made her relevant. It would make her a witness to whatever was about to be said. She'd probably eventually have to testify. The symphony would not be happy. Thomas would not be happy. *She* would not be happy. And she really couldn't help anyway. She wasn't Nate's sister, and she wasn't a crafty little lawyer. Her ten-day trip to the Hamptons was supposed to have ended with her flight back to Houston yesterday, but she couldn't imagine letting the two of them do this alone. She told Thomas a friend needed her help in the city so she was extending her trip. He said she was a good friend and that he'd meet her at the airport when she said the word.

Now that they were about to follow through on their plan, Lauren could see her role clearly. She had to get Kelsey to play *her* role. And Lauren was one of the few people May and Kelsey would allow to boss them around.

"No time for bickering, you guys. Here's what we are going to do. We will make one very small martini and place it in three glasses. That gives you a little nip to calm your nerves, Kelsey, and Nate will think we're already one round in. Fair enough?"

The lack of an argument felt like a consensus.

"And, May, everything is all set upstairs?"

"Yeah, they'll text me as soon as we have enough—*if* we get enough."

May had met Carter Decker and Danny Brennan in her hallway after the doorman let them up. It had only taken a few minutes for Decker to place the recording equipment in her living room before proceeding to the roof to make sure the sound came through clearly. They had wanted to wait in the bedroom in case things fell apart, but after Nate had refused to help her fold the laundry in his apartment, May was worried that he might find a reason to scope out her place for any surprises. The rooftop garden was only three floors up, accessible through a staircase directly across the hallway from May's apartment. It was close enough if anything went wrong.

The doorman called May at exactly five-thirty. Nate was right on time.

44

May kept her well-practiced smile pasted to her face as Nate fumbled with the lock to the terrace door. "Wow, we were all too shell-shocked the first time I was here to pay much attention to your apartment. This view alone is worth the price of admission."

She reached past him and flicked the latch to the left. "It's sticky."

He took a quick step outside before turning right back. "And, yep, I'm still weird about heights."

"This was my sanctuary during the shutdown," she said, allowing herself a few breaths of fresh air from the twentieth-floor view.

"I can imagine," he said.

He was wearing a lightweight button-down, khaki shorts, and loafers. Kelsey had been the first to greet him, welcoming him inside with a classic Kelsey hug. Watching her arms wrapped around Nate was different now, and May had tried not to think of the two of them together. She was, however, confident that Kelsey had accomplished goal one with that hug—make sure there was no gun in his waistband.

It was a good thing that Carter and Danny hadn't parked themselves in her bedroom. The first thing Nate asked for once May poured him a glass of red wine was the tour he didn't get when they'd come here after Kelsey's arraignment. She could feel him studying her during the quick walk-through. Did he know she suspected him?

That moment when he walked into his apartment with Kelsey's laundry—she was replaying it another time, questioning every second of the interaction. Saying *Don't you need to get that?* when her phone rang. Was that a normal thing to say? His keys in the lock only seconds earlier. It took time to put a key in a lock, and she had been talking to Kelsey's father until that very second. He could have heard her.

That was the phone call that broke everything open for May, when she asked Bill Ellis why he and Jeanie had gotten divorced. He didn't want to answer at first. "Not everything has to become a public matter, May. Some families have secrets."

She told him she thought she knew what their secret was. Kelsey and Nate.

"Jeanie and I . . . well, we would find them. At first, they were just little kids, holding hands and rolling around together. We were thrilled the children loved each other. It was everything we hoped for—a way to make a family after we'd each lost a spouse and our children lost a parent. But then we saw them kissing in the backyard, and not like siblings. They swore they were just curious. Jeanie's therapist friend said it wasn't unusual, even for real siblings, to experiment out of curiosity. We were told that it might be scarring if we made a bigger deal out of it than it was. So we kept an eye out for any other warning signs, but over the years it didn't really seem to be an issue. Then one time when Kelsey was staying the weekend to get a break from her freshman roommate, Jeanie and I came home early from some horrible movie. We heard them in Kelsey's room. Then saw them. We were horrified. I still feel sick when I think about it."

"And that's why you got divorced?" He was confirming what she had suspected about Kelsey and Nate, but it didn't fully explain how it split up the family.

"I blamed Nate because he was the boy and I know how boys are. He took advantage of his own sister. But Jeanie blamed Kelsey. Apparently she had known that Kelsey had been sexually active for years already. I most certainly wasn't aware of that. She made Kelsey out to be the predator. After something like that—it just changed how we saw our children, and that had been a big part of what made us a family. There was no fixing it. Why are you digging all this up?"

She had started to explain when she heard Nate's keys in the door and hung up. How much—if any—of that phone call had he overheard?

Nate bent over and scooped Gomez from his dog bed. "Hi, Mr. Gomez. Nice to see you again, pudgy puggy." Gomez began wiggling and jumped back to the floor. "I guess someone's not a cuddler." Nate took the seat next to Kelsey on the sofa, setting his glass of wine on the coffee table. "Kelsey said your fiancé's out of town?"

"Yeah. Corporate boondoggle in Napa." She was becoming an excellent liar.

"Nice."

She pushed any thought of Josh to the side. Once they all got through today, working things out between them would be her top priority. That morning, he called to remind her about the calendar entry for this Friday, the drop-dead date before their deposit became nonrefundable. Apparently he thought they might be calling things off in the next three days, but she couldn't think about that now.

She made sure to sip her wine spritzer slowly—much more spritz than wine—as Kelsey talked about having to reschedule all her meetings and the shows they'd supposedly been binging since they'd become court-ordered roommates.

"How long is this supposed to go on?" Nate asked. "Kelsey said you were trying to get clarification from the court and instead the judge let slip that he was listening in on gossip from Boston."

They had agreed that if at all possible, they'd wait until Nate was the one to bring up the investigation. They didn't want to make it obvious that they were trying to get him to talk about the case.

"Right. Well, I'm glad you and Kelsey are here together, because the news isn't very good. So you know I've been trying to get that detective in East Hampton to see that Bill may have done this on his own, without Kelsey having any idea. But he's telling me the Boston police are convinced that Kelsey had to be involved, because even if Bill knew about David Smith, he wouldn't have known where to find him in East Hampton unless Kelsey told him."

"Unless he was having him tailed," Nate said.

"Two months after they broke up? They're not buying it. Kelsey called her dad Saturday morning on the way back from Montauk to get Josh's car, and they're convinced she told him about her run-in with Dave."

"That's ridiculous," Kelsey said. "I called him because if I don't, he calls me, and I wanted to get it out of the way."

The only person Kelsey had talked about David Smith with was Nate. It was another piece of evidence that Lauren and May kept emphasizing.

"Well, I think they're just trying to intimidate you," Nate said, swallowing the rest of his wine and reaching for the bottle on the coffee table. "They can speculate all they want, but they can't prove you were involved, because you weren't. Hell, they can't even prove the two cases are related."

"Oh, turns out that there's new information on that," May said, her tone growing sharper. "I've been meaning to tell you, Kelsey."

"Tell me what?"

"The latest update from my detective friend. They got the ballistics evidence back on David Smith." She looked at Kelsey with the expression she used to wear when cross-examining a defendant. "He was shot with the same gun that was used to kill Luke—"

"That's bullshit," Nate interrupted. "I mean, don't cops do that all the time? Make up some evidence they don't have, hoping to get you to confess? I think that cop's playing head games with you, May."

She shook her head. "Nope. I thought the same thing. I told him to send me the results. Cashed in a favor with a guy who used to testify for me at the DA's Office. It's solid, Kelsey. And when I was prepping you to talk to that detective, I asked you point-blank about any phone calls you made. You never told me about calling your dad Saturday morning."

"I probably forgot."

"Stop lying," May said, keeping her gaze aimed directly at Kelsey. "How could you have dragged all of us into this? Are you ever going to start telling us the truth?"

"What are you talking about? Oh my god, are you accusing me again? I thought you were finally on my side."

Lauren was walking out of the kitchen with a bowl of chips. "May, this is really screwed up. Is that why you brought us all here, to interrogate Kelsey in front of us?"

"You're supposed to be my lawyer." Kelsey's voice was filled with the pain of betrayal. Nate wasn't the only actor in the Ellis family.

Nate set his wineglass down on the table. "May, this feels straight-up unethical. What are you doing?"

"Honestly, after what she's pulled, I don't care. I'm not even a practicing lawyer anymore and she tricked me into representing her. Why, Kelsey? So I wouldn't figure out the truth, or because I wouldn't be able to tell anyone once I did?"

"Hey," Lauren said sharply, "don't put that on her. That was Nate and me."

"Well, she shouldn't have let me hitch my horse to her wagon. And what about you, Lauren? You've spent years feeling sorry for her, when she's an entitled little Veruca Salt rich girl who got her daddy to kill two men all because she can't stand being rejected. Daddy always buys you what you want. Your spot at Wildwood. Prep school. College admission. Your job. Isn't it that simple, Kelsey? It wasn't about the embryos or wanting to be a mom. You just hate being dumped."

May had been worried she wouldn't be able to pull off her monologue, but it turned out she still had enough built-up resentment to deliver the lines convincingly.

"Stop it," Kelsey said, her shoulders beginning to shake. "I swear I didn't do it."

"It's okay," Nate said, reaching to wrap an arm around Kelsey. "It's not even true. She's lying to you."

"About what?" Kelsey asked beneath what sounded like actual tears.

"The test results. Luke and Dave weren't killed by the same gun."

May had been fiddling with her phone the whole time and snuck a glance at the screen, waiting for the text message from Decker. They all knew more now than they did three days ago. Carter had found the Hertz reservation to prove that before Nate arrived in East Hampton by train on Monday, he had rented a white Chevy Malibu in downtown Manhattan on Saturday, returning it early Sunday morning with 272 miles added to the odometer, more than enough to get to the East End of Long Island and back.

Boston police had learned that the night Luke was killed, Nate called in sick for the small role he had in an indie play in the East Village.

And May was pretty proud that she was the one who found a cashier at the Jersey City AutoZone who recognized Nate as a customer from the previous weekend. He couldn't confirm what he purchased, but the store did sell the kind of LED lights a driver could mount on a dash. Unless Nate had gotten rid of them already, she was confident Decker would find the lights and a police uniform in his apartment once he could enter with a search warrant.

"I'm not lying," May said. "Why would I do that?"

"I don't know, but you are definitely lying about the guns."

"How can you possibly know that?" she pressed.

Kelsey was slumped on the sofa. She was no longer playing a role in this setup. When tears began to form, May could see that they were real. She was crying because she knew the truth now.

"Because it was two different guns," Nate said. "I know I saw that somewhere on the internet."

It had been public knowledge that Luke was killed with a .38, but the police had not yet released the fact that David Smith was shot with a 9mm.

A new text from Decker. *That'll do it.* The evidence they had, combined with Nate's apparent certainty that two different guns were used in the murders, would suffice. Carter could get his search warrant. And from there, they could make an arrest. The plan had been May's idea. Carter went along with it only after she promised that she would not push Nate any further once they had the bare minimum for a probable cause affidavit.

The room fell silent as Nate realized what he had let slip. "I mean, it couldn't possibly be, right? Because you didn't do this, Kelsey. And even if some hit man was hired to kill two different men five years apart, they wouldn't use the same gun. It just doesn't make sense. That cop's messing with you, Hanover."

May nodded as if she was taking in new information. "I guess it's possible he sent me a ballistics match from a different case and told me it was from Luke and Dave?"

He pointed an index finger toward her. "Bingo. I bet that's exactly what he did."

Lauren moved behind May's chair to give her a quick shoulder squeeze. "It's been a stressful week. We have to stop hauling out accusations against each other, okay? We need to stick together."

"I can't believe I fell for it," May said. "I'm so sorry, Kelsey. For him to make up something like that? It probably means they don't have any evidence at all."

It was exactly as they had planned it. Lower the temperature, continue with drinks, pretend everything was normal. Keep Nate occupied while Carter got a search warrant and went to Nate's apartment.

But Kelsey was still crying. Nate rubbed her back. "It's going to be okay. Did you hear her? There's no evidence."

When Kelsey looked up, she turned to face her brother. "When I called you earlier, I told you that if my father did this, he did it for me, and yet it only ruined my life."

"But he didn't. Nobody we know did this."

"You did," she said. "And you ruined my life. Can't you see that?"

"Kelsey, no—" He reached as if to hug her, but she leapt from the sofa, upending the coffee table. A glass shattered. Wine began to spread its way across the rug. So much red.

"I'm a pariah now, Nate. I order food under fake names. I have to keep working for my father for the rest of my life, who pays me just enough to have a good life but not have actual freedom, because no other employer will touch me. Men—you certainly made sure I'd never have a relationship again, didn't you? Luke and Dave didn't deserve to die. And Marnie? Did you really kill Marnie, just because she heard your crazy talk that night?"

"I didn't kill anyone, Kelsey. May's gotten all up in your head."

May was trying to stem the flow of the wine, worried it might spread under the sofa, where the recording device was planted. "It's like Lauren said. We need to stop accusing each other—"

"They know about the Hertz rental, Nate."

May bit her lower lip. There was no way to walk that back. She had to hope Carter and Danny were still listening.

"I have no idea what you're talking about," Nate said defiantly. "They won't be able to prove anything, because I didn't do it."

"They'll try to prove it, though. The trial will be front-page news. I'll have to testify about my surgery, my embryos, lying to Dave about my own name—everyone will find out everything. You may or may not go to prison for the rest of your life, but any hope I have at a normal life will be gone forever. This whole time I've been standing by you, you've been a murderer—since college."

Nate was facing Kelsey, his hands on her knees, as if no one else was in the room. "With Marnie, I didn't mean to. I was grabbing her arm to get her to understand why she couldn't tell anyone. She pulled away and tripped. Her head was bleeding."

"So you drowned her?"

"I thought she was dead and I freaked out. That's not murder. And Luke? Fuck that guy. He dumped you and was going to keep you from having children."

"No, don't you dare. Don't you *dare* convince yourself you did this for me. I hate you. Do you hear me? I fucking hate you."

Their heads all turned in the direction of a door slamming in the hallway outside the apartment. It had to be the door from the stairwell. They were here.

It happened so fast, Carter pushing through the apartment door first, Danny right behind him, as Nate jumped from the sofa, looking back once to Kelsey before reaching for the terrace door.

Why hadn't May locked it when he stepped back inside? The sticky latch would have stopped him. Carter and Brennan would have gotten to him.

"No!" Carter leapt over the upended coffee table in an attempt to close the distance.

May felt a gush of hot, humid air as the door opened. She watched as Nate hiked his sockless, loafered right foot over the metal railing. "She didn't know," he yelled. "She didn't know anything."

He was gone.

May began to scream—that shrill, ear-splitting, panicked noise she had no idea could come out of her little body until last year.

And then she decided to stop. She was in control of herself again.

EPILOGUE

THIRTEEN MONTHS LATER

May applied a new layer of SPF 50, her third of the day. She was always serious about protecting her skin, but law school classes were starting in two weeks and it seemed obnoxious to show up with an obvious vacation tan. She tinkered with the floppy brim of her straw hat until it was just right and leaned back in her chaise longue, gazing out at the turquoise water between their beach and the lush, rolling hills of St. Barts.

"You guys, do you think I can convince the Anguillan government to open an American law school here? Maybe I could be the inaugural dean."

"I'm in," Lauren said. "I'll teach music at the high school and get a standing gig crushing it at one of the resorts."

On the other side of Lauren, Kelsey flipped another page of the trashy gossip magazine perched on the top of her cute little belly bump. "I'll develop commercial real estate projects." She took a loud sip of her virgin rum punch, which she derisively referred to as boo-juice because "no alcohol is *boo.*"

"No fair," May said. "Your idea would actually work."

May was the one who'd proposed the idea of another summer beach trip. Kelsey kept saying she was worried they were cursed, but May and Lauren finally convinced her that they needed to prove to themselves that they could go on a perfectly uneventful vacation. She and Kelsey initially balked when Lauren suggested a trip to the Caribbean in August, but apparently the first week of the month in Anguilla was known as Carnival, a celebration of Emancipation Day filled with parades, boat races, and live music.

It was only when they arrived on the island that it became clear Lauren was a known quantity there. She used first names with the resort staff and ran into someone she knew at the wine store. It turned out she and Thomas had been coming here at least once a year for more than a decade.

"How come you never talk about him with us?" May had asked. "He's obviously important to you."

"Because I see no reason to take up the valuable time of other women talking about a man unless I really need to talk about him. And part of why Thomas and I work is that he doesn't do anything that makes me need to talk about him outside his presence."

It made perfect sense. May, on the other hand, had taken up plenty of Lauren's and Kelsey's valuable time talking about Josh in the months after Nate had jumped from their terrace. Initially, they had opted to take back their deposit on the reception hall while it was still fully refundable—just to have one less thing to worry about in the aftermath of Nate's death and the investigation that followed. Then she saw Josh's laptop open to apartment rentals. He let her believe that it was because May felt queasy every time she had to walk past the terrace door, but by October, he had signed a lease for his own place on the Upper East Side.

She had gotten a message from Carter a few minutes ago asking if they could meet in the city for dinner the night after she got home. So far it wasn't serious, which was exactly what she needed right now. She had been planning to tell Kelsey and Lauren, but decided there was no reason to. She'd talk about him with the Crew if the time ever came when she needed to.

Kelsey set her magazine aside and began scrolling through her phone. "You guys, good news. Luke's murder case is finally officially closed. My lawyers convinced them to put out a statement saying that they have concluded that Nate was responsible and acted completely alone."

The East Hampton police had done the same with David Smith's murder last November, but they had the advantage of stronger evidence. When they tracked down the car that Nate had rented the day David Smith was shot, they conducted a thorough forensic search for DNA evidence. The car had been cleaned multiple times since the murder, but the search found a small amount of blood inside the hard plastic casing in which the driver's-side seat belt retracted. It was a match for David Smith.

May had seen Kelsey a half dozen times in person over the last year. With each visit, she noticed Kelsey grow more comfortable saying Nate's name. She was still in therapy, but the really bad days were behind her.

So far, they had managed to withhold the truth behind Nate's motive for the murders. The recording from May's apartment made it clear that he thought he had done it to help his sister, but so far everyone seemed to accept the explanation that he was protective of Kelsey because she was the Ellis who had continued to take care of him after their families divorced.

Explaining Nate's reason for killing Marnie had been trickier. That day in May's apartment, when Kelsey asked Nate if he did it because Marnie had overheard his "crazy talk," he claimed that he had grabbed Marnie's arm "to get her to understand why she couldn't tell anyone." Kelsey had wanted to tell the police the entire truth, even if it meant reliving the shame from what had transpired between her and Nate when they were children. May had persuaded her that she could give Marnie's family closure without disclosing that piece of the story. Instead, Kelsey told the police that Nate's "crazy talk" was an admission that he had been cheating on May and that Nate was scared that Marnie would run to May with her newly gleaned information. It was close enough to the truth.

May didn't tell Kelsey, but the usual lookie-loos on the Killer-Insights board were still convinced she was in on Luke's and Dave's murders with her brother, and nothing the police said was likely to change that. But some of the same people also believed in pizza places that were human trafficking hubs, that the moon landing was faked, and that 9/11 was an inside job. There was nothing Kelsey could do about it, so why did she even need to know?

"To new beginnings," Kelsey said, raising her glass.

"To new beginnings." Lauren and May joined in the toast.

The twins were due before Christmas.

ACKNOWLEDGMENTS

Writing is solitary work, but this writer is not a solitary person. The title of "editor" does not begin to capture the from-beginning-to-end-and-beyond role that Jennifer Barth has served to advance my work for more than twenty years now, but thank you, Jennifer, for helping my books be the best they can be. And thank you, Reagan Arthur, for welcoming me to Knopf, and to Elora Weil, Abby Endler, Brian Etling, Erinn Hartman, Laura Keefe, Todd Doughty, Kristin Fassler, Chris Dufault, Valerie Walley, and Ruth Liebmann. I am also so grateful to my agents, Sloan Harris at CAA and Jody Hotchkiss at Hotchkiss, Daily & Associates; to Alison Gaylin, Megan Abbott, Michael Koryta, Angie Kim, and Janelle Brown for valuable feedback on this one; and to Harvey O'Brien at Sandh & Co for much-needed website design and support.

And a huge thank-you to readers. I completed this book shortly after celebrating the twentieth anniversary of my first novel. I thought I'd write one book for Professor Burke to keep on her office shelf. The editors who wanted to acquire it all assumed it was a series, so I said, "Yes! A series, just as I planned." I never thought I'd write or coauthor twenty books in the twenty years that followed, and I hope for another twenty-plus more. Thank you, thank you, thank you to the readers who have given me this chance to have a career and live my life as a storyteller. Many of you have taken the time to connect with me in person at events or online through social media. You have become friends, default event photographers, and voluntary word-of-mouth publicists. I appreciate you so very much.

The most common question writers are asked is where they get their ideas. *The Note* is the culmination of three inchoate ideas I was playing with.

Idea One: A stupid practical joke. Profuse apologies to the person who found a similar note on a car windshield. I won't disclose the vacation town where it happened, the person who wrote the note, or how it ended up where it did. But, admit it, you brazenly stole that parking spot. The note existed only because a group of reunited friends wanted to make each other laugh. On the ride home, the friends realized they were ridiculous and began to wonder what happened when the note was found.

Idea Two: A homicide investigation I have followed for years. I won't identify it out of consideration for the victim's family, but it's enough to say that the victim was making someone so unhappy that someone seeking to protect the unhappy person may have decided to end the unhappiness. It's a case that got me thinking about how intense and potentially deadly loyalty can be.

Idea Three: Faraway friendships. We collectively went through a bizarre, traumatic time a few years ago. We sought connection to the people we really needed. Many of us became even closer to friends who lived hundreds or even thousands of miles away. Those friendships stick. These friends are family. They're the folks who show up for you when others won't. Are there any limits to how far we'll go to support each other?

I hope everyone who reads this book has a May or a Lauren or a Kelsey in their life. So another thank-you here, this time to the long-distance, 24/7 group-chat friends who are my real-life Canceled Crews (but without arrests and criminal investigations): The Vacation Besties, The Pizza Posse, The Puzzle Guild, The Petty Pals, The FlimFlam Hive, and Karin/Lisa (how do we not have a nickname?).

And finally, I do nothing in this world without also feeling tremendous love and gratitude for Sean, forever and ever.

If you would like to see and/or hear more from me, you can connect on

Instagram @alafair.burke
Twitter (I still call it Twitter) @alafairburke
Facebook @alafairburkebooks
Threads @alafair.burke
Bluesky @alafairburke

A NOTE ABOUT THE AUTHOR

Alafair Burke is the Edgar-nominated, *New York Times* bestselling author of fifteen novels of suspense, including *The Ex, The Wife, The Better Sister,* and *Find Me,* and coauthor of the bestselling Under Suspicion series. A former prosecutor, she is now a professor of criminal law. She lives in New York.

A NOTE ON THE TYPE

This book was set in Adobe Garamond. Designed for the Adobe Corporation by Robert Slimbach, the fonts are based on types first cut by Claude Garamond (ca. 1480–1561). Garamond was a pupil of Geoffroy Tory and is believed to have followed the Venetian models, although he introduced a number of important differences, and it is to him that we owe the letter we now know as "old style." He gave to his letters a certain elegance and feeling of movement that won their creator an immediate reputation and the patronage of Francis I of France.

Typeset by Scribe,
Philadelphia, Pennsylvania

Printed and bound by Berryville Graphics,
Berryville, Virginia

Designed by Casey Hampton